# Skeads

## A Decent Sort of Man

## Dave Pistorese

Copyright 2019

Daniel Wetta Publishing

Table of Contents

Acknowledgments

# Acknowledgments

I never thought seriously about writing a book until an unintended consequence slowed me down. I kept a journal for decades, more as an activity to enjoy a little solitude with a glass of bourbon.

Over the years, I had acquired the impression that literature and writing graced individuals with special genomes imparting both grammatical and storytelling gifts.

Pure serendipity pushed me to this book. I entered a combined bookstore and coffee shop with the intention of buying a cup of coffee, smuggling it to the bathroom, and mixing in it a few shots of bourbon for my afternoon sabbatical.

This I accomplished.

On exiting the store, I passed the outside patio and saw a fella in a wheelchair and his elegant female companion sitting next to him. For no reason, an empty chair next to theirs called me over, and I sat down. We talked, we laughed a little, I sipped my doctored coffee, and they, Rick and Emeline Bailey, invited me, a perfect stranger, to a Thursday afternoon writers' meeting. After attending for about a year, I dabbled a few paragraphs and observations. More a solitary man, I discovered enjoyment in the hodgepodge conversations of the group.

A person of minimal ambition, I put together over time a novel only with the help of the people I met in this group. From them, I learned that writing often is a collective endeavor, a union of effort, care and concern, and a shared appreciation for words, storytelling, and the miracle of language.

So exercising a little humility, a difficult sentiment for me to summon, I tip my hat to this community of companionship. Vanity tempts me to take all the credit, but too soon someone would call me on it, revealing that the credit goes to...

Rick and Emeline Bailey
Cindy Bowser, my wife
Jack Bray
Sharon Dillon
Cindy Freeman
Carl Gillen
Lou Hamilton
Elizabeth Compton Lee
Jack Lott
Barbara McClellan
Patricia Parquette
Christian Pascale
Peter Stiper
Jim Tobin
Daniel Wetta
Susan Williamson

They are a collage of decent people, and I am sincerely indebted to them for sharing their knowledge of our astonishing language and for an optimism countering my customary skeptical view of life and humans in general. Last, but not least, I wish to thank anyone who takes their time to read this story. If my gratitude has missed anyone, which I'm sure it has, please accept my apologies.

# Part I: Skeads and the Fishing Vessel, *Faith*

# Chapter 1: The Fishing Vessel, *Faith*

Onboard the F/V *Faith,* ignored and stored with little care in a dusty old shoebox, rested black and white photographs. Taken after the Great Depression and before the Vietnam Conflict, they were dog-eared, blurred and faded. One was of three fishermen wearing heavy wool suits, work boots, and rakish derby hats. In the middle of a North Pacific winter, they calmly stood on a dock; their hands stuck into their pockets. These men stared at the frozen deck of the *Faith* and its unlikely cargo of ice, snow, and, stacked in orderly rows from bow to stern and deep into the hold, frozen corpses. The dead were once tourists, adventurers, mothers, fathers, and children. This picture showed the remains of a passenger ferry that had gone down in the middle of a winter storm. Another photo haunted the box, that of a mother and her child stacked on deck, glazed in ice, captured in their final twisted and petrified embrace, the silent child's lips locked open in a colorless icy howl.

Our rig worked for many decades in the fishery. The original owner built three of the same design, naming the other two *Hope* and *Charity*. Over the years the sea had claimed both, and our *Faith* was the lone survivor.

The beauty of line stretched simply across its overall length of 90 feet. A narrow beam with heavy wooden rails made it appear less stable than its actual performance in rough weather. Rising above the shear only a few feet, a modest bow added the humble gracefulness old wooden boats seem to hold over their more stern and steel sisters.

More than forty years have passed since I was the new guy on the *Faith*. I had arrived from down south, dropping out of college, having lost in a jungle any meaning or interest in art, history, literature, or even knowledge. I had lost the grace of hope, and the loss was so subtle, I failed to notice its void, instead of considering it a condition of nature and myself. For a week, begging for work on the cannery docks, I landed a job as an inexperienced deckhand on the *Faith*, a responsibility to help pull in the gear at the end of the season. That's how I met Skeads, one of the most remarkable humans I would ever meet. He gave me the job. On a chance edge of the Aleutian Chain, through a chance meeting on a chance dock, he became a chance event in my chance life. We both had lost in a jungle something missing we couldn't describe.

I wasn't a half bad cook and ended up staying on more as a respite from my own pilgrimage.

Before the sea finally claimed the *Faith*, its galley and stoic living quarters provided a pleasant place to sit and drink, to talk and smoke. After four decades, I can still recall this place of subtle details that appeared almost as an afterthought by the shipwrights who had built and created a modest beauty of hardy strength. From the thick joinery of the structural members to the dovetailed drawers beneath the bunks, these details combined to lend a gentle elegance that was less boastful than an implied humility. Embracing you in arms of comfort, it felt secure. Pushed aft, this space tucked behind the holding tank under the work deck and above the guts of the clattering engine room. Bunk beds built against the wooden hull surrounded a worn, pitted galley table. All the other necessities, for the rig had few wants and all the needs, had been plumbed and wired wherever space permitted, and function demanded.

Heavy scarred wood, much of it virgin oak and mahogany, collected and held the heat from the diesel fired stove and mellowed the yellow light cast by electric lamps. Over the decades, many an exhausted engine and pump saw a bewildering assortment of their gaskets, housings, impellers, and various other organs spread across

2

the galley table. The soul of the *Faith* had been probed, explored, and lamented by crews with names now long forgotten, if not dead, bracing themselves against the extremes of an angry and indifferent sea. Up to this point, their unsung history of the effort to govern the machinery, to overhaul, to persuade, and to cajole the noble craft, had succeeded keeping it alive before the luck ran out and nature grew impatient and lethal.

The struggle never ended; it was the way of life. Perhaps now a little imprecise in details and events, the people and places I worked with have become a pure memory to me, as if still immediate and present rather than burred by four decades. This remembrance is absent those midnight ravens, glaring and clawed on to winter leafless limbs, cawing out my shames and regrets, absent the melancholy when my mental sweats fail to make sense of a life that is now more reflective and in evening decline.

While working on the *Faith*, I would learn that the rig had never abandoned a crew, though a crew had abandoned her.

With pleasant ease, I remember the February afternoon when a Northwest gale moaned and howled across the town and through the masts and rigging of the fleet. The *Faith* was secure to a cannery dock, and our crew huddled around the scruffy galley table, sharing nothing more exciting than a bottle of whiskey, what in the future would be called second-hand smoke, and no ambition to venture beyond the diesel-burning comfort of the time-worn stove.

It was a time before onboard television and VCR, and crews still entertained one another with conversation. In his own world, Skeads played cards. Sitting nearby, Mallary, with the face of a mummified baby and hands like claws, flicked through the rustling pages of a quarter sheet journal. On our old and dependable wooden boat, he had worked many seasons, and in his outlandish syntax and dialect said he could hear voices moaning from the hold that once held the frozen bodies from that tragic ferry.

"Ghosts exist as certain as the sea and heaven, but if you ignore them they ... if you don't believe ... to their own they keep." He said this as seriously as if it were his last breath on earth. Of course, we laughed at him. Our skepticism meant nothing to him. On cold nights, when stretched out alone in his bunk, he swore he could hear a mother and child wailing as loud and clear as any of us seated at the table, louder even than the storm.

Having taken an hour earlier Mallary's monthly gambling budget, Skeads, a solitary man, his face creased older than his years, played solo cribbage. He studied his cards through drugstore reading glasses and rubbed his tobacco-stained finger into one of the deep furrows cascading down his pale cheeks. The board on which he played had a history. A few years before, that date now escapes me, he had been herring tendering in the Norton Sound. Early one morning he took a private walk on the beach. In those flat light northern latitudes, obscurities form just before the sun rises. An unusual silhouette sticking out of the gray sand and stones caught his eye. Very little driftwood washes ashore that far north, and on closer inspection he saw, draped in seaweed, a limb thrusting up from the beach, a tombstone of sorts, attached to a creature buried from some Aleutian storm. Issuing from a deceased and wave-buried walrus, a tusk protruded into the pale morning. With a few judicious strokes of a saw, Skeads claimed it from its deceased owner, and with some artistic license, turned it from a clam shovel into a scrimshawed cribbage board, a work of art, a one of a kind. Skeads never said where exactly he found the tusk, leaving its counterpart, the other tusk and worth a considerable amount of money, with the walrus in its final resting place beneath the sand and rocks.

Mallary, reading his tattered fishing journal, commented with a "grunt and harrumph" regarding an article with which he disagreed and debated.

4

With a touch of ceremony, with a thud when heels hit the ironbark deck, the fourth of our crew could be heard making his entrance with sledgehammer-like footfall. In your mind's eye, you saw the boots kicking off the snow and icy mud, kicking vigorously enough to send vibrations through the thick wooden hull, trembling galley light bulbs in their sturdy holders, shivering their yellow light. When the hatch opened, a ball of frigid fresh air tumbled down the vertical stairs wounding the warmth. Boots quickly followed, surrounded by a fleece, a billowing full-length silver fox fur coat. Rantlings, our skipper, materialized; he entered from the cold like one of the essential elements.

In one move, he secured the hatch behind him, cursed God and His Creation, and stated the obvious, "There is no answer for the weather out there. Why should the Heavenly Father create such weather? Poor Adam and Eve couldn't have been all that bad. No worse, at least, than myself."

Removing his coat, he rolled it into a ball and like a bundle of laundry throwing it on his bunk. Rubbing his uncut beard and wind-burned cheeks, he leaned over the table towards the bottle, cocked an eyebrow, and shot out two questions of only rhetorical importance, "I'm not breaking up anything important?" and, "So, what are we drinking?" He knew the answer to both.

With his pale blue eyes floating over the rims of his glasses, Skeads, his concentration temporarily interrupted, looked up from his cards. "You are a disturbing and ambitious man."

"I am a man of ambition," our skipper replied with muscular confidence.

Mallary poured whiskey into a coffee cup, feigned handing it to Rantlings, took a sip, ignored our skipper, and turned another page of the journal, saying, "If you freeze to death out there, can I have the fur?"

"Mallary," our skipper replied, "out of respect for your age, if we catch a million pounds this season, I'll give you the coat. Then you can freeze in it."

"My honor it would be," he replied.

Though under thirty years, Rantlings' reputation was earned from a critical peer group. He was only a few years older than I but was born on these cruel waters and carried the attitude of a man bred knowing nature cared less about reputation than life, that in its brutal eyes competence was more honored than confidence. While bearing the laurels of one of the young titans in the fishing fleet, he was a youth of prudence and moderation, and a man who held well his liquor.

As for me, I studied a book of casserole recipes, trying to find some galley synthesis for the freezer-burned caribou and root vegetables whose vigor had grown spongy. A culinary trick I would fail to achieve, regardless of braising, or slow cooking, or all the limp carrots, celery, and onions in the fleet. The skipper squeezed out an engine manual from a shelf tight with books, eased into a corner of the bench, and began to leaf through the pages pursuing the resolution to an oil leak in the generator engine. Besides being a good skipper, he was a superb engineer.

We settled into a comfortable silence but for the staccato vibrations rising from the engine room below us, or the occasional furious animus of wind stampeding across the frozen deck, shaking and throttling the rigging above us. A winter storm bound us.

Mallary, with his strange syntax like none other I have heard since, read an article in a year old journal. He said to no one in particular, "Hard to believe ... believe, we the living ... skedaddling not unlike cockroaches, nasty critters in this tatty pantry of plenty ... that a crew abandoned ... abandoned this noble vessel."

6

Our baby-faced reader added, "This rig, the *Faith* ... in this bay, united to this frigid earth by twisted lines of a hope forsaken ... an' this unearthly hull once pregnant with lost souls from the tragic ferry forever crossing eternal water ... this very ark of a crew numbering a mere four who then abandoned her. Ah-ha, then fate obliged a single survivor."

Skeads peered up from his cards. Mallary took a breath and a sip saying, "Yes, one among us. Not to, in my experience, cudgel the only Rachel of a rig to then survive and fully function without a crew. It's a testament to a seaworthy design surviving in solitude, content to witness three of four of its crew drown, lost to the unavoidable elements. Harsh. Very harsh. Less, of course, the one alone retched up not unlike a living hairball, a fisherman in our very midst and this sacred hull united by the absurdities, the insanities of life." He avoided looking at Skeads and applied another sip of whiskey to his word-parched tongue.

Skeads returned to playing his solo two-hand game, moving a peg down one side of his walrus tusk, settling on a hole near a scrimshaw detailed in thin lines of black ink, depicting a limit seiner pulling a purse sein. He said, "Insanity. Sanity. They're carved of the same bone."

Skeads paused for a minute, not so much for effect, but thinking and studying his cards. In a muffled vibrato below us, the dissonant engine generator clattered. "But two made shore," he whispered. Adding in words as sure as a heart attack, "Two."

Mallary, his tongue wetted, sipped another taste of whiskey, and looking at Skeads said, "But you are the lone survivor. The soul-mate. My Skeadsman saved from the seaweed's grip."

We all became very attentive.

The Coast Guard had towed in the *Faith* empty of the crew,

securing it to the transit dock. The vessel was found abandoned, floating in open water. Tied to the dock, it became an instant attraction, finding day or night a group of fishermen standing around studying its "return from the dead." In a way, another echo from its dense history, or perhaps, an addendum to the photographs of the dead and frozen bodies of the passenger ferry. You couldn't go into a bar without hearing the rig's name mentioned and its mystery repeated.

As early as the next day of the tragedy, a server at Polly's waited her tables with a heart staggered by the nightmare that her son was one of the missing, she trying to fill this horrid abyss with work while the customers sat numbly in the knowledge of her grief. The labyrinth of this ruin was yet to find order. To this point, the sea and the *Faith* rendered only speculation. Skeads and the entire crew were still missing and assumed dead. The empty vessel floated tied securely to the dock.

Skeads studied us sitting around the table, "Like a string of sausage," he replied. His hand reached for a peg and moved it another dozen holes, this to an inked etching of a beached walrus, half-resurrected, its front fins caught clawing madly out of a rocky beach, its mouth gaping in a muted bawl, its single tusk ascending into an ivory ether.

Sometimes Skeads spoke in conundrums, and his reply about "sausages" meant nothing to us gathered around the table. He added, "But for the Grace of God, so go us all ... all of us eventually ... if ... there is a place to go." Rearranging the cards in his hand, with a cigarette smoldering between his stained mahogany fingertips, he crossed himself like a Catholic lacking conviction.

With his mug, he gave a toast, "To the living. To the new guy, to Wronski who made shore alive." He did not laugh. He took the sip of whiskey, his eyes fixed to his cards.

Rantlings peered over the manual, "I know nothing about Grace or God, but that-there's a skipper's nightmare, and I'll work my soul to squat to avoid it." He closed the manual. "You always stay with the boat. It's common sense. You should have stuck to the *Faith* like a maggot to a corpse."

Skeads replied, "Nothing's common about common sense. Stupid happens all the time. What we did is what we did. The rig could have easily rolled over and floated for days with us hanging on ... hanging on like your maggots on a corpse. Then again, it could have easily sunk, sending us to the deep ... to that what's littered by the likes of those that's gone before us."

Skeads buried his cards between his forearms, the left one bore a tattoo on skin that looked more like parchment, the blue-green veins visible and coursing beneath an iconic dagger wrapped in the remains of a faded scroll reading, "Death Before," the rest of the avowal having been burned to a waxy patch of scar tissue.

He paused and looked at the tusk, "We're blind to our insanities. Hell, old men never cease to convince young men to kill and die for causes that within a breath of history are forgotten. Not a lick of difference from a lemming jumping its cliff."

I looked at his defaced tattoo, wondering if he had torched it.

Skeads said, "Our awareness, our greatness blinds us. We don't see nothing. Damn if the same madness that creates the nature of leaping a lemming's cliff, creates the vanity for dying, for giving up life for a cause. I tell you what ... both disregard life only from different insanities." He stopped talking and sucked on his cigarette.

At the time, to me, he seemed to be making no sense at all.

Nightmares govern a skipper's sleep, and Rantlings spoke with a healthy respect and loathing for the dead-night demons. He put down the manual and grabbing an idle coffee mug, peered impatiently into

9

it as if searching for resolutions rather than the random nastiness he found at the bottom. With less than a spotless finger, he scraped out something foreign, pushing the mug towards Mallary who always seemed closest to the bottle.

Our skipper argued, "As it was, damn, as it is, the *Faith* did what it was designed to do. It's a fact. It floated. You can't tell me that not one of you had the wit to stick with the boat? It makes no sense at all. What got hold of you?"

"Sense? Facts? Facts never fail to prove you're right until the same facts prove you wrong," replied Skeads.

Skeads had been the lone survivor. Within hours after the rescue, and against the protest of the medical staff, he walked out of the infirmary. He returned to clean up the *Faith*. He said nothing and would say nothing. Without his surviving, the *Faith* would have been a perfect mystery; a vessel found empty of a crew floating on open water. A ghost ship. He said he didn't remember, but he did in infinite detail. Survivors make stories.

Skeads said, "The crew was equal to any here. All good. All sound. All."

Rantlings, having opened the manual again, peered over the top of the frayed and oil-stained guide, "You know, it was a nothing storm. I've known this rig longer than any of you. *Faith* has weathered a thousand storms with nothing more than a few teeth getting knocked loose." He stopped and shook his head, less in disgust than a stomach-bile reaction to the idea of abandonment. He belched, took a sip of whiskey. "It makes no sense. It's not what you make of it. It's what you make it."

Skeads replied, "You didn't make the wave. You didn't see the wave. It was something else that happened ... luck ... odds gave out. But ... I saw something else beyond a wave."

Skeads murmured around his cigarette sticking in his mouth, "Impossible happens all the time. Hell, life is impossible. We squat here dumb and stupid animals, taking it for granted, but it's a miracle reeking under our noses. Life's a miracle, the only miracle. What's death? Pass the bottle."

Mallary had moved the bottle closer to his reach. He glanced up from the journal, "Well, has not my Skeadsman waxed the philosophical?" Mallary pushed the bottle to Skeads and waited, knowing he had finally bated his friend.

The whiskey rested an inch from the bottom of the bottle. Skeads poured half an inch, hesitated for less than half a thought, and drained the other half. "There's still another half left in the bottle," he said, "and on a night like this, when sitting here in comfort, you can believe in the infinite good as easily as an infinite number of halves in a bottle of whiskey. Don't bet against another survivor making shore. Call him Wronski. Call him a miracle. Call him a sausage."

I could understand what Skeads was saying. Order presented itself as a natural condition from the nested and cozy living quarters on the *Faith*. The unthinkable is unthinkable for a reason. The unthinkable is the blood of hope. Nature is reasonable when hearing it from a warm distance kick snow across the ice-covered deck. It seemed impossible and improbable that a crew would collectively abandon a seaworthy floating boat. However, that crew, that night, took their chances in January seas. They abandoned the *Faith*.

Skeads had never talked about that night, but this evening the time had arrived. He was a man who did not live in the past yet could not escape it. The reticent and quiet man was ready to talk. Retiring his game, he pulled his pegs, slipping them into a small hand-carved ironwood box.

Looking at Mallary, he frowned, his thin lips disappearing into

11

his pale face: "The night started out like any other night. Many boats lay anchored as the season was grinding to a close. But a few still worked their gear, and we were one of them. Trusting the weather report, we pushed out into the storm toward our gear. Had we waited just a few more hours ... but bad luck," he paused looking at the tusk, "Luck. Had we waited just a few hours, a few minutes maybe, and we would have missed the wave. But we jogged slowly out of town into a swell, comfortable with the forecast predicting the storm blowing out by morning."

He sipped his whiskey, leaned an elbow on the table with his rolled cigarette pinned between two fingers, "The *Faith* is strong. A great boat. The engine's dependable. Radar and Loran dependable. We knew our position and our place. It was a typical black sea with nothing bigger than a Beaufort Four. Our work lights divided the night from the sea.

"The skipper stood the wheel. We settled into our bunks for a little more sleep. We figured by early morning to be on the grounds ... after the storm settled.

"Wronski had worked the *Faith* for several seasons. He checked the engine room, stuck his washboard into his bunk and his head under a pillow. The new guy seemed to be on his game. He had a kind mother who always found us a table at Polly's and served us lunch like we were big shooters. I can't even look at her now. She was proud of him."

Skeads' cigarette was burned to a nub. He looked at its tobacco-saturated scrap, placed it in his mouth, ate it, and pulled a leaf from his papers. Taking his index finger to form a trough, gently tapping tobacco into it from a tooled leather pouch and pressing the leaf into the pocket, he slowly created another cigarette by rolling the dark brown shreds into a cylinder. Even after all these years, I can still remember Skeads' beautiful hands while rolling his tobacco.

Athletic hands. Hands fashioned for a musical instrument, like in those Renaissance ink sketches, revealing and capturing a moment, perhaps a miracle, detailing a life of brutal work, a testament to a life in the midst of life, fingers long and graceful, with unbroken nails in perfect ovals, a lost destiny for a violin or piano perhaps, but annealed by the fishery, soiled with tobacco resins and a thin gray grime under the cuticles.

His eyes resting on the cigarette he had just rolled, Skeads continued: "The wind changed. The tide turned. The waves changed to face and break hard. One of them might slam into the hull. Here, right here, where we sit in this place, that night, in my head, I could see this force breaking into white foam beneath the work lights. It would shake us in the bunks. I put in my washboard.

"The skipper backed down the engines, slowed and kept his heading, riding the waves. The privacy curtains across the bunks shook back and forth without any rhythm. I remember I got up and checked to see if the refrigerator door was dogged down tight. The rig rolled, lunging and jerking. I stumbled, holding on to the table and other handholds, aided by the single nightlight. The storm was a little bigger than expected. Its personality changed."

I still can hear Skeads' soft voice describe, or instead list, the next series of waves. I learned that storms often ignore the best of forecasts, indifferent to our estimates. I could imagine these waves forcing themselves across the deck, bigger than before, small mountains of boiling black beneath the sheen of the work lights, and, on occasion, one pushing the bow to lose its heading, and for the *Faith* to hesitate for a minute to find the course again, rising to the next wave.

A wave, a huge and unnatural wave, forced them into the trough.

With the smell of diesel burning quietly in our stove, its heat

13

filling our living space, and while I searched for a recipe for a hunk of tasteless caribou, Skeads studied his cigarette, rolling it around inspecting its form. In his pale eyes, you could see the movie in his mind return to that night. "I could feel the skipper bring the rudder hard-over to correct. You could hear the hydraulics straining and whining through the pressure bypass, rudder clanking hard to starboard, the sudden increase in engine speed, the skipper trying to kick the *Faith* out of the trough. We were all awake by then and could feel the rig coming around for the next wave. But it hit us, and she broached. Then all turned against us. Hell, our illusions of life broached.

"In a way," said Skeads, "it's so simple. It's like falling flat on your face to find you're stumbling around with a face full of floor. When you realize what's happened, you're down. We twisted to beam, our lights fell off the waves. That rogue, that damn monster wave came out of the sea. The *Faith* shuddered. She trembled like a small animal in the hand of a god."

I knew rogue waves can be found in any storm. They exist hidden in probabilities and possibilities, three or four times greater than any previous wave, deformed assaults of nature. This monster disregarded both expectation and imagination, arousing that most primitive of denial that "this can't be happening."

"The rogue came out of nowhere. Should've wiped the wheelhouse off the deck." Skeads studied his cigarette, perfect in form, and as if made by an artist.

I could see in Skeads' description this paranormal wave rolling out of the night and slamming into the *Faith*, knocking out the wheelhouse windows. Within that instant, in this unexpected defilement, the character of the boat shut down, and perhaps it was then that they, the crew, in the words of Mallary, "lost faith in the *Faith*."

14

I remember Skeads, sitting there at the table assessing his handcrafted cigarette, saying that by the time the skipper found his feet they all believed the sea had overcome them. It blasted the wheelhouse with the force of a shattered dam. The boat, on its port rail, struggled to right itself, only to have a second rogue wave roll across its entire length, smothering the engine exhaust ports, nulling the capacity of the crippled boat to breathe. The *Faith* was drowning.

A wave that buried them alive threw the crew from their bunks, the darkness wreaking havoc, havoc dispelling all the touchstones that make life explicable, the explicable redefined by dense chaos. Steering seized, radars and radios instantly shorted, the *Faith* disfigured to flotsam, to a piece of driftwood, to a tusk on a beached dead walrus.

No radio, no mayday.

"We were sausage," Skeads said, glancing at to his walrus tusk, meticulously placing the unlit cigarette on it. "Our tools turned to toys. We were headed for the bottom, trapped alive in our own tomb wandering to the center of the earth."

Skeads said something that would take on a darker meaning later. In our shared lives together, years later his statement would malice into a terror. That evening when sitting around the galley table of the *Faith,* he said, "I don't believe in God. But that night I saw the face of a cruel force. Better to believe in the cruelty of life than a sadistic god. But it don't mean nothing. If you live life long enough, it will take its revenge. That's what it's meant to do."

Skeads' testimonial seethed, the muscles in his face contorted, and even Mallary remained silent. None of us looked at him. I had never heard someone talk with this intensity, a quiet and respected man unveiling the moment when he saw the incomprehensible. I can see now, but not back then, this account was not about the storm Skeads endured that night on the *Faith*, but about something he saw

15

within himself, within his life. He saw something that night we avoided or were incapable of seeing. He saw in that endless night void a meaninglessness to life's core from which he could find no rescue.

The silence around our table became embarrassing for men living with indifference about anything beyond what we could see, grasp, and smell. It made Skeads different from the rest of us. He had experienced something beyond the senses.

While I sat in the galley listening to Skeads, it triggered the story when Saul stepped on the road to Damascus. The story of a spiritual revelation, divine light and spiritual intervention, and I remembered when I was a boy and still a believer, with the Sunday morning sunlight streaming through a window into a small room of children sitting in a circle, listening to the story of perhaps the most famous road story in history, a road story of a miracle. I can still remember wondering what such a miracle might be like. And years later, after seeing life refracted through a jungle, I recalled having been introduced to Caravaggio's *Paul on the Road to Damascus*, the saint flat on his back, the 3D illusion of the Apostle's head thrusting out of the picture toward me, his arms outstretched, and I, older, more skeptical, wondering if the sinner-turned-believer was blinded by the light of his God or was reaching out into terror, into a terror of an overwhelming void. But now, sitting around the galley table, hearing the engine rattle, listening to Skeads onboard the *Faith* failing to find the Apostle's transcendent light; instead, flooded by a great darkness, a spiritual inversion, and this metamorphic moment darkening him as surely as Saint Paul was graced, I realized that perhaps in that night, Skeads saw something more real than found in any nightmare hours, discovering not divine light but the vision of the eternal darkness that only prophets, seers, and the babbling insane experience.

Skeads continued. "When the rogue hit, our connection to

everything we trusted, disconnected. A lightbulb feeds the fantasy of our control over the sea.

"Our galley turned into a coffin. The sea turned into a beast so fierce it tore my soul empty." He stopped, searching for words, "I saw a force howling without the need of lungs, of air, of flesh." He looked around the table at us, and said, "I saw what waits on the other side as sure as you sit here."

Rantlings started to say something, but Mallary silenced him with a glance.

"The rogue tried to sink us, and the *Faith* defied it. She wanted to find her keel. Me ... I found my boots and, without thinking, pulled on another pair of long johns over the pair I was wearing. All instinct. I pulled a flashlight I kept under the mattress and opened the hatch. The sea fell down the stairwell with a lump behind it. It was the skipper gasping for air, tangled in a coil of line. He fell on me, his face bleeding from a gash across his forehead and a smashed nose. His gash grinned into the beam of my flashlight."

Skeads picked up his cigarette and with a steady hand put it between his pale lips. Years of use had rubbed down the chrome surface of the Zippo lighter to jaundiced brass. He placed two fingers on its lid, his thumb on its bottom, and quickly squeezed, their opposed friction snapped open the top. With another snap of his fingers against the striking wheel, the wick burst into a yellow flame. It was the only nod to theatrics I ever saw him exhibit. He continued. "Wronski, an able engineer, far more able than me, opened the hatch to the engine room, shined his flashlight down the stairs and entered into the center of a wound."

With Skeads words swirling in the cigarette smoke, "Hanging onto this table, the new crewman asked, 'Why are we laid over? What happened to the lights? There's something wrong?' None of us had enough hold on the situation to simply answer, 'We're going

17

down.'

"We were sure the *Faith* was sinking. Wronski poked his head out of the hatch of the engine room and pointed the beam of his flashlight into the galley. With bloodshot eyes jacked-open to where the whites glowed, he stammered, 'The engines are dead.'

"Maybe if we gave it five more minutes ... maybe ... had we stayed with her and waited for the engines to rest a little ... maybe. But life is all maybes." He exhaled, the dirty air swirling from his mouth as if his lungs smoldered.

"We abandoned what floated. That's it. Our guts seemed to demand it. We crawled into our life suits. We crawled out onto the deck. We crawled through the black night. We could hear the waves rumble across the deck, the surface of hell bound boiling cold. We grabbed the rail and tied ourselves together with the line that once coiled around the skipper. We deployed the life raft. I remember staring for a moment at the broken wheelhouse windows and their broken glass grinned."

Rapping his knuckles on the galley table, answering Rantlings' unasked question, Skeads said, "It's easy to judge being stupid. We sit here in the galley, and it's easy to believe ourselves smart. Hope gives courage to our arrogance. Arrogance gives faith to our illusions."

His experience held an authority none of us argued with, not even Rantlings. Skeads continued, "We climbed over the rail. The sea swallowed us like a string of sausage."

Skeads described how another wave rolled through, popped the painter line connecting the *Faith* to the raft, and buried their last hope that might protect them from the elements. He sipped his whiskey and again filled his lungs with smoke. "Once in the sea, the flashlights shorted. We drifted in the pitch black and became nothing

18

but voices with bodies settling quickly into silence. No bearings, no stars, no land. We drifted, in suspension. It was perfected terror. The new guy's lifesuit leaked. He babbled about his mother. He grew silent. He became a drogue. I cut the line off of him. The skipper prayed aloud only to finally cut himself free and drift silently away. Wronski and I stuck together. We waited for death.

"And then serendipity arrived. Fulfilling the forecast, the storm subsided, the sea turning into a heavy swell. It had taken half of the crew."

For some reason, I blurted, "Zemblanity. Zemblanity, not serendipity. Boyd, maybe Nobokov?"

Skeads stared at me. Mallary took a sip of whiskey, his baby-faced eyes steady in their wrinkled sockets. Rantlings listened.

Skeads finally added, "Call it malicious, call it feral serendipity. I knew I was going to die but wanted to live for just one more moment. To live in pain and fear is to live. I feared that night and what I witnessed in the galley more than I feared all ... creation.

"You don't need to see angels or a man walk on water to believe a miracle. Breathing is the miracle. Being alive ... the will to live. That's the miracle of all miracles. Even when life pulls those curtains back to reveal only an abyss, enigma, nothing. And in nothing, you still want to live, and that is the miracle lurking in your ... zemblanity, serendipity."

We sat around the galley table without saying a word.

In the north, winter light is born flighty, knowing it must expire in a few hours. It loiters more than prevails. I can't comprehend drifting alone in a stormy sea, suspended between dawn and sea. I don't want to comprehend waiting for the unintended consequences of hypothermic peace. Nature unearths cruel handiworks to murder us, but Skeads' and Wronski's physical endurance held off death.

19

Two men, tethered together in life suits, drifted side-by-each, and like an exhausted audience waiting for the night's macabre final-curtain, the dawn arrived introducing the vertical cliffs of black prehistoric rock rising like a fortress wall.

I wanted to ask Skeads what he had been thinking about, the expected cliché thoughts about whom he loved, or about his mother. Stupid. Any questions coming to mind seemed intrusive, voyeuristic, silly, particularly when asked of such an insular man. Regardless, he never mentioned anything about such human deathbed sentimentalities. After surviving hours in the sea, after cutting loose two still living crewmen, what that first manifestation must have been like when he appreciated current, wind, and luck, pushed them not to any sanctuary, not to a safe beach, but toward a more rude end.

A hundred yards off, emerging from the dawn like a sulking black-toothed monster, Skeads saw in the overcast sky the pure majesty of the island cliff, carved and jagged by eons of conflicting forces. For thousands of years, a sea had shattered its energies against the rocks in a crescendo of nature, a malevolent monophony in wait for the coda.

This power of the waves ignored gravity, taking the shore-break fifteen feet vertically up the volcanic cliffs to linger and dwell in a boiling crest to then collapse in undercurrent at the jagged base. Skeads and Wronski knew this was not their refuge, but another variation of suicide.

Another swell rolled under them, this wave revealing a ragged reef, an otherwise serrated contusion just beneath the water. If they hit the reef, it would shred them before even reaching the shore.

For more than eight hours, both of the men had survived the night in cold waters capable of shutting the body down in minutes. Even with the protection of the lifesuits, their endurance neared the impossible. It was here they parted company. Skeads cut himself loose from their tether and slowly began to back-stroke toward the shore. Wronski back-stroked away from the beach. They said nothing to one another; they had decided to die alone. Words seemed as absurd as life.

* * *

That morning, flying from the mainland, a bush pilot changed his usual course. Within this chance, he spotted an anomaly bobbing between the overcast gray horizon and the black morning sea. As he approached, his study of this irregularity changed into a black-hull vessel rolling around in the trough. He almost decided to ignore it and fly off, but curiosity inspired him to turn around and approach it again. This time he flew much closer, close enough to see who might be onboard. He saw no one on deck. He made a sizeable lazy turn and dropped lower, approaching the vessel from the bow to see if there might be a crew in the wheelhouse. No humans hailed him. He spotted the aft hatch open. The bush pilot radioed the Coast Guard.

Within a couple of hours, a Coast Guard helicopter lowered two rescue swimmers to the deck of the *Faith*.

Rescuers discovered an abandoned vessel. Waves slapped against the hull. In the trough, smelling of oil and salt air, the rig rolled gently. Entering the living quarters through the open hatch, morning light slipped in loitering in the corners. A seabird nesting in a bunk greeted them. Blinking, yawning, stretching its stubby wings and legs, it rose up, squawked, flapped its wings, and shot out of the hatch like a feathered missile, forcing one of the men to duck to avoid the bird's flight path. The rescuers laughed. One asked: "Where's the crew? That can't be the only crew on board?" Their dark humor echoed in the emptiness of the *Faith*.

In the engine room, deck plates lay scattered from the violence of the storm. Even with flashlights, like a dirty pond, sea in the bilges sloshed around. The men checked the battery connections and tried turning over the main engine to see if it might start. The engine turned but resisted firing. Finding some starting fluid, they sprayed it into the intake manifold, cranking it again. It belched and rattled until breaking loose from its limbo, and in its resurrection, kicked over, filling the vessel with life and hope.

While an intense search for the missing crew proceeded, by nightfall, the *Faith* was sea lore, tied to the transit dock of our island town.

* * *

At the galley table, after a long silence, after rolling another cigarette, Skeads said, "Wronski. When he untied himself and backstroked away mumbling a prayer. There wasn't enough life between us to make spit. But he didn't quit. He kept paddling."

Mallary closed his journal, Rantlings ignored his tattered and oily manual, and we all looked at the Skeads with his cards and walrus tusk cribbage board. Skeads smoked his cigarette, pouring a shot from a fresh bottle of the skipper's stash. With his hand-rolled cigarette, he continued the lifetime nightmare.

Skeads said, "Somehow I drifted over the reef. I lucked the wave right. I didn't want to die in the sea. Drowning never appealed to me. The cliff called me. The rising tide and swell lifted me, or, at least, what was left of me, so that I floated over the reef. Ten minutes earlier, I would have been cut into crab bait. But I drifted over the reef separated by inches as sure as a mile. Serendipity.

"Another set of waves pushed me toward shore and somehow rolled me up the face of the cliff and left me hanging onto an entrance to a small cave filled with nesting seagulls. The impossible happened. The gulls looked at me and then each other. I wanted to live a little longer and talk to the birds I believed had been expecting

22

me. They never stirred a feather. Impossible. Feral serendipity. Zemblanity. Perhaps my own insanity."

Skeads grew silent, took a deep breath, "I passed out, and when I woke it was night and Wronski stood over me in the cave smiling at me with what was left of a face. As real as any of you, I could see him like it was twelve noon. He was torn to raw flesh, and half his head was missing. I figured, at first, he gave up finding another landing, and turned around and followed me and hit the reef. There in the cave, he crouched beside me, no less or no more than any of you around this table. He sat down beside me, and we talked about life, about living. That maybe we had made it. Then he stood and said, 'Piece of cake. The hard part's over.' He walked off the cliff and into the night like he owned the universe, like it might be a stroll across a path made of clouds. I swear, he was in that cave with me as sure as any of you sitting around this table."

We didn't argue with Skeads vision. Thin is the line that separates a vision, a nightmare, a tall tale, or truth. Luck and happenstance dance together. A day later fishermen saw seagulls swarming in the air, cawing in chorus. With binoculars they saw Skeads crazy from hypothermia and thirst, hanging onto the side of an outcropping, licking the water off the face of the rocks, screaming into the sky. Skeads believed the gulls promised they'd find him rescue, this from the lips of a skeptical man. He believed it. We, sitting around the table, believing he believed. Who was I to question what he saw or heard, or any of us for that matter?

Rantlings raised his mug, "It's good to be alive."

Mallary poured a generous shot into his mug, pushed away his journal, saying, "I tell all that ghosts live. But wait a minute. That same storm the *Faith* survived by sturdy design and no help of the crew. That same storm that lifted my Skeadsman like a swaddled pup and involuntary swimmer of the sea, and then gentle carried him an impossible distance to save his body and soul from an unassailable Poseidon. A fact, we are incapable of seeing God's Plan. Ah-ha. To place my Skeadsman in one terrific and complete piece? Say not that a miracle. Ah, but poor Wronski, he disappeared forever. Tombed by the sea." His baby-blue eyes scrutinized Skeads as he added, "Now if a miracle is nothing more than a momentary and mysterious dismissal of my blessed Lord's laws ... by which, I might add we all are subjects ... this nature demands ..." He stopped.

Skeads looked over his drugstore reading glasses at Mallary, "Last spring, I read where a couple hunters found—just north of where I found shore—the ripped remains of a lifesuit. I tell you, Wronski made shore. But he also met at the same time and place a hungry bear taking a break from a winter's sleep."

Sitting quietly there in the galley, listening to this tale, I could imagine the other survivor, Wronski, struggling onto a safe beach, having bounced through a break in the shore, having crawled and clawed across the cold rocks and gray sand, to rest not unlike a piece of driftwood—or a walrus perhaps, taking that deep breath and treasuring the hope that rescue was possible, that happenstance and circumstance favored him. To only see the sleepy hairy predator seize him by the leg or head, to maul and drag him into the scrubby tree line, and end Wronski's adventure of a lifetime, his second shot at a precarious life, abridged to nothing more than a bear's winter snack.

Skeads picked up the cards, reset his pegs, and started shuffling. The starting position on the board was etched with a beached walrus with two tusks, howling in the sand and little comical x's over its eyes.

Skeads smiled, "When I returned to the *Faith* to clean it up, my cribbage board ... a bird had shit on it."

With that, as I recall, the conversation drifted away, and we

24

continued to search for the infinite halves remaining in a bottle of timeless whiskey.

* * *

I finished the season to wander out west to look for what I had not seen. About a year later, I returned. The rig I worked delivered to town and arrived early in the morning. Heading for Polly's Bar and Grill, I walked down the graveled and potholed cannery row, toward the town square and through dawn, a dawn gently balanced in the crisp air and sweet with those scents bursting from the sea and its salty affluence, and almost divine beauty. I walked with my youth, a wad of cash in my pocket, and on that day in love with the act of living. I sometimes now forget how terrific it was to be young. I wondered if the *Faith* might be tied to some cannery dock and if Mallary could still hear the haunting voices escaping from the hold. I definitely wanted to see Skeads. We had exchanged a couple of letters, unusual for fishermen. Somewhere in his past, he learned to write a decent letter.

Polly's was a terrific booze and food establishment. Fifty-nine minutes earlier, the noble bar had just closed to tidy herself from 23 hours of drinking and eating, to exhale the randy confluences of the previous day and night, to inhale a deep breath for the next day, to then open her doors for another morning of uninhibited drinkers. What a wonderful cycle. I entered into this bouquet of booze and tobacco and artificial light. I felt at home. At the bar, fellow fishermen sat like crows on a telephone wire. A silver fox fur coat wrapped around one of them who in the dim light read a natty journal.

The baby-faced man himself ruled like a prince on a throne, his blue eyes fixed and steady in their weathered sockets, his face burrowed into newsprint. By luck, an open stool waited beside him. I joined these brethren searching early morning booze-inspired

25

revelations.

Unnoticed, I slipped beside him, ordered a beer and a shot, and asked the bartender if I could order breakfast and if she had ever heard of an overdressed sort of fisherman named Mallary, a showboat sort, though in most ways, a singular guy.

She smiled. I realized only then, and I pretended not to notice, she was the mother of the 'new guy' who had abandoned the *Faith* and was lost at sea and never found.

Mallary's head remained fixed over the journal, but his right eye performed a ninety-degree avian pivot to see who might be the source of such a summary.

"If you care to check it," he said in his unique, raspy jargon, "I'm the one wearing the big-shot coat suitable for any able-bodied movie star." Within several more rounds, three eggs over easy, a pile of sausage gravy over a heap of hash browns—it was a time before cholesterol counted—we tallied months of adventures. Rantlings had moved up another rug on the ladder of success to a bigger and more modern rig. Skeads was now an engineer on the F/V *Ambrosia* and was setting up a herring operation.

I had not heard, but Mallary related how the *Faith* had suffered an engine failure in the straits on the other side of the island. Its inline diesel gave up for unknown reasons. A light storm and a full moon current had pushed the *Faith* to shore. While the crew tried setting both a sea anchor and the main anchor, neither found a holding bottom, and both dragged until the old loyal wooden boat nested hard aground. Kind and forgiving, the dependable old rig safely put the crew ashore. As Mallary waded through the freezing break, our baby-faced crewman related how he held high over his head the foxes he now wore. A week later another storm raged through. This storm pulled the *Faith* from the shore, burying her in the deep, in the forever. She, at last, joined the *Hope* and *Charity*.

26

Ruffling the collar of the soft skins of the dead foxes coddling him, his voice tense in his conviction, Mallary swore filthily. His troubled blue eyes rose from his newsprint, and flecks of spittle like sparks shot from his mouth. He cursed, saying, "With this furry testament of Rantlings' generosity raised high over my head, I slipped off her deck and waded through crying waves to shore. To you and all and in our Baby Jesus's name, I swear as true as midnight graves seethe in evil hours and where the dead breathe rank and foul, I heard the precious woman weep and her hallowed baby howl."

# Part II: Skeads, Neal and the *Ambrosia*

## Chapter 2: The Fishing Vessel, *Ambrosia*

Wanderers are both driven and drawn. It was not unusual to find wanderers roaming the docks during this part of the year, people between a job and an address, between the waypoints in life wherein people can find themselves. Often unaware of their exploration, they found in the outlands of the Aleutian Chain a haven, a quest for money, an adventure, an escape from themselves, and not a few discovered a refuge, a resolution in this cold, inhospitable territory. Our deck boss, Skeads, and I were no different from those fitting this description, except that we had a bunk on the F/V *Ambrosia*. He offered me a job. Without hesitation, I took it.

Before Neal ever approached the *Ambrosia*, you could not help seeing this strange young man prowling the docks, a shadow-man who seemed entirely banished, scurrying like a feral cat, approaching rigs, talking briefly to crewmen, then leaving without amendment to his destitute situation—finding a job. Like a gymnast, Neal was coiled and muscular. An unruly, dark brown beard bound his face and pushed towards his black-rimmed, military-style glasses. A matrix of scratches covered the lenses. These scarred disks framed strange blue eyes with spikes of gray, and his eyelids blinked so physically you thought you could hear them click. He rarely looked anyone in the face, preferring to look at objects behind you, at a place beyond your presence and to wherever he journeyed next. Like Skeads, when talking, he never raised his voice. Like Skeads, his eccentricities left him unperturbed.

With a duffle bag hanging off a shoulder, and his cheeks and forehead burned red by the wind, he drove himself like a blunt tool into the aloof cold with total indifference our winters offer. Our present skipper would be leaving soon for another rig, regardless, one afternoon invited this feral entity to eat dinner with us, but this stranger said little and returned to the docks to wander. For the days we were in Dutch Harbor (forty years ago a bleak place, at best), he never gave up shuffling across the worn, dirty, withering cover of snow. Where he slept was a mystery.

One day, as we untied from the dock and set course for No Cannery Bay, Neal appeared, threw his duffle bag aboard, and leaped onto the deck of the *Ambrosia*. The skipper had given him a berth. I suspect Skeads put in a good word. We later learned both Neal and the skipper shared time in the nuclear submarine service. There have been stranger tickets to a berth, and though he had no deck skills, he was hired to help cook and work on gear for what could have been no more than meals and a warm, dry place to sleep. Someone described him as "poor as Job's turkey." I've never heard that description since.

After a short passage, we anchored in No Cannery Bay, and the *Ambrosia* looked pleased with itself. Steel made up 90 percent of her character. She rested on the calm and blue-green water and cut a clean line. Its bright red hull ran ninety feet along the water, while its bow flared a good fifteen feet in a graceful arch and to a sheer that blended toward the stern and superstructure of the aft house. The boat looked built for hardy motion across the water. Mischievous, it seemed to be ready for life, desiring to break the anchor's hold to the bottom and head out, with or without us. The aft house rose more than twenty feet above the deck, with the wheelhouse raked slightly forward, giving the illusion of lightness; its bank of window gazed out on an expansive view of the work deck below. The boat possessed less the sense of a brute workboat than a strange form of privilege. Don't ask me to explain that—I can't.

We were the first vessel ready to buy salmon. The former skipper flew out, and we waited for the new skipper, Monroe, to arrive.

* * *

Pushed into a fringe of gray scrabble shoreline squatted a small village, a northern oasis of about two dozen single-story houses, weathered tough as driftwood by an indomitable chronicle of arctic winds, gasps of summers, and those short sighs of spring and fall. With the aid of binoculars and from the perspective of the *Ambrosia's* deck, the curious buildings that might be considered to represent civilized society revealed the dome and cross of a modest Russian Orthodox Church and the long shed of a cannery. The cannery shed proved the name on the navigation chart of No Cannery Bay a misnomer; if not, some unidentified cartographer's idea of a joke.

The morning breathed cold, clean and almost sweet. The sun had just appeared over the eastern side of mountains forming a protected anchorage. I can still remember being anchored on days like this because the harsh elements of both the fishing life and the abysmal weather seldom coalesced into pacific splendor; the memory of these rare conjunctions making gentle and beautiful touchstones too often forgotten or taken for granted. For as early as it was in our petite spring, the morning preened over the bay and village with its iridescent hues, painting a tentative faith that winter could feign occasional tranquility, if not artificial and temporary relief. In the distance, rising behind the village, a somnolent volcanic mountain hosted a few patches of snow hiding in the shadows of its treeless and lichen-covered moonscape. In the last week, on its ruddy skin, shrouds of browns and grays changed to blankets of emerald green. For those familiar with these seasons and their abrupt changes, it became merely the eternal ebb and flow of this extraordinary, brutal place. The suspended sun, not so much warm as empty of the vicious winter absolutes, saturated a sky painted with cobalt blues, and had Gauguin chosen the north to explore his vision

33

of color, I still wonder how he would have marveled at the light in the northern latitudes, how he might have painted a crazy, methed-out Borealis.

Five crab pots had been kept onboard and tied forward of the holding tanks. One was lying flat across two wooden crates, raising it about a foot off the deck so that it was easier to repair. The crab pots were constructed of a massive, welded rebar frame about seven feet square and better than three feet high. This frame surrounded and gave protection to a tarred nylon web, with smaller mesh entrances called tunnels designed to invite the crab to enter and eat bait hanging in the pot's center. After living life in the fishery, it seemed given how one omnivore can make its final exit as the food for another.

Three of us, Skeads, Falin, and I, worked on the crab gear, and Neal was in the galley cooking breakfast.

Skeads used a shuttle wrapped with tarred nylon line and re-wove the torn mesh along one length of the pot. He had pale skin with just a few weathered freckles. Though around thirty, he seemed aged beyond his years, his face something of a road map, lines censoring his eyes and high-ridged cheeks, with his rangy body of sinew and vein forming with no fat on his frame a musculature stretching from joint to ridge. His eyes, like a fighter's, were cold and without sympathies, but he had a restrained nature, the kind that when it does show irritation or anger, it's unexpected, focused, and could prove fearless. He was the deck boss and respected enough by the owners that they felt comfortable with him, would permit a day or two without a formal skipper. More than once he'd been offered the job, but for unknown, private reasons, turned it down. I think at the time, he found contentment in where he lived.

I repaired a pile of lines, cutting out the frays and splicing their running ends. Falin held a cup of coffee and leaned against the rail

34

looking across the bay. He looked like he might start helping in a minute or two. He was an exceptional deckhand, good-sized, and lean. Even after several months in the Bering Sea, he wore his dark hair stylishly combed, framing a clean, chiseled face ready to camera-joust with male models. He wasn't prim as much as conscious of style, a man aware of appearances and their significances. His thick turtleneck sweater could have been featured in an outdoor magazine but bore none of the coarseness imposed by this work or the fishery. His denim fit his torso a little tight for real physical work, suited more for a tavern line dance. Sporting Euro sunglasses, our fellow crewman had the look about him of taking a day off, the casual, the chic man about town, sipping a mug of java, waiting for the joy of life to mutually embrace hail fellows prepared for a "well-met" social bat of the breeze with his equals. In the still air, steam lazily rolled off the surface of his coffee cup, and he watched Skeads place another hitch into the panel of the torn web. Falin was a man satisfied with himself. For a time, I envied him.

"Man, wasn't this a great season? I never wanted it to end. A piece of cake. You know, this might be the easiest season in a long time." Falin scrutinized us over his coffee mug, waiting less than a breath for our negative reaction. From the opening day of any season a crab pot hits the water, an endurance-experience begins; from that instant, I think it's safe to say fishermen start looking forward to storing the gear and ending the season. This crab season had exhausted our collective mind and body.

Skeads, a self-taught man, a man who had a reservoir of words but reserved them, shook his head in quiet disagreement. When on the F/V *Faith*, teaching me the various forms of splices, he might have used ten words in explanation, instead of putting the line in my hands and silently correcting me as I learned the splice. The only time I ever heard him say much beyond telling a brief story or relating an anecdote was when the *Faith* still floated. But that was

35

the last he ever talked about that event in his life. He never talked about Vietnam.

"Come on Skeads," continued Falin, "We had days when you could confuse the weather report for Hawaii's ... sunshine on babe-filled beaches."

The five pots needing repair waited on deck. Without stopping his weaving, Skeads glanced up at Falin, then to the stylish turtleneck sweater. "Should drop another pot and get it ready?" The comment was less of a question than an invitation.

Falin replied, "Ahh ... right. Let me finish this cup of coffee. Those pots aren't going anywhere. Man, let me live in the moment. When's the new skipper coming in? You think he could find me a job further out west pulling another thousand pots? What you think, Skeady, you an' me pulling another couple of months' gear ... show these new guys how it used to be?" Falin looked at me when he referred to "new guys."

"Maybe," said Skeads. He changed the subject. "New skipper's supposed to be in today. Heard last night. On the radio."

Skeads finished repairing the panel of web and then inspected a tunnel for a hole. He sat on the edge of the pot and reached into to hitch it secure.

Falin took another sip of coffee. "Let's go ashore and check the place out?"

"Nope. The boat comes first. Got the forward hold full of lines that need repairs. Towns never change."

"When you figure that the season's going to open for reds?" Falin referred to red salmon that would be the season's opener. Skeads stood up and stretched a little. He looked at the shore, took a deep breath of the strong salt air.

"Don't really matter. We're ready. Need to take care of the gear, though." He looked briefly at Falin, tried to smile, but it withered. Returning his concentration to the pot, he inspected its lid. The hinge-lines securing it to the pot were frayed, and he cut them loose with his survival knife.

Falin peered into his coffee cup, "I'm going for another cup of coffee and see how breakfast is coming along. Neal will need help ... no doubt. Want anything?"

Skeads tried to smile again, but it lacked sincerity.

* * *

For a few days, we had been anchored in No Cannery Bay. Counting the passage, Neal had worked five or six days on the *Ambrosia*. Skeads was the first to notice that this quiet and strange man understood engines and pumps, bearings and drive shafts, and he intuitively and technically grasped all the thousands of mechanical parts keeping the *Ambrosia* making money and a crew from an unintended swim. In this mechanical world, this new crewman held an extraordinary competence. Whatever he experienced on the submarines, he had made part of his knowledge. Within those few days, the eccentric crewman, often muttering to himself, searched the holds and the engine room with unnatural energy and penetrating intellect and curiosity. It would be difficult to say if Neal adopted the *Ambrosia*, or if the boat had embraced him. This strange crewman devoured facts, the very nature of the rig, in the same way that a starving dog eats gratefully from any offered hand - or as we would discover later, how a lover embraces and protects his beloved.

Besides talking to himself and his nervous blinking eyes, Neal had two other strange behaviors. He appeared not to need sleep. For the first three days on board, he never slept. Instead, he studied and familiarized himself with the *Ambrosia*. The other trait that made him unique was his reading choices. Before television made its appearance on the boats, the entertainment center was a bookshelf and a deck of cards. On those days, we were anchored and hiding in the bays from the giant low-pressure systems falling off the ledges of the Arctic; we read detective stories and westerns; we read the great books. We even read the Bible. All these reads left behind by previous crews could be found on any given boat. Great writers waited on the unlikely bookshelves - a Tolstoy, a Ross MacDonald or Chandler, a Grey, or even a dog-eared Conrad, these thumb-worn old texts corroded by salt air and diesel fumes, these literary sweats stacked side by side, each awaiting the companionship of a crewman stretched out on a bunk beneath his reading light, lip-synching the words spilling out life and lives in unfamiliar worlds, worlds with resolutions often more forgiving than ours - all this couched in the soft roll of the rig and the immense relief of a quiet anchorage.

Skeads read them all when not playing his cribbage, and it was in the fishery I discovered his favorite authors, Farley Mowat and Melville (the delight of his unique voice), tucked together on bookshelves of the *Faith* and the *Ambrosia*.

But again, Neal was different. From Ketchikan to Adak Island, for relaxation and recreation, no other living soul in the fleet peered into a thick raggedy book of prime numbers or integrated calculus; no one contentedly chewed on the end of a wooden pencil while chuckling and communing with the symbolic nuisances. No one, that is, except Neal.

It left me curious, Skeads fascinated, and Falin, at first just shaking his head, saying, "The dude's weird."

Falin entered from the deck and poured himself another cup of coffee. Watching Neal destroy breakfast, he sat down at the table. If Neal might be nearer extraterrestrial, Falin was a firm terrestrial. Through gut-born instinct and neighborhood culture, he couldn't help but appraise Neal as a strange being in his homeland.

Our crew rotated cooking meals. This morning it was Neal's turn to cook, and he was turning breakfast into carnage. This unassuming mathematician and exceptional mechanic practiced the culinary skills of a lead in a chainsaw massacre movie.

Coffee, brewed by Falin (he would not let Neal touch even one ground of coffee), filled the air of the galley. A table built into a corner against the bulkhead was surrounded by shelves and cupboards for books and manuals. Hanging above the table was a thick plank of cedar with the name *Ambrosia* carved into the grain and brush-varnished to where it glowed. Its reflection grabbed the eye and was a work of great skill with its letters sculpted in a firm gothic font large enough to read from thirty yards. Some previous crewman had carved away much of his leisure time to make this homage to the rig. In a relief, the woodcarver left a knot in the board in the top right-hand corner, a relief cut into an illusion of an eye in perfect detail, painting the iris sea-green, the sclera a crystalline white, and the eyelid and its dark lashes such that you looked twice to see if it might not be real. This single eye was carved with such skill and illusion that regardless the perspective angle and plane from which it was viewed, it appeared to be looking at the observer like Mona Lisa's, only it was the *Ambrosia's*.

I entered the galley to get another cup of coffee and refill Skeads' mug only to find contents from the refrigerator lying like a shattered cornucopia across the galley countertops. Pots and pans and various kitchen utensils merged into chaos. Neal's meticulous skills in the engine room unhinged, spinning centrifugal in the galley. An egg had rolled off the counter, breaking on the light-green linoleum. With its bright yellow yoke nested near the broken shell and resting in a small pool of clear protein, it stared at the ceiling. Muttering to himself, Neal stepped vigilantly around it, as if squishing the egg would blind it. Strips of bacon curled, sizzled and popped on a seething griddle. An egg carton lay in the sink along with the gutted, greasy package of bacon. A bowl of leftover mashed potatoes rested nearby waiting incineration. With a fork, our chef de *Ambrosia* abused a pale yellow puddle of scrambled eggs. In another bowl, retrieved from shady corners of the refrigerator, ambiguous chopped up animal proteins and vegetables waited to be fired on a lethal skillet. There would be no sauté here.

Falin, the best cook onboard, saw half a dozen ways of doing a better job but enjoyed Neal's struggle. "What's up boss? Can I help clean up before you step in it?" He wiggled his finger at the egg on the floor.

Neal looked up and blinked in the direction of Falin, "What? Breakfast?"

"No. Egg. On the floor. It would be tough to step on the breakfast, though it looks like you're trying. You know, I wouldn't mind helping, but this experiment may be too far gone for help." Falin spoke easily about the meal. "You got any idea what you're doing?" He winked at me, smiled his beautiful smile, and leaned against the back of the padded bench.

Neal remained quiet, or maybe he was just oblivious. "I'm still learning," he said, his eyes blinking vigorously behind his scarred glasses.

"Kid, you got to have good humor when you got no idea what you're doing. But I got to admit, I've seen stranger things come up from the bottom of the sea than you." Falin dropped his sunglasses over his eyes and smiled at me again. I shrugged in agreement.

Cleaning the egg off the floor, I grabbed some plates and flatware. I still knew very little of our new crewman, and outside of passing introductions, Neal had said very little to me.

Falin continued to play the moment. "Let's give your breakfast a

40

name. Let's call it *No Cannery Bay Fry*."

"What? The eggs?" asked Neal.

Tweaking his sunglasses and giving me another friendly smile, Falin replied, "Yeah, Neal, the eggs. Who taught you how to cook? Hope it wasn't the guy who showed you so much about the engine room?"

"Taught myself," said Neal. "Eggs ..." He peered at Falin as if he were now trying to have a conversation. "... their character turns to different properties with very little heat or application. Almost pure ... I'm still learning. It's the beginning of life."

"That's an understatement. I'll pray for you and the guy who tried to teach you." Falin sipped his coffee.

With the bacon moderately carbonized, Neal moved it to the oven and scooped the potatoes into the smoking skillet.

"I'll tell you what ... next time you cook, I'll try to show you a few tricks."

I respected Falin, an intelligent man who could be impressive. He was an accomplished crewman and by family born into the fishery. He understood navigation and grew up with machinery, though it was one occupation he seemed to avoid. I suspected he knew his way around the engine room. I also noticed girls liked him, that he had an eye for them and they for him, and he dated beautiful women, all of which inspired envy in me. In those days, it was so easy to confuse envy with respect.

But his views seemed accurate about Neal. Our crewman was strange and was a stranger. Our crewman was an alien creature lifted from a different depth. In our atmosphere, he saw the light from our shared perceptions inversely, this foreign man perceived another world. He, too, wandered.

# Chapter 3: Culinary skills, eccentricity, brilliance

Even after forty years, I can still remember mornings anchored-up on some now-forgotten bay. I was stretched out in my bunk, semi-sleep, semi-awake, not unlike a drug-induced stupor, when my mind more than body sensed the vibrations solely from the diesel generator. I imagined, while in this semi-dream place, these tremors like the cadences of a heart, not the lump-thump human heart, but the racing heart of a small creature, a sparrow or a ground squirrel, terrified and trembling, its life seized in a fist.

Skeads heard seawater from the holding tanks cascading through the scuppers and back into the bay. A seagull cawed its place into the sky. To him, these sounds demanded only unconscious awareness, a white noise striking no pitch, but filled with a cadence, an order, producing contentment. The ancients woke to the quiet solitude of the earth, hearing their own thoughts long before the modern cacophonies of human inventions dulled the voices of nature. Skeads noticed these solitudes, these serene moments, and I would sometimes catch him listening.

A dissonance introduced itself. Skeads looked up from his work to search the horizon and found a floating speck within a slow and lazy circle framed by the cobalt blue sky. As it grew near, this speck loomed larger, forming into an airplane. Skeads watched and heard boisterous props pulling a stubby Albatross aircraft over the west end of the bay.

Rigged with pontoons for a water landing, the Albatross disproved any doubts that an absurd aeronautical design could play with the demands of gravity. Heading to the beach, it banked and dropped toward the bay. Its wings leveled and faced the light offshore wind. Leveling a few feet above the placid water, it yielded to this separation, bouncing twice and like a winged plow deceived into believing it could fly, cut a furrow into the water. Skeads murmured, "Only birds fly. We fake it," and returned to his work.

Less than half an hour later, with its two-stroke engine sneering and its hull slapping the water surface, a skiff approached, skippered by an Aleut impervious to the cold, wearing a tee shirt, Carhartt bibs, and a wool stocking cap with a black ponytail flapping from beneath its fold. The bow of the skiff gently tapped the hull. Skeads caught the line the operator threw, and two passengers climbed aboard.

The first man came aboard handcuffed to an aluminum briefcase raised high over his head like it might be more valuable than his own life. Two duffle bags followed. Skeads recognized the second man. Without saying a word, the operator retrieved the line, pirouetted on the kicker, and as indifferent to the cold as a caribou's hoof, skimmed away never once looking back, his ponytail bouncing behind his head in the wake of the wind.

They entered the galley. Falin stood up when the pair of strangers entered. The guy handcuffed to the aluminum briefcase wore a heavy coat over a flannel button-down shirt, and a pair of pressed khakis punctuated by hiking boots. All these apparel seemed to be experiencing the great outdoors for the first time. He sniffed the air, extended his hand to Falin and said, "Good morning. You the skipper?" His tone was abrupt, his words clipped, almost an interrogation, and without waiting for a response, he added, "I'm the buyer. Dan Phillips." He sniffed the air again. He raised the aluminum case anchored to his hand as if it would make its own introduction.

"What's that smell? What's burning?" Phillips asked. Falin seemed pleased with the mistaken promotion.

The other guy introduced himself to Falin, "I'm Monroe."

Skeads entered the galley and said, "Monroe. So, you're the new

43

skipper?" Monroe was as quiet as wallpaper, had dark hair, trimmed business-like, no beard, and wore spotless coveralls.

Monroe said, "Yeah, I'm taking a shot at the wheelhouse."

"You're ready as anybody," replied Skeads, and shook his hand.

"How about that. When flying out you never told me," said Phillips to Monroe.

Taking a deep breath, our new skipper looked uncomfortable, his social camouflage lacking the fine-tuning necessary to hide the illusions and delusions of his ambition. "I'm still getting used to the idea."

Without first unlocking the handcuff, Phillips tried to take his coat off. He looked to see if anyone noticed. We all did. He was not a man who laughed at himself. He unlocked his source of embarrassment, and wrestling with his coat, appeared close to being pinned. Falin jumped to the rescue and helped him off the imaginary mat.

Phillips reverently placed the case on the galley table, and with another key tethered around his neck, he unlocked and opened it so we could view his source of anxiety, or purpose, or perhaps the pair they formed. When we saw the briefcase's contents, we could understand his angst, for if this cargo had been lost overboard, he would have been better off going down with it.

Paranormal vibrations, in a manner greater than from *Ambrosia's* generator, set the contents squirming and throbbing into their moment of celebrity. With no doubt, we, gaping, as firm believers in Mammon—though Skeads seemed less interested—congregated rather than gathered around the galley table.

Inside the aluminum case, wrapped bundles of cash snuggled with the intimacy of a starlet spooning her producer.

Neal heard the silence and suspended his torching of breakfast. Peering around Skeads' shoulder, he murmured, "Gosh." Neal never cursed, but took another involuntary breath, repeating, "Gosh. How much is there?"

"Three hundred and fifty thousand," whispered Phillips. A small handgun nestled on top of the cash. As an aside, the *Ambrosia* was loaded with several heavy pistols and scoped hunting rifles capable of hitting a heart at a thousand yards. Now, the rig's arsenal hosted a peashooter, though nonetheless deadly.

Phillips added more plasma to pulse our piety to Mammon. "It seems several buyers over the last few years failed to honor their checks. So now we're paying in cash. It will be interesting by the end of the week how much money will be floating around in this bay. Enough to finance a revolution." He chuckled, and his cheeks and shoulders shook in unison.

Falin guided our guest to a place at the table. "Hey Neal, let's get out some plates and eat breakfast. Sorry about the meal," he consoled our guest, "but Neal's still learning how to cook." Skeads and I served the food. The galley smelled like we might have just put out a grease fire.

We sat down to breakfast, munching without complaint based on the code that he who complains—cooks. Neal's meal endorsed the stoic dictum that one should eat to live, rather than live to eat.

The table conversation never left business. Phillips said, "The early salmon are running east of here, and I expect any day for a price to settle. It will be fast and furious. The boat ready?"

Monroe and I looked at Skeads, but Falin in the excitement of the social occasion answered, "We can be ready. No problem."

We sat around the galley table. With his fork, our guest picked out what resembled once edible calories. Pushing and adjusting these to the rim of his plate, he took a skeptical bite from the opposite side of his plate. As Monroe remained quiet and ate, Falin salvaged the breakfast by keeping Phillips in small talk about life in Vancouver. Adjusting his sunglasses resting on his combed hair, he crafted the conversation well. Skeads ate silently, and Monroe, our new skipper, listened.

Skeads pointed upstairs to the wheelhouse and said, "Your bunk's topside." It was the only thing he said to Phillips, letting Falin do all the talking.

"We can't have problems," said Phillips. "This must be all high-quality product. The roe is going to Japan. Its profit margins are better than cocaine." He smiled and looked around the table for effect. Falin smiled. The reference glanced off our sophistication, though in future years the allusion would find significance. "The salmon is gourmet-pack for France." This reference we understood.

The plan was for the *Ambrosia* to deliver to a cannery in Canada, requiring a passage down the coast. When considering it in terms of time and distance rather than unintended consequences, this passage seemed dressed in the casual fashions designed for a pleasure cruise.

Falin said, "I'll cook this afternoon." With his white teeth sparkling, he owned the gift of familiarity, as if he had known the buyer for years. Falin enjoyed that knack of never having met a stranger. He smiled at Phillips. "Here, let me get your stuff," and slipping out from the table he grabbed Phillips' bags, for some reason ignoring the new skipper. Falin and Phillips made fast friends. For the few days Phillips was onboard, Falin cooked. No one complained.

* * *

The seiners arrived. The tenders arrived. The salmon danced in

46

a huge ensemble, returning from their ocean cycle, a raw, obsessed resolution of nature reconnecting to their birthplace of No Cannery Bay. I can still recall, after decades, the miracle of the run, of this being, of this entity, of this force. They had been returning like this before markets existed, before money, before humans had invented a net or hook, before our ancestors had even painted a cave wall. Like flashing strikes of lightning through the cold dark waters, tens of thousands of salmon returned from the ocean, slipping beneath the hull of the *Ambrosia*. While we played the role of predators and masters of the universe, we peered at the massed schools of salmon racing with beautiful energy to breed and die in the frigid waters of the river. To us, pieces of silver.

Skeads had five years of tendering seasons behind him, and this depth of competence made our operation smooth. He had shown Neal how to seal off the tanks and make the brine with bags of salt to lower the freezing temperature of the seawater. This brine recirculated in a closed system with the refrigeration pumps taking the brine without freezing down to 32 degrees Fahrenheit, a temperature necessary to maintain optimum quality for the fish.

Day and night, Phillips unloaded his briefcase of cash to the fishermen as they emptied their catch of salmon into the bowels of the *Ambrosia*. Late into the evening, the sodium vapor lights burned a bright white, turning the deck into a stage, abstracting the fishermen into shadowed players dancing free-form across the screen of night.

Neal's gifts stood out. His ability to absorb information, details, systems, was extraordinary, truly beyond comparison. In mechanics, he was smarter and quicker than any of us. He checked the pumps circulating brine through the refrigeration chillers. It was critical to keep brine within two degrees of optimum temperature. More than just familiar with the machines, he understood the principles behind them. The process of learning appeared unnecessary. I wish now that

47

I had the gifted ability, the talent, that bizarre a priori, no different than breathing, no different than how the salmon run. He was one with the *Ambrosia.*

Falin, with incredible skill, used the crane to load the brailers of salmon like it might be an extension of his hands. I tried to learn this skill from him, but I lacked experience and the nuances requiring months to get to half his ability.

This primordial hunt ignored time and fatigue. Above No Cannery Bay, heavy dark clouds crowned the peak of the sleeping volcano. Dimpling a bay as flat as a cast iron skillet, a cold drizzle fell on us and the frenzied commerce beneath the mountain's gaze. The overcast might break up, and with a little imagination, you could see faces and figures shaped and shifted in the clouds. The ancients must have observed this, their subconscious mind in an endless search for form and order.

We lived life on the edge of a rational and profitable universe.

As can and should be expected, something unintended occurred. A hydraulic line on the crane ruptured. Though it was Neal's first shot at such a task, Falin stood on the sidelines and watched. And strangely, so did Skeads, but Neal repaired the line with the sureness of a man who had done it a hundred times.

Within two midnights, we loaded more than three hundred thousand pounds of salmon into the tanks of the *Ambrosia,* the hatches secured. Phillips made his exit on the morning Albatross. "Take care," he said. To Falin, he added, "Good luck. Let's get together in the city; I'll show you the town when you get in."

Though four in the morning, Monroe pulled anchor and headed from the bay for our town, our first stop before Canada.

Recalling and considering this journey decades later, the friction between Neal and Falin had started beneath our noses, and our failing to see it, or worse, our avoiding it, proved tragic. An event as simple as the repair of a hydraulic line set the conflict, and though it produced no smoke at this point, it began to scar their opposed surfaces. Falin could not abide by a stranger. Neal had no idea he was part of a process. However, as Skeads cryptically would later say, "We're all too proud of ourselves."

# Chapter 4: Complications

Weaving slowly out of No Cannery Bay, Monroe guided the *Ambrosia* between the anchored seiners and through a quiet labyrinth. Waiting like hunters hungry for dawn, the boats were floating shadows leaning against the night. Mist struggled to turn into rain.

In the dark wheelhouse, the hood was off the radar, and the cursor swept in silent circles across a pale green screen showing squiggles and blips of the land mass surrounding our course. Dials on the console glowed red, and between these two sheens, they cast Monroe's smooth face with surreal patinas.

Falin stood beside Monroe talking about getting back to town and how well we handled the salmon. In the darkness of the wheelhouse, he was merely a thick outline. Jubilant, he said, "The boat performed well. Good job, Skipper." He couldn't find enough compliments concerning the buyer, Phillips, "What a great guy. A real heavy-hitter. That guy's got some ideas on how to make money." He patted Monroe on the back, and our new skipper seemed to appreciate the reinforcement.

Another voice entered the dark. You could hear Neal climbing up the ladder to the wheelhouse, talking more to himself than anyone else. "I pulled the filters on the chillers." He held a baking pan containing a refrigeration filter that had been cut in half. "Been checking them, and I don't understand why there's reddish powder in them. They're some kind of ..." In the meager light, Neal raised his reddish-brown smudged fingers. The fine particles were like red talc. The words could have been expressed by anyone in the darkness, but when uttered by Neal, an ordinarily muted crewman, from him the words were the equivalent of a dissertation. No one replied.

As we pulled from the bay, it had felt like a done job, but in reality, the unintended business had just started. Neal became a messenger. While we were sane men and cynical of omens, we had yet to understand what the fine power meant. The residue on Neal's fingertips would flatten any bubbles of a champagne voyage to Canada.

Our strange crewman had read the manual on refrigeration as if it might be a chapter out of the *Ambrosia's* memoir, and he listened to the rig as if its sounds and movements were the murmurs and stirrings of a living creature.

"Powder?" Monroe poised the first question.

"Yes, like the color base artists use for acrylics."

"Acrylics?" Monroe found a question for every response of our impromptu engineer, and every answer rutched into another unrehearsed question. Our skipper had yet to appreciate Neal.

"Yes, like what you use in paint, like for a picture on a wall," Neal blinked and looked towards the skipper, his focus about a foot behind Monroe's head.

"So, you're saying that our filters are forming a pigment?"

"Yes. No. Not exactly. Maybe catching one." Neal seemed animated, also thrilled, and began asking questions more of himself than of us. "But, where does that stuff come from? It can't be natural to be there? There's nothing in the troubleshooting section in the manual." The darkness etched a vague outline of our engineer's face, and his glasses intermittently caught a little green or red depending on the radar cursor's sweep and how he turned his head.

Falin had stopped talking about getting to town and said, "Hey kid, you're not natural. What do you know about what's natural?" He laughed easily, a man who enjoyed a good laugh regardless of the humor.

As though Falin didn't exist, Neal ignored the comment and continued, "So far the chillers seem to keep the brine at the right temperature. I guess you could say that nothing's broken."

Falin said, still finding humor, "You keep seeing gremlins and sure as sunshine you'll talk to them. You're not going to cook up that filter for breakfast are you?"

"Have you talked to Skeads?" asked Monroe.

"Yes. He wanted me to talk to you. He's finishing up the deck. He's not sure what's going on."

"Well. All we can do is keep an eye on it." Monroe checked the radar screen as we cleared the bay, stood over it as if studying a crystal ball, then added, "We'll have the cannery techs take a look at it when we get into town."

Falin could not stay out of the conversation. "What do you know about refrigeration that Skeads doesn't?"

Neal replied, "I'm not sure about anything. I know a little about atmosphere control on a submarine. The brine is a different atmosphere, but it's still an atmosphere."

"So, you're saying that brine in the tank is the same as air?"

"It depends on your needs. I'm saying they're related. Connected."

"So, salt water and air are the same?"

"Maybe not to us humans, but ..." Neal was solemn and quiet. He'd been on the boat for a couple of weeks and maybe smiled once, and this was a long conversation for him. For him, the conversation lay within his element.

"They share certain natures." Neal's voice complemented the blurred lines formed by the darkness inside the wheelhouse, lines rendering solids obscure profiles. "*Ambrosia* talks to us if we listen.

52

Everything has its voice. Even if we don't know exactly what she's saying ... a wordless communication. She's talking to us. How we listen...."

Because we were blind and deaf, we were unable to consider it at the time, but Neal could see in his mind the language of the machinery, hear the vibrations of the *Ambrosia*, and later would see in his book of math the writing being written across the rig's steel bulkheads. Never understanding his inscrutable world, I failed to appreciate Neal's ability to see unique abstractions nonetheless concrete.

Skeads saw this singularity from the beginning. He could appreciate in Neal, the peculiarities in the man, and how our strange engineer could see through time, through the past and the present, weaving these insights into a future. Falin turned to Monroe, shrugging, granting his confident smile. "You know he don't make no sense."

Skeads had entered the wheelhouse and overhearing Falin, replied, "Don't mean that he's wrong."

"Well." Monroe shook his head like a stymied student overwhelmed by a conundrum before his professor. "We have the right water temperature now. Keep an eye on it, and we'll get it checked out on our way through town."

Falin shook his head and said to Neal, "You have no idea what you're talking about. You're nuts." At the time, we didn't know it, but the former observation was inaccurate, but the latter prescient. We never doubted that maybe we were irrational.

* * *

Between the two main diesel engines, more than 900 horsepower produced incredible noise, shaking the brain in its socket. In this environment, Skeads would find Neal oblivious, in his

53

own world, inside the bowels of the *Ambrosia,* communing with an engine manual on his lap, or tracing out the electrical, hydraulic, and plumbing lines like they were arteries, ganglia, a pulsing creature of steel and technology. Neal obsessively cleaned tools that might have but a speck of oil and dirt, placing them carefully back into their drawers and shelves. Our deck boss, Skeads, let him run free, trying to answer what questions he could, but the obsessive and remarkable new crewman continued to absorb knowledge in greater amounts to anything we in our lives had experienced. It was unnatural. Skeads would shake his head, the skeptic in him fixing his face, but he still enjoyed their talks about salinity or torques, flow rates, foot-pounds, and operating temperatures of engines. However, Neal was beyond our league; in any given space we might notice five qualities, he would see twenty.

Trading off wheel watches, we had slept through the morning and the afternoon and the night. Sleep, an interest taking second place to work when loading the *Ambrosia*, became an addiction after three days of its absence. When the hope of this attractive opportunity arrived, the craving became drug-like. When this corpse-like state arrived, when lying on your arms, the weight of your body would numb them, and the pain would wake you to find your limbs aching and your pillow damp from your drooling mouth. You'd stir, interrupting this un-world enough to roll off your arms and plunge back into the muddled labyrinth. But work would consume your dreams, appearing like a silent movie flicking across the mind, framing the life lived in a moment on a boat and on a sea. In these flash-images, the exhausted mind watched surreal brailers rise from the ghostly salmon boats, swing across the rail and with the burst of a million fish disappear into bottomless holds and evaporate into the abyss, leaving only the frustration that your efforts meant nothing.

A need to relieve myself broke my sleep, forcing me to visit the head. In the galley, a single light shined over the table. Playing

54

without conviction solo cribbage, waiting unconvinced for more sleep to arrive, Skeads sat beneath the light over the table. Now awake, I decided to stay up, doodling around with little conviction for cleaning the refrigerator.

Falin climbed down the ladder from the wheelhouse, interrupting our shared solitude. Entering the galley, he turned on all the lights and refilled his coffee cup. He looked at me and said, "You know, you do good work. I like working with you." Sunglasses rested on his nest of dark hair.

He glanced at Skeads. "Skipper's got the wheel for a minute. How's your card game going?"

Skeads replied, "You can't win when you play against yourself."

"Stack the game if you have to. Winning is everything. Who in their right mind wants to lose?" He paused for a minute, whether it was for effect was hard to tell. "We got one loser here. That's for sure." He took a sip of the coffee, and I'm not sure if he asked me or told me, "You made the coffee? Did good." Then returned his attention to Skeads. "Is the zombie still asleep?"

I couldn't help thinking about what he might be saying about me behind my back.

Skeads remained silent and shifted two cards in his hand. "He's forward, looking at the chillers."

"Have you taken a look at them? You hear what he was saying to Monroe when we pulled out of No Cannery? I mean, what does he know? Who says the filters aren't doing their job? He even says he can't find nothing wrong. They're 'talking' to him."

Skeads placed his cards face-down and looked at the sunglasses resting on Falin's tossed hair.

"Moon must be awful bright off the water." Skeads stretched by arching his back. He started rolling a cigarette.

"I forgot they were even there." He pulled them off his head, folded the temples, and hooked one of them on his neckline. "I don't get him. Hell, is there anything to get?"

"Get who or get what?" asked Skeads.

"Where'd he come from?"

"If you're talking about Neal, I don't know. Mars? Out of a bilge of a submarine? Where did you come from? Considering the alternatives thirty latitudes south of here, this is an edge of the last place any normal person might want to find a future. Or, it might be the last chance. Besides, who wears swanky sunglasses on top of their head?"

Falin nodded in agreement, "You got me there." He slid behind the table and leaned over it, resting on his forearms, "When this guy sleeps, he's like a zombie. We all sleep hard, but there's something wrong with him. Hell to pay, has he slept since we left? You could set him on fire, and he wouldn't wake up."

Skeads studied Falin. "On fire? I wonder how many BTU's you can get from that experience?"

Falin ignored the question. "He lacks the experience to be in the engine room ... by himself."

Skeads replied, "Maybe. He seems capable to me. Let it be. He's smarter than me and you combined." Skeads put the unlit cigarette between his lips. He only smoked on deck. "Well, maybe not as smart as you. But it's my responsibility ..." Skeads leaned back and waited as if it might be a card game, or maybe staring at a pair of sunglasses, "... unless you want the job?"

With his great teeth, Falin smiled like a model in a magazine,

"No. Of course not. You know I trust you and your judgment. You've paid your dues."

Leaning on the table and again lowering his voice, Falin replied, "I've got nothing against him. He's a good enough guy, only he has no business being on this rig. This rig's too good for a guy with his little experience. He just showed up. That loony heard about us and just showed up. Nobody even knows who this guy is."

"You seem to know a lot about him. How? You never seen him in your life," replied Skeads.

"Yeah, well, I've checked around. It's kind of my responsibility to my uncle."

"Uncle?" asked Skeads.

"Yeah, my uncle owns part of this boat."

"I see." Skeads smiled, and his washed-out face opened enough to show those tobacco-veneered teeth.

Falin sat silently sipping his coffee. "What do you think of the new skipper?" He studied Skeads' road map face, a face that collapsed into its pale folder.

"What is this? Twenty questions? What kind of skipper Monroe will be ..." He stopped and looked at his cards on the table, "What kind of skipper you'll be, or anybody will be only time knows." The cigarette wiggled between his lips.

Falin replied, "Truth is, I make no apologies for my ambition. I'm going to run a rig someday. I'm not going to sit here and work on deck until my teeth start to fall out of my face and I'm so busted and bent over I can't walk without staring at cracks in a sidewalk. I tell you what, when I'm a skipper, I'd hire you in a minute. But Neal is another deal. You know it. He doesn't fit."

Falin paused, crafting his next words, "Truth is, you should be

57

the skipper. You know it. You should feel downright offended. Why, it's disrespectful for you to be ignored. I ought to tell my uncle about it. You got more talent than anyone on board." He cocked his head a little, looking from under a ledge of groomed eyebrows, waiting for a reaction from Skeads.

Skeads' reply came measured like his words had been taken apart, reshuffled, and dealt again. "I'm not sure you're bullshitting yourself more than me. It don't really matter. I will live with my own failures. I'm content where I'm at, my place. But I'll standby Neal as long as he's trying. I suggest you leave the guy alone."

Skeads took a long drag off the unlit cigarette and started to fold his cards together. You could smell the tobacco reeking off his clothes and body. "But I guess that pretty well states your call. Leastways, nobody can say you don't have one." Weariness clouded his Skeads' face. "I'm ready for a smoke and a good sleep. Anything is better than this. If you can make it more perfect, go the head on. Then again, you're free to leave when we hit the dock. I'm not leaving, leastways, not yet. Neal's okay in my book. But then again that don't mean nothing neither. I suspect he's never hurt a fly. With any luck, he never will."

The galley seemed quiet even with the engines rattling below us. I had pulled a jar of mayonnaise from the refrigerator and cleaned the threads on the cap as if this con dodged playing in the conversation while still remaining a player.

Falin glanced at me and then to Skeads, "Any way you want to make it, we got a fruit cake who thinks the boat talks to him, mumbles to himself, sleeps like a dead monkey. We got a greenhorn skipper who doesn't have enough confidence to walk across the deck without a chart. You know it. You seen it. In No Cannery Bay, Monroe was lost, and I tried to help Neal. I tried to teach him the crane, and he was a disaster."

58

This again was accurate. Falin had tried to teach Neal the crane, skills in which Falin excelled. In unskilled hands, it was a monster. In the wrong hands, hydraulics and steel turned lethal by the equal pressure given to a piano key. Feather touches of the levers required both knowledge and intuition and concentration crafted from hundreds of hours of work. Calculations in the mind of the operator could easily become miscalculations tearing off a leg or arm like a plucked piece of lint. Falin had stood beside Neal acting the mother hen, and his student had severe difficulties. At least, when Neal was cooking, only indigestion could result.

"You know what could be the problem?" he whispered to Skeads but loud enough for me to hear, "I heard ... I got a real fear he's a cokehead. You know that's why he can work the way he does and sleeps like he's brain dead. You've seen it."

Putting his cards in their sleeve, Skeads folded the conversation and slid out from behind the galley table. When he stood up he looked down at Falin and studied him, holding his gaze for what seemed a long time, he said, "I don't like you. I've worked with a lot who I don't like, but it seems important I tell you. Don't take it too seriously. In the long run, sooner-or-later, it don't mean nothing."

I pretended not to hear anything and finished cleaning the refrigerator. Silenced, Falin sat for a while longer. Skeads' gaze never left Falin's face, and then he said, "I've had my fill of suits preaching facts, lying to themselves for themselves, turning what little truth might exist to kill zones. If you can, try to remember there's no kind of good found in this. Leave it rest."

I turned around when he said this and noticed the sign of the *Ambrosia*, and that eye carved of a knot shifted.

# Chapter 5: How we dance and drink

By midmorning, we were pulling into town and expecting anything on the hard and somewhat civilized ground to provide relief from months of work. Monroe headed the bow of the *Ambrosia* toward the dock, took the rudder hard to port, reversed the engines for a few seconds to slow us, and setting the engines to idle, used the current to push her 500 tons to the pilings. In this management of the rig, we could see he was getting a feel for her.

With the long winter behind us, the hope of spring cheered us. Above our town, ascended another sleeping volcano, not unlike No Cannery Bay, and like a pyramid built by gods, it crowded the sky with its summit lost in the thin unthreatening gray cloud cover. Though first impressions encourage false positives, inside the body and mind, you can feel a strange sense of deliverance when arriving into the arms of an outpost of civilization.

In the background, a two-story cannery loomed, and a couple of forklifts rumbled around the dock. Two young women waited in the foreground. How they knew we were pulling in at this precise time seemed unusual because Monroe had called only the manager at the cannery. But there they stood, in stark contrast to one another. One with her face featuring an exotic beauty, a little dark, native twice or three times removed but bred and charmed into her features the islands, the aboriginal and the Anglo. Like cuts of black diamond, her eyes flashed in the morning light. A billowing collar of silver fox fur coat framed her countenance, and columns of the luckless creatures cascaded down her body. She ruled the austere dock like a Siren of the lost heart.

Beside this northern goddess, stood a cannery girl with a dark round face, a round nose, her round dark eyes fixed on Neal. She dressed like a field soldier with a blue knitted watch cap, an olive drab military field jacket, and olive drab cargo pants tucked into military jungle boots. Native to the blood and stoic to the bone, in her military haute couture she appeared exfiltrated from an island garrison more remote than Cannery Bay—straight from a world subsisting on a couple of island freighters a year. My imagination could see her eating with little complaint, perhaps contentment, seal and dried fish all winter long. A wispy little thing, innocent and simple, she gave a shy smile, the waffle soles of her jungle boots planted on the edge of the fish dock.

"There's my baby." Less an observation than an ovation, Falin shouted to the girl in the fox fur coat. At these words, a black leather glove peeked out from the furry sleeve and waved slowly. Faint, cool, understated, her smile appeared with a hint of perfect radiant teeth. For some reason, I thought of a perfect martini, chilling and inviting and floating on the surface of an exquisite glaze of flecked ice summoning the palate.

The cannery girl smiled without parting her lips, embarrassed even to stand on the dock, an improbability wedged between awkward apprehensions. Raising a bare hand briefly, this gesture disappeared as quickly.

Visibly brightened, pleased, blinking profusely, Neal returned her smile and waved awkwardly, looked at Skeads and me and seemed embarrassed, as if this manifested a fleeting unexpected mystery.

From the second floor of the cannery, a round and clean-shaven man with a fringe for hair poked his head outside a window and waved, pointing at Monroe in the wheelhouse.

Monroe was the second to climb onto the dock and head to the cannery office. Falin, a leap faster, had embraced the fox, their synergy like two elemental forces colliding into a furry singularity.

The cannery girl waited, with her hands holding one another in front of her until Skeads motioned her down to the deck. Neal seemed unsure if he had the authority. Agile as a wharf cat, she climbed down the vertical ladder hanging from the dock.

Skeads and I left Neal with his friend on the boat, and we went to buy groceries. Not without a little self-interest and a minor detour, Polly's Bar and Grill happened to intersect the means of the cannery and end of the grocery store.

Polly's still provided a refuge for wanderers and uninhibited drinkers. Without windows, this retreat lived its life in artificial light. Obscurity bonded with the smoky air to craft what a more hip society might discerningly describe as "inverted-ambiance." Our eyes took a few moments to adjust. Smoke congealed around table lamps, their timid yellow light fearing the black holes in the corners waiting to absorb their essence. Immediately on entering, Skeads lit a hand-rolled cigarette, the flame from his Zippo yellowing his pale skin.

Falin was already having lunch with his silver fox. On a leash, like a portico statuary, a long, slinky dog with a long snout and longer hair, spread its considerable length beneath their table. Together, they formed an enviable trifecta. He waved us over— Falin, not the canine lounge lizard—and with his usual triumphant attitude, he motioned in a sweep of his hand that we should have a drink with them.

Which we did. All the tensions which can exist on a boat during the long season discharged with the first sip. Falin's friend—he didn't introduce us—granted us her eyes, unveiling a faint, distant smile on her lips; her body subtly shifted inside the folds of fur. He, with his sunglasses riding on wavy hair, she, with her arresting arctic beauty, they conjoined into a nonpareil couple that at the time confirmed the aphorism that the grass can be greener on the other side of the universe. Not to mention—or at least as an aside—I silently asked what kind of nature blessed Falin with such good fortune but then spited with a galactic disregard—Skeads and me? What insights blessed her to appreciate his astral endowments, while we, as mere mortal space cadets, muffed it completely? Regardless, Skeads appeared indifferent, not one flicker of interest coming from his washed-out eyes. I then noticed sewn into the shoulder of the coat the head of the dead fox with its two ebony eyes eyeing me in a steady and paranormal stare.

"Man. It's great to get off the boat for a while." Falin reached under the table and held her hand and seemed genuinely pleased and fortunate. "You know? It's been 99 days."

Skeads took the drink, replying, "Better than 66." He turned on his silence and said nothing more.

I thanked Falin for the drink, and Falin's girlfriend turned her head, her black hair shifted and shimmered, her raptor eyes flashed, and her lips brushed his smooth cheek. She glanced at me, and for a moment I thought her eyes vulnerable, that I could see a young girl playing a role, but it disappeared.

The eyes of the fox head sewn into her collar changed and twinkled in the unnatural light.

I felt vulnerable, needing to say something but ended up mumbling, "Thanks." Under the table, I petted the dog who had rested his head on my lap and seemed to appreciate my attention.

"I'll get down to the boat, but ..." Falin looked at his girl, "we need to make up for lost time." He smiled, and across his lips and eyes, you could see embedded an uncharacteristic humility and appreciation.

The cannery manager appeared at the table, and Falin introduced us. We shook hands. "Skeads is one of the best I've worked with," Falin said, adding, "This is my uncle."

"Keep your seats," he said, then turning to Falin, "We'll talk later." He familiarly nodded to Skeads and moved to another table.

Our conversation flapped around for a few minutes, mostly about fishing, and it ended when Falin said he would return shortly to the boat. The fox looked into the back of our skulls and gave another smile reminding me again of flecks of ice floes shimmering on a martini. Skeads and I both knew this meant in several hours, odds-on when the *Ambrosia* was pulling away from the dock. The dog raised its shoe-shaped head, slobbered on my hand, gazed at me with its big brown-lashy eyes, and said, "Woof."

We excused ourselves to give them their privacy, or publicity, or both, and we sat at the bar for one more. We bought doubles to steady our nerves for the rigors of grocery shopping. It turned into another round enriched into a buzz invisibly working its magic, reaffirming it was good to be alive.

During our second double, from one of the black-hole corners, a lanky man emerged wearing insulated coveralls and a red storm of a beard. He lumbered across the worn dark carpet to greet Skeads. This stranger gave me a nod.

"Haven't seen you in months. Got time to play a board or two?" He referred to cribbage, as Skeads was known as a money player who gambled for big stakes.

"No, not this time. Maybe when I get back."

"Yeah, I heard you have your hands full. Are you looking for a crewman?" The eyes above the rangy face looked like they expected an answer.

Skeads' eyes tightened a little, and a suspicioned tone in his voice loaded rather than an answered a question. "What do you mean by that?"

64

"I heard you got some crazy who's screwing up your refrigeration."

"Interesting," replied Skeads, "Where'd you hear that?"

"Naw, it ain't important," his watery eyes hovering above a moonscape nose, "I don't want to spread any crap around if it's not so. But you're not looking for a crewman?"

Skeads replied that we had a sound crew. I shrugged, gesturing something to the same effect.

Still wanting another, we finished our shots and went to the grocery store. There, yet another fisherman came up to Skeads, this time asking about Monroe. "I hear he's having his problems?"

"Not so," replied Skeads, "he seems capable and's getting his feet under him." A big endorsement from somebody like Skeads, as he kept his own counsel when there was nothing good to say and handed out fewer compliments.

The source of this gossip remained our mystery. We both knew that we were not the cause, and it seemed unlikely Falin could not have sown such seeds this fast. Regardless, the seeds of weeds are meant to grow.

After buying groceries, we stopped again at Polly's to see if it was still there. The faithful old place had not moved. After another round, we walked back silently through the town on the rutty cannery road to the *Ambrosia*. The delivery truck with our groceries arrived as we climbed aboard. Neal shared a sandwich with his friend, and together they waited for the refrigeration technician.

The tide had dropped several feet while we were gone, and the *Ambrosia* seemed to be almost aground. Climbing down the ladder, in words plain and understated, Skeads said, "Falin's a real piece of work." That's all he would say about him until our return from Canada.

The technician arrived as we took the last cardboard box of supplies into the galley. Monroe and Neal met him on deck. He was medium height, and medium build with a dodgy baseball hat skewed a little off center and its bill disintegrating around the edges. Wisps of long reddish hair dangled from under the headband and framed his round red cheeks. Chuckles burst from his bright constitution. "Hello, my name's Chuck." His demeanor inferred no one needed to ask if he saw the glass brimming, indeed tasty, and confident the next day's libations of life would prove more delicious.

Neal showed him the refrigeration system crowding the tight space of the fo'c'sle. Chilling tanks the size of coffins were jammed and secured against both sides of the bulkhead. Pushed into the forward peak were pumps, more cylindrical tanks, and to my ignorant eyes, all this twisting into a plumbed mystery. Keeping the brine and salmon at a steady temperature of thirty-two degrees Fahrenheit, the purpose of the system was to circulate brine from the fish tanks through this mechanical labyrinth, cool it, and return it to the fish tanks.

The cannery manager stood with his hands in his pockets and watched. The tech secured the pressure gauges to the refrigerant pump, studied the dials, scratched his nose, and put his hand on various sections of the plumbing, pumps, and tanks to feel for heat. As Neal told him about the powder found in the filters, he picked his nose and chuckled. A puzzled expression assumed the technician's face, Neal's question spawned curlicues wiggling across the tech's face; another chuckle popped out from between his rosy cheeks. "I've never heard nor seen this before. What I think we might have here ... what is it called? Ah. What we might have here is a ... fa-nom-e-na."

He pulled at a thread hanging from his cap, finding an answer.

"Simple. Change the filters."

"I've been trying that. But I'm not sure that's the answer," said Neal. Taking off his glasses and rubbing his eyes, he looked at a used filter where the powder had penetrated the ceramic cells, "What is this stuff? What causes it? It's a corruption, isn't it?" He took a knife and scraped some off, rubbing it between his fingers.

More question marks scurried across the tech's face. He picked and scratched his nose this time without humor, replying, "Well, if the temperature is holding, if the system is doing its job, then nothing is broken that we can fix. Keep changing the filters to clean the system out until the stuff disappears ...

"Right? Make sense?" The tech looked at Monroe and the manager, continuing, "Everything's working normally. You got the pressures. You got the temps. They're all in spec. What's here to fix except the heebie-jeebies? I can't fix those. I mean ... we can't fix the future. It hasn't happened. Yes?" He grinned shyly and shifted his ball cap and plucked at another thread dangling off the bill.

The technician was correct. To break down the entire system and inspect it might take several days to discover self-inflicted anxiety. Odds and fate weighted against attempting to prevent that which hadn't happened. A third of a million dollars of salmon needed to get to Vancouver. The goal was more immediate than the uncertainties of replacing a refrigeration system and waiting several days for the parts (if any were needed) to arrive from the states. It might be more an exercise of waiting for a future as an end in itself that then never arrives. The longer the delay, the odds of selling the fish for anything more than cat food increased. The technician left with the manager and Monroe.

On the dock, we could see the manager talking, and a finger pointed into the third button of Monroe's shirt. It was a one-sided, heated conversation with our skipper standing quietly listening. Even from our distance, a few phrases fell loud enough to the deck that we could get the message. "He's your responsibility ... no further damage ... that guy has a screw loose." Somehow, the manager had already formed an opinion of Neal and made his judgment. We would leave on the midnight tide for Vancouver. The seeds had sprouted.

* * *

We had expected to take Neal to a movie and maybe meet up with Monroe somewhere, but our strange crewman had disappeared with his cannery friend, and the *Ambrosia* seized chain-to-collar around Monroe.

We went to Polly's. Falin had not shown up to work all day. We could appreciate why, but it nursed my witless envy and resentment. When I said, "It's not right." Skeads replied, "Yeah, we got it real tough." Then he ordered another round and rolled a cigarette. When he exhaled, the smoke seethed from between his stained teeth. "Besides," he added, "it's in the past."

In the theatre, the sticky carpets joined with the smell of moist exhaled booze and popcorn. An empty bottle rolled under a seat in the middle of the feature, and someone snored softly. Images blazed across the screen as a bunch of cowboys protected a village from seven hundred evil marauders. The ambiance felt terrific. We drank our surreptitious pints in soda cups from theatre canteen.

Yet again, Skeads and I ended up at Polly's surrounded by more booze and smoke. Concealed in the darkest corner of the bar, we listened from across the floor to an outlaw western band from the lower 48 twanging and riffing about horses and soulless gin mills (like the one we stood in which seemed an oasis to us). We watched without comment a northern noir of locals chase the liquid in their highball glasses, laugh over the long necks and stubbies of brew, lean across tables with their faces etched by light and shadowed into

68

three-dimensional compositions washed pale yellow by the meek candles. In shadowy plateaus, the tables floated. We saw Neal, and then, like voyeurs, we watched him dancing with his friend. Time back peddled to a 1960's high school innocence, their hips modestly apart and their cheeks pressed into one another's, their hands together curled and tucked into themselves. They blended into the smoky firmament, the dance floor sealed inside their dreamlike world.

Others jumped and bounced in rudimentary dance across the floor. Neal with his friend never left it. Skeads and I, neither of us ladies men, watched the strange Neal and the cannery girl enjoy an intimate, innocent, interlude, holding one another indifferent about the difference between a two-step or line dance, holding onto one another in their own way. For the second time that day I experienced envy, though the sources proved poles apart. Maybe it wasn't envy as much as loneliness, but then again, jealousy may be the most intense loneliness. Skeads said nothing about dancing or women. I'm not sure he experienced loneliness or envy, perhaps given up on such emotions. "Neal's not a bad sort," he said, more to himself than to me. Then adding, "He might have found a place to fit in."

We returned to the *Ambrosia* and found Monroe on his game: the main engines were up and idling, the deck lights flaring into a white light canopied hovering over the dark deck. A few crab pots were left onboard, tied to the forward port rail. Filled with restless energy and yet to express any further mischief, our *Ambrosia* seemed ready to share the sea with us. In the wheelhouse, Monroe was roaring to leave, leaning and looking out the wheelhouse window as we climbed aboard. Neal appeared a few minutes behind us holding hands with his friend, and parting with a self-conscious kiss—one of those little pecks—he climbed on to the deck and headed for the engine room. His friend waited motionless on the dock, plain-faced, quiet, solitary, garbed in her fatigues and jungle

69

boots like she was waiting for a foxhole, her hands in front of her holding one another. The cannery in the background belched lustrous steam from the cookers, sending this heated mist swirling against night's canvas.

Five minutes passed, then ten. We waited for Falin's arrival. Maybe because Monroe was a new skipper and felt uncertain about leaving a crewman whom he didn't hire, and the politics of this crewman a relative to one of the owners, we didn't pack up and go. Skeads would later say he had thought about that lost moment of opportunity. "We could've left Falin at the dock," he said. Tragedy hangs from hidden hinges.

Both the *Ambrosia* and Monroe waited fifteen minutes for Falin to appear. He arrived by truck, red and chrome, the silver fox hidden in the cab, with their duo keeping us waiting another five minutes until he emerged with a cough of neon white fog issuing from his perfectly crafted lips. He glanced at us, smiled sheepishly, shrugged his shoulders, and entered the aft house.

The drizzle started to fall. After Falin climbed aboard, we untied from the pilings and slipped into the channel. The fox drove off, and the cannery girl stood in the rain beside a crane on the cannery dock.

As the *Ambrosia* pushed farther into the dark channel, Neal returned to the deck to stand by the starboard rail to watch his friend surrounded by the steam belching from the cannery.

# Chapter 6: Irises, passage to Vancouver

The morning welcomed us with an endless drizzle, a sea polished blue-black, and a lazy following swell. This swell ran beneath the hull, gently raising our stern first. Water surrounded the *Ambrosia* giving the sentience of solitude and isolation, that conscious peace and unconscious angst open water summons regardless of the number of passages.

A few hours out of town, the *Ambrosia* again began to speak to Neal. Our engineer listened and touched the various moving parts searching for the meanings in vibration and heat. Placing the tip of a long shaft screwdriver on a pump housing or a bearing cover, he would rest the knob of the handle against his cheek or chin, picking up the vibration signature. To us, it may have been an act of showmanship, but through this exchange, Neal could hear the voices of our vessel. Throughout the night, he had stayed in the fo'c'sle or the engine room, and you could see him appearing to query various parts of the machinery, scratching his head, squatting on his haunches, sniffing around the chillers, engines, and pumps. He acquired knowledge through sweat.

He changed the filters again, again finding that infection of brown powder. When Neal reported this to Monroe, our new skipper inspected them himself, shaking his head and saying, "Just do the best you can. Our course is set. There's no turning back. We'll have to deal with what happens next."

By late morning, Neal informed Monroe the chillers were not keeping the tanks at the necessary 32 degrees. They had risen to 36. The *Ambrosia's* schizophrenic refrigeration system seemed to mock Monroe, to taunt an expectation of a smooth voyage. Once, we added a few bags of salt, a false palliative, hoping that by adjusting salinity, it might hold the seawater in the tanks to 32 degrees.

However, the mystery of the fouled filters forewarned the inescapable. It became easy for all of us to imagine tons of rotten salmon stinking in the hold.

At the galley table, when Monroe ate, I could see the skin across his face pulled a little tighter, reflecting the stress the vessel doled out with paranormal joy. The *Ambrosia* tested both possibilities and ambiguities, assembling its trials and tribulations, testing his mettle, assembling a set of problems not created by his malfeasance, but regardless for which he would be held answerable. At one point he asked Skeads—indeed stated—he was not up to the job. Our deck boss replied with tranquility, "It's too early to tell. Don't forget, you asked for it. You lose when you quit or die."

Routine on the *Ambrosia* fell into not-unpleasant, disciplined side work. We deep-cleaned the boat. We shined cupboards, the stove, and head. Falin scrubbed the refrigerator. He worked with meticulous attention to detail; he accomplished well anywhere he applied himself. I never understood how he took so little interest in the engine room, and it wasn't because of Neal, for when Skeads had pulled the maintenance, Falin showed no interest. Regardless, Neal watched the vital signs of the rig like a concerned lover for its beloved, and I should have watched more closely, as I now respect his brilliance. Sadly, to my shame and loss, I found him, as did Falin, too strange.

We pulled wheel-watches; we cooked unhurried meals; we lay in our bunks reading. While refusing to teach me cribbage (I was terrible at it), Skeads threw a copy of Farley Mowat's, *People of the Deer* on my bunk, and after browsing a few pages (generally speaking I cared little for tree-hugging books), I began to read it, turning its pages, finally seduced by a writer who had been a spy in WWII. I would never again read more contentedly than when onboard a fishing vessel.

72

On the open water, when pulling wheel watch, the elements of the night isolated the wheelhouse from what might be called "the real world," creating a cocoon, an encapsulation woven out of the sounds and substance of the *Ambrosia*. With the night-safe dials on the console confirming the engines' faithful performance, with the green glow of the radar screen searching for an echo of what lay in the unseen, this black sea and thick night surrounded us in a surreal cavern as our work lights carved shadows from its nocturnal walls. The radio finder, connected with a distant rock'n'roll or Mozart, voices so abstract and imperishable, fading in and out, formed into a remarkable memory spun by darkness, by the sea, by the abstract light, by a 2 a.m. simplicity and a momentary sense of peace and safety.

Looking back over some four decades, in trying to understand this passage comprised of ignored incidents that seemed inconsequential and unconnected, I failed to see how they collectively grew no less than any malignancy. It should have been apparent that the friction between Falin and Neal demanded discharge, that Neal was not your average personality, nor Falin, and for sure not Skeads. Had Falin taken the trip off and communed with his fox-fur apparition, our strange engineer could have been a hero. But the two of them together at the same time and place—as Skeads foretold, no good could come from it.

* * *

One afternoon, we worked on the crab pots and lines. The bow churned the wind currents. Beside the boat, seagulls flew in a loose formation. How they had moved this far offshore was anyone's guess. Bouncing around in the wake of the wind, the tireless stroke of their wings slipped through the air. A bold gull might land and spread its white wings to catch the wind slipping over the whaleback; its yellow beak jacked open in cawed bravado hailing its comrades.

73

Skeads had pulled out an old block of frozen herring from the bait freezer and would occasionally stab off with his survival knife a chunk of the fish, tossing the pieces over the side of the rail. The birds would fall off their flight and dive on it, raucous and screeching, turning flight into a scrimmage.

Neal sat on an upturned five-gallon bucket and struggled to splice a line into the eye of a buoy. He would stop, look at the gulls and return to the task. A renegade gust of wind scurried over the starboard rail and across the deck, to vault over the port rail.

Neal asked a question only he could muster, "What does a seagull think flying over something like us?"

Skeads peered at Neal, scratched his bony nose, pulled a cigarette from his pouch, and said something to the effect of "Harrumph."

No one answered. Though Neal well may have been talking to himself, he asked another question, "Do they think about the land over the horizon? Do they fear losing sight of land?"

Skeads answered this one. "They can fly high enough to see land. I think they can smell land if the wind's offshore. All things equal, they're sure to the sea. They're bred with the tools they need."

"Do they fear?"

"Fear what? Their tools? I doubt it," replied Skeads, still true to his skepticism. After a pause, he added, "They react. Not much different than us."

Neal struggled with the fid, confusing where to insert into the lay of the line. "Do they see us as gods?"

Falin shook his head and staring at Neal like he might need a straitjacket, "Christ on a crutch. They're birds."

Skeads watched a seagull release its little white bomb lobbing through the breeze and splattered on the deck. He "harrumphed" again. "Maybe they're out expressing themselves. Letting us know who's boss." With a cigarette stuck between his lips, he canted his head, so that the smoke caught the wind and avoided his eyes. "No. I suspect they're more like artists painting a canvas." To this he grinned, the smile more a crack in the seams patterning his face. He threw out more herring. A swirl of white splinters, the gulls fell on it. "If they found us dead and floating, they'd feed on us no different than the herring. We're not gods; we're just part of the food chain with grand illusions."

Shaking his head, Falin fell to his knees and shouted at the gulls, "Do you think we're gods?" He looked at Neal shaking his head, stood up, and returned to repairing the crab pot. Working with speed and craftsmanship, he mended the web, cut from the door the frayed line making the hinges, and in adroit moves quickly replaced them. He turned to Neal, "Birds don't see God."

Neal struggled with the splice. The talents he had with machinery failed to transfer to gear work. He would take a strand and get lost in the lay of the line, confusing the order of the splice. He had yet to develop this skill. Falin watched him for a while saying, "You having trouble? Job too tricky? You got to be smarter than the line." Lifting his sunglasses to rest on his hair, he took the line through the buoy eye and set the splice in a few moves. He looked at Skeads, shook his head and returned his sunglasses. The wind ruffled his hair. "Stick to that cannery chick. She's easier to wrestle than a line. Probably not as smart."

Neal blinked at Falin.

This work continued for half an hour until Falin left the deck. A few minutes later, we could see him with Monroe in the wheelhouse, and like a silent movie lacking subtitles, the windows framed their silent conversation, Falin laughing, Monroe grim.

It was not unusual to shoot seagulls. Some believed these birds made good bait for the crabs. Prolific as rabbits, no one wept over the creatures, as more often than not, they were seen as pests. As humans, as self-appointed paragons of the animal kingdom, we discounted their tenacity, boldness, and endurance; we disassociated from those virtues the creatures took for granted and we esteemed in ourselves. In our youth, we were confident we were the suzerains of the sea, ignoring both that we required a fortune in equipment to prove it and often died as quickly as a seagull.

Falin returned to the deck with a rifle. An exquisite piece of craftsmanship, the breech, bolt, and barrel had been tooled, the grip and shoulder stock ornately carved and illustrated with forests and fauna. He locked and loaded a round and brought the weapon to his shoulder, spread his stance, timed the roll, sighted, and blew a seagull out of the air. Twirling and descending like a shattered kite through the wind, it retired into the sea, its golden-yellow eyes open, its wings distended, and its white body left an undulating X on the wake. Its brethren shifted a little and flew on indifferent. Skeads looked up from his work. Neal began to talk, arguing with an unseen person.

"I just hit one of our worshipers." Falin pulled off another round and missed. This time, cawing, the gulls scattered in a strong and assured rhythm as innate to flying as to dying.

His marksmanship created a euphoria, and Falin fired two more rounds *spinning* another bird into a white puff. "Did you see that shot?" A bliss seized him, his face lighting up, his brilliant teeth ... more brilliant than his sense of success. He extended the rifle to Neal asking, "Have you ever fired a gun like this? It's one of the best. Go ahead. Try it ... I want you to try it."

It was a strange exchange to watch. Living in close quarters threatens social delusions, and once the veneer—perhaps envy might be a truer word—wore off Falin's fox-fur woman and red truck, he began to strike me as a confused man, not that much different than myself. He lacked the interest to see beyond himself, but in this simple gesture to Neal, this sudden graciousness seemed sincere, void of any ulterior motive. I now wonder if Neal had accepted this offer, if capable playing the game, maybe his fate would have changed, that the invisible friction would have somehow abated, and all Falin needed was some affirmation. However, our strange engineer looked up from his splice to the weapon and then to the joyful face above it. He frowned, his eyes blinking behind his square black-framed glasses. Shaking his head, he returned to the splice. "I heard about them, but I think I'll take a pass."

"Oh, come on, take a shot." A small wave broke against the beam and the debris of spray shot across the deck. Falin turned his back on it to protect the weapon.

Neal struggled with the fid, opening the lay of the line. "No. No thanks. I got no interest ... I need to learn this stuff." Shaking his head again, biting his lip, he murmured loud enough for Falin to hear, "Why would anybody want to kill for target practice?" The comment was not said in spite, but Neal was asking a question from one of his other-selves. Unfortunately, the introspection may as well have been shouted through a bullhorn. Even Skeads looked at him, his pale-blue eyes squinting between pink-rimmed eyelids.

Falin's camaraderie collapsed. "You kidding me? With tons of dead fish on board? You got a problem with me killing a bird dumber than a shoe? We're not out here stumbling around in this forsaken place to hug each other. If you care to check it, we make a living killing and selling fish."

Oblivious to the tenor of the conversation, Neal replied, "But the fish aren't target practice."

"No. You're right ... for once. They're a product that we sell,

77

and then we buy other stuff. Let's put it another way. If we hunt good, we eat good. We hunt like bunnies, we eat grass and sleep in holes. We're not scavengers. We're predators."

"But it doesn't make it right."

Both certainty and disgust framed Falin's face. His movie star appearance played well and benefited his viewpoint if not logic. Skeads watched but said nothing.

Neal continued to wrestle with his splice while waiting for the next rebuke. Another wave broke across the beam, and cloud-diffused sunlight filled the spray, sending a chilling heavy mist across the deck, this time dousing the hand-tooled weapon.

Looking at the rifle, Falin swore. "We make things; we make money ... I didn't make me a predator ... it's our nature, you bunny.

"I brought this out to show you, to be nice to you. Now it's soaked. Besides, what's 'right' got to do with it?" He wiped off the weapon with his sleeve and put his face an inch from Neal's, "You're not in touch. You know that? This is the last time I'm going to help you out. I brought this out for you to try. You're probably afraid of it, aren't you?"

Neal looked into his antagonist's eyes and answered in a surprisingly calm voice, "I know. I am different, but it doesn't mean I don't have a place."

"Place? No place? What's that got to do with squat?"

"Falin," Skeads said, "If you're not careful your sunglasses are going to fog up. Go shoot some filthy birds or get back to work." His voice lowered, "Let it go before...."

Falin blazed off the deck, the hand tooled weapon carried in his hands like an injured bird.

\* \* \*

The evening seemed more to ascend from the sea than descend over us, and from inside the galley, you could feel the *Ambrosia* slip down a slow roller. There must have been a storm farther out to sea, its energy forming the big fat humps of sea. Skeads played solo-cribbage with two hands of cards, peering over his drug store glasses, picking up one hand, studying it, then picking up the other with the same contentment, for him, I guess, a form of meditation. From four feet away, you could smell his sulfuric breath and body-stink of tobacco. The dishwater in the sink rolled back and forth, and a free bottle shifted in the refrigerator. Skeads interrupted his game, opened the door and secured the bottle by wedging a head of lettuce against it. The vibrations from the main engines sent tremors through the steel like a pulse through flesh, this beat finding mien in the concentric circles expanding across the surface of his coffee. To no one in particular, he commented, "I suppose Neal could figure out some math formula for how this coffee's vibrating."

We assumed Neal was forward communing with the chillers. Falin cooked supper. I sat near Skeads trying again to figure out how to play cribbage.

"I got no mood for this ..." Falin paused, turning the frying potatoes, "I should have blown off this trip and just worked on gear in town, camped out with Sabrina. You all didn't need me this trip." He added wistfully, "I had a great time in town. Man, I miss her."

"So, her name is Sabrina?" Skeads asked without looking up from his cards, and not waiting for an answer, he added, "But it's your fate to be the best cook onboard. The only one who knows how to cook without having to serve baking soda for dessert. Your gifts keep Neal from turning our guts to concrete. Besides you got an interesting way with Monroe. Maybe it keeps him from jumping overboard or having a heart attack."

"So, what's up with that girl Neal latched on to?" asked Falin.

79

"Seems like that would have been way down on your list. I'm surprised you noticed, considering in town how fast you disappeared." Counting in a whisper, Skeads moved a peg and picked up the other hand, adding, "Stick to cooking meat and potatoes. You're a pretty smart guy, but a dumbass when it comes to what you're sure of." He stared at Falin, "I suggest you keep commonsense close by and best leave Neal's private life alone."

Falin almost said something, maybe a few words that might have an edge to them, but he remained silent, laid out two packages of hamburger and began forming patties. "I mean nothing by it."

"I'd like to believe that." Skeads rearranged his hand.

Falin continued. "Did you see the movie in town? Do feet still stick to the carpet?"

"Yeah..." Skeads looked up from his cards. "Yeah. The good guys won. And that's what it's all about. White hats and black hats. What's winning? There's no difference between the two except black hats are bloodthirsty but could care less, and white hats grieve over their bloodthirst. Leastways, that's the story we like to tell ourselves."

"What do you mean by that?" Falin asked.

Staring at the cards, Skeads replied, "I'm not sure. However, I'll bet you seagull hunters would find it a lot less interesting if the feathered bastards could return fire."

"What? How the hell you know? You a bird?"

Skeads actually laughed. "I'm more screwed up than you. But I know it. That's why I like the cards better than you. They make more sense than either one of us."

"I got no idea what you are talking about." Falin slid a skillet to a burner.

"Good ... at least we're in the same game," replied Skeads.

Falin pulled out three cans of different beans, drained them, and shook them into a bowl, adding the remaining contents of a bottle of salad dressing. "What do you think Neal sees in that cannery chick?"

Skeads looked up from his cards, "I wonder what questions you got about me when my back's turned?" He moved a peg, leaning back into the cushioned seat. "I guess he sees a lot more in her than he sees in you. Is that what bothers you?" His lips twisted across his face, and his features looked strangely atavistic, his skin reptilian.

"Come on man; I mean nothing by it. This afternoon I blew it. I should'a never got mad like that. But that gal's been passed around more than a basketball. You know it. There's nothing you can say about her she hasn't done to herself. She's a cannery whore. She'll go through him like shit through a goose."

"Gander," replied Skeads.

The *Ambrosia* shifted off trim, and a spatula fell to the floor. We had thought Neal was forward inspecting the refrigeration, but he appeared like he had been there longer than anyone wanted, standing in the borders formed by the bean salad and the frying potatoes. The "whore" comment lingered within the life of its own. It echoed in the space. The galley crowded into a smaller space; the eye in the sign above the table rocked back and forth, and with the roll of the rig, the black pupil flicked from the ceiling to the galley table. Neal may not have heard anything, or, he may have heard everything but not known of whom Falin spoke. An anxious silence stumbled into the background noise of the engines and the frying hamburgers.

"I'm going to check the chillers." Neal's eyes settled on Falin, hardening behind the scratched lenses of his glasses. "Interesting," he said.

When Neal returned, he brought his math book. Sliding into the

81

bench seat of the galley table, he dropped his face into its pages. We tried to pretend that the word "whore" had stopped echoing.

Falin asked Neal, "Did you see the movie in town with your friend?"

"My friend?"

"Yeah, that chick on the dock who had eyes for you."

"No," replied Neal.

Skeads put down his cards and said, "Falin ... stick to cooking."

"How'd you meet her?" asked Falin, touching in the middle the burger patties, testing for doneness: "How do you want your burger?"

Neal looked up from his math book. I noticed it was about prime numbers. "I like her. How she lives her life is her business."

*Ambrosia* rose from the port stern and passed under us. She did a little twist. Skeads slid his cards into their sleeve and took a deep breath; you could smell the burgers and frying potatoes; together they became a confusion of odors. Between them, tobacco reeked.

"Oh," Falin replied, "Yeah." The "yeah" grew shoulders and sat at the galley table. "They're all nice in their way."

Skeads looked at his etchings on the tusk, "You can't help yourself, can you?"

"You know," Falin continued, "you might want to be careful about her." The tone of his conversation cradled its own sincerity.

Neal looked up from his math. "What do you mean by 'passed around like a basketball'?"

"Oh. I wasn't talking about your chick."

You could see Neal thinking, the eyes pacing a process, "I

didn't say you were. I never heard the expression before."

Skeads replied slowly, "Falin ... a sheet of toilet paper could wipe up all the common sense you got."

"Hey, Neal can handle his own."

"That's what I'm afraid of."

Neal studied Falin who quickly said, "Look, I was making conversation. I've never met the girl." His face filled with apology, and he said, "Really, I'm sorry about this afternoon. If I've hurt your feelings, if I've offended you or your friend, I'm sorry." Falin seemed apologetic, and across his face passed sincere regret. "I was wrong. I don't know why I did it."

Neal closed his book, studied the cover, and asked what seemed at the time removed from any sequence of events. "If you can see something bad is going to happen are you obliged to stop it?"

"What? The refrigeration?" asked Falin.

"Can you solve immorality with immorality?" replied Neal.

Confused and growing impatient, Falin replied, "You need to rest."

Skeads, putting down his cards and visibly inhaling, replied, "I've found morality depends on who holds the cards. Plenty of humans have been killed in the name of humanity. It's sick. Situational ethics."

"So, an action can be moral and immoral at the same time?" replied Neal.

Skeads said, "If you hold the cards."

At the time, it held no consequence to any of us, perhaps the mindless riddling of a strange man in search of refuge or escape, beating his head like a fly against a window pane.

Falin looked at Neal and said, "Man, you need to get some sleep."

Again, the stern of the *Ambrosia* rose, and you could hear the prop catch a little air. I started to wash a few pans lying in the sink. Falin wore an aftershave that smelled piney, a definite contrast to Skeads. While the hamburgers sizzled on the griddle, I pulled out some dishes and flatware to set the table.

His finger traced the black line of etched tears on the tusk. Skeads said, "An illusion."

I saw the eye on the sign over the table. It must have been a reflection, an artifice cast in the play between the galley lights and the roll of the *Ambrosia,* but the wooden sign rocked and the eye blinked.

# Chapter 7: The Failed Engine

We kept our heading and hoped changing the filters would correct the refrigeration problem. As the temperature in the tanks rose, in our mind's eye we could see the salmon spoiling, the high-quality red meat and fine, sweet, clear oil corrupting into rancid venoms fit only for unloved cats.

Monroe, in his bunk, tried to get some sleep. Peering into the night, Falin took watch at the wheel. In a lethargic posture, he stretched out his legs, resting his feet on the console. About three hours had passed. His turn to take the watch, climbing the stairs, Skeads held a mug of coffee and balanced a peanut butter and jelly sandwich on its rim.

"Is it fresh?"

Skeads replied, "It doesn't matter." Skeads didn't offer to get him coffee, and Falin remained in his chair still peering straight ahead.

"Have you checked the engine room lately?" asked Skeads. The procedure required checking the engine room every two hours.

"Yeah, when I came on," Falin paused for a moment, adding, "I rechecked it about half an hour ago."

Skeads considered the response, saying, "I'll check again when I finish my coffee."

A silence waited to introduce its prelude. After several minutes, Falin said, "We need to have a serious talk."

"You sure you don't mean that you need to have a serious talk? I had enough serious talk. Why another?"

"Yeah ... I was wrong to blow up, but you know things aren't running right. Back in No Cannery Bay, I could see that you should be running this rig."

Sitting across the wheelhouse in the port chair, Skeads dipped the donut in his coffee and slurped a little of it. The coffee was bitter and old. "Monroe's learning. I'll do my end and leave management to others. I know where I belong. Do you?"

Falin replied, "Monroe's not a bad guy, but he lacks your experience. He should have never trusted that nut-case near the engine room. Big mistake. You know that."

"I don't know that. Maybe you should be running the boat," said Skeads, "You ..."

Falin interrupted, "Yup. I'm getting ready for it. I've never wanted to be anything else. But, somebody needs to tell management what's going on."

Skeads continued, "...got uncanny confidence. Most any man could mistake it for competence."

After a minute more of silence, Falin rose from his chair. "You know, and I mean no disrespect, but if the fishery depended on guys like you, we'd still be using spears and cast nets. There's a new kind of business coming to the fishery. You need to catch up."

Skeads slurped his coffee, and whispered more to himself, "You're right. However, I've come as far as I can, and I can't get no farther away. I know that much about myself. Besides, what's that got to do with this conversation?"

Monroe entered the wheelhouse, vigorously pushing a toothbrush against his teeth. "An old skipper I worked for told me that brushing your teeth wakes you up. I'm not sure I slept any, so I guess I don't need to brush my teeth. Damn if I wasn't eating rotten fish. I hate to think what that means."

Falin moved from his chair for Monroe to sit down. An open magazine rested on the console.

Unable to sleep, I entered the wheelhouse and sipped coffee.

"Can I get a cup of coffee for you?" asked Falin.

"Please." Monroe took the magazine off the console and handed it to him, asking, "When was the last time you checked the engine room?"

"About fifteen minutes ago. I'll get you some coffee, and I'll make it fresh."

Monroe inspected the night around him, felt the roll of the *Ambrosia*, and listened to the rhythm of the engines. Life appeared routine until his mental checklist focused on an oil-pressure gauge on the console. At first, what he saw he failed to see. Comprehension favors denying reality. Little white bubbles burst from around his toothbrush, and he said, "This can't be happening."

Each main engine had its own oil-pressure gauge, and the port indicator fluctuated like a metronome. Within the red glow of the nightlight, its needle waved at Monroe, bouncing insanely between normal operating pressure and zero. A jolt of reality took the last of the peppermint from his mouth. The *Ambrosia* shifted.

Monroe slowed the engines to idle, told Skeads to take the wheel, and as if on fire, he jumped from the chair taking steps two at a time, the engine room calling him like a three-alarm.

The engine room smelled and sounded normal. When Monroe approached the erratic engine, its indicator mimicked the one in the wheelhouse. "What next?" he asked. The port engine was failing.

He pulled the dipstick and saw that the oil, the blood of the engine, rested considerably above the full mark.

Falin had followed him, and shouted above the racket of the

engines, "I'll bet Neal put in too much oil. He overfilled it. I'll get him down here."

From when the *Ambrosia* had slipped her lines and pulled away from the dock, Neal had only eaten his meals, drunk a few coffees, and then worked with the *Ambrosia*. Considering his time in town, Neal may have been up and working for over two days before hitting the rack. Sleep, for him, often seemed an inconvenience. However, when asleep, the boat could sink beneath him without his even adjusting his pillow.

Falin lunged into the small stateroom and switched on the lights.

He started shaking Neal and poking at him until the man finally emerged from his sleepy bindings. He blinked, closed his eyes slowly, and then opened his eyes again, but he could only see his dream.

Falin said, "Hey bud, you screwed the engine up."

"Engine?" asked Neal. His hand reached out and found his glasses.

"Yeah. Engine. That hunk of metal that makes the rig move."

"What's wrong with my *Ambrosia*?"

"We're going to lose this load of fish. It's all cat food or fertilizer because of you. You screwed up the chillers and now an engine. Wake up." Falin slapped his head, knocking a leg off his glasses. "Wake up."

Neal fell from his bunk. Falin slapped him again, pushing him. Neal grabbed his glasses and stumbled to the engine room.

Monroe, his face an icon to both panic and despair, searched for answers to stick on unasked questions. He stared at the dipstick like it might find a voice and tell him the problem. Over the racket of the other engines, he shouted at Neal, "Did you overfill the engine with oil and blow some kind of seal?"

Neal's face shifted into thought. He started to ask the *Ambrosia* questions. With one leg missing off his glasses, the lens listed across his face. He ignored our skipper's question. His mouth twisted, then untwisted, and behind scarred glasses, his eyes blinked with metered rhythm. Panic may not have been emotion in him. He took the dipstick from Monroe and reinserted it into its port, let it rest, and pulled it to see the oil level far above the full line. He cleaned it off with his fingers and smelled the amber fluid, pausing, saying to himself, "You've got diesel in you. Fuel is being dumped into your oil. It's thinned with fuel and lost its viscosity."

Neal turned off the engine. Rattling, shuddering to rest, it appeared to have given up. He put his palm near the engine casing, and then slowly placed it against its side. "You haven't overheated. That's good."

Falin interrupted this analysis, "Man, if this don't prove you don't know the difference between salad oil and diesel, nothing will."

Dropping into his strange world, Neal ignored him and went to the bottom drawer of the tool cabinet. Pulling out a manual, he started to study. He talked to himself out loud, but the noise from the generator and the other main engine reduced his words to chant.

Monroe knew he had lost control of the *Ambrosia*. Any hope of success in his life vanished. He labored up one step at a time to the wheelhouse confident in the knowledge that with one engine, the passage would take eight days rather than four. This engine failure stymied his ability to think. He would later admit, he had panicked. If lucky, the salmon would arrive as a suitable fertilizer, selling for 10 cents on the dollar, and his validation as a skipper would be known in town as a failure. He knew, or thought he knew, that no one onboard was capable of repairing the engine. Sitting on his

89

throne, the skipper's chair in the wheelhouse, he gave up. The gauge of the engine now rested, mocking him. He may have questioned whether swimming in the surrounding sea seemed more agreeable than facing the humility of failure.

"I'll cook you some breakfast," said Falin.

"It looks like this could be a long trip," said Skeads.

"Have you any ideas?" asked Monroe.

Silence murdered any reply. Skeads, figuring he might check the engine room, replied before leaving, "We could call the cannery and see if they have any ideas."

Monroe called, explained the "situation," which left the listener stunned and silent on the other end of the radio transmission. Into a third of a million dollars for the fish, the news that the refrigeration and the engine were failing left the other man with few words on his end of the ether. "Give me ten minutes," returned the voice. He called Vancouver.

Ten minutes later, the transmission crackled through the distance, a man named "Phillips" had called back. This man said to change course, and they would have a crew to meet us. Our heading was set due east. With one engine it might take two days to find the port, but it was better than eight. Nasty options exacted nasty choices.

The *Ambrosia* changed course.

* * *

"Which way we headed?" Skeads had returned from the engine room.

"Iris ... Harbor," muttered the skipper. None of us had heard of the place and had no idea where on the alien coastline it existed. With no pun intended, the strange name for a northern harbor lacked both aboriginal and botanical roots.

Falin consoled Monroe. His sincerity purred. "This is tough luck for you, skipper. You don't deserve this."

Monroe opened the back hatch of the wheelhouse and threw the plate, fork, and breakfast overboard and returned to his chair asking, "Where's Neal?"

"Neal ... Neal?" Skeads replied, "Ohhh, he's still down below stripping the engine to the block."

It would take little imagination in the dark wheelhouse to see Monroe's face turn as pale as Skeads', which could be a nifty competition. At the moment, our skipper may have had more blood circulating in his fingernails than his face. "What? He's taking the engine apart?" He choked on its perceived madness. What little of his breakfast he had eaten, voluntarily returned in one belch.

"He's drained the oil, and taken the valve covers off the engine. Last I saw, he was pulling the rocker arms." Skeads cocked his head and put an unlit cigarette between his lips. "It's time for a smoke."

Monroe's face captured the visage of existential despair you might find on the face of a Golden Gate jumper. Had our newbie skipper been an older man, a heart attack would have made its grand entrance jangling with bells and whistles. Now, for sure, his career sank. He had not found rock bottom; instead, rock bottom had found him. He could easily see himself the laughing stock of every fishing town from the tip of the Aleutian Chain to the Dungeness Grounds of Northern California. He could envision in the *Fisherman's Journal* a front-page article screaming in the silent headline "INCAPABLE" ... he then ceremoniously awarded a gigantic crown "INC" to wear on his forehead the rest of his life. For the second time that night, our skipper was two feet off the seat and halfway to the engine room in about the time it takes to have a stroke. He could

91

see himself arriving in Iris Harbor with a madman who had parted out and salvaged the boat while still underway.

Monroe found a sweating Neal—ignoring the high decibels that danced around in a merry jig in the engine room—with his glasses taped to the bridge of his nose. He was in the process of stripping an engine block of its head, the valve covers, the rocker arms, and the list went on, those essentials neatly aligned forming a jigsaw puzzle across a tarp placed on the deck plates. Neal embraced an activity only for skilled mechanics, and well beyond any talents possessed or assumed by anyone onboard. Neal was deconstructing an engine.

With the other engines rattling in the contrapuntal chorus, Monroe shrieked over their clatter, "What are you doing? Do you know what you're doing?"

To the broken engine, Neal whispered. In deep concentration, our engineer ignored Monroe, for him a non-essential player. It was all about the *Ambrosia*. His eyes passed over our skipper and he continued his work, an alleged mad man in his alleged mad world.

Monroe retreated, ascending the two flights of stairs to the wheelhouse.

"He's gone crazy. I don't know how to stop him." Monroe squeaked.

"We need to get him out of the engine room before he sinks the boat," said Falin.

From Skeads corner, you could hear, "Waste of time. The engine's broken."

"We need to tie him up," said Falin.

"Bull. The engine is broken. You can break what isn't broken. You can't fix what's not broken. For sure, you can't fix what's broken by doing nothing. That's all we're doing. We're doing

92

nothing while he's in the engine room trying. He might fail, but it won't mean nothin' in the long run. At least he's doing something. It don't matter if he talks to the boat and drinks diesel."

Falin, now fired up, said, "I tell you he's nuts and I'm going down to stop him."

Skeads replied, "No you're not. You're doing nothing - like you always do. Can you fix the engine? You won't even try. You're leaving things be." Darkness covered any signals in his face, but you could hear his conviction, and this particular imperative was the first of two he marked before the *Ambrosia* would carry us back home.

Another hour passed before Neal climbed into the wheelhouse, still in bare feet and shorts, his hands remarkably clean considering that he had torn into a diesel engine. Exhaustion smearing his face, staining his eyes red, he was unaware that he sported a bruised face from where Falin had struck him. He held a stainless steel rod not much bigger than a thick pencil, bent about eight degrees from true. He said simply, "This is it." Neal's eyes were steady behind his lopsided glasses, both lenses reflecting what little light existed in the wheelhouse.

"What?" asked Monroe.

Falin laughed, but without conviction. Envy finds its forms of expression, and you could see them cutting across his face.

"This pushrod failed. When it bent, the injector started misfiring, losing the combustion cycle, dumping raw fuel into the crankcase, diluting the oil, lowering the oil pressure. That's what the gauge showed us. The engine's no different from everything else. It's all tied together. If one connection fails, the system disconnects. You got to figure out the connections. She hasn't failed us after all. She's testing us to see if we honor her ... connections." You could hear everyone thinking.

Falin said, but now with far less conviction, "Connections? Great. You got an engine scattered in a thousand different parts, and you're standing here with a bent rod. I should've never come on this trip."

"I will fix it," said Neal, ignoring all of us, "With the torch, I can straighten the rod out. Anneal it. Put the engine back together."

Falin turned to Monroe, "You got no business putting him in the engine room. Management will go crazy."

Skeads picked up the magazine that had covered the console and handed it to Falin. "Here. Take this connection. It was covering the gauges during your wheel watch."

Neal then for the second time confronted Falin, "You cook breakfast good. You're the best on the crane. I took the engine apart, and I can put it together. Can anyone else here?"

"I can't," said Skeads.

"The *Ambrosia* reveals herself ... She knows to deliver the fish. I know it. She's told me."

If lungs could suck a molecule of hope from doom, Monroe, after holding his breath for a long while, exhaled a bleak question, "So you're saying you might be able to get the engine running?"

"Yes," said Neal as he turned to descend the stairs. "It's my *Ambrosia,* and she wants to deliver the fish, no matter how little we believe in her."

Through the night and into the morning, Skeads and I beheld how talent and intelligence express itself. While we shined the various parts, our strange engineer stripped off the engine. His madness repaired the bent push rod with baffling ability, annealing with a torch the steel, peening it straight. Then over several hours in whispered self-discussion, assembling the engine, pointing out to us

94

what parts to hand him, fitting the pieces together, our strange engineer somehow knew how each element worked with the other, confident in his knowledge and intuitions. In this small cauldron of expressions, Skeads saw Neal as a hero who had arrived from the wasteland.

Only then, did the engineer return to the manual, studying how to set the timing, and after several other procedures that lay beyond our ken, he cranked the engine to listen to the heart of the *Ambrosia* beat again.

We headed for Iris Harbor under two engines. No one disturbed Neal this time when he slept.

Years later, Monroe would recall that hopeless night; it was the wisest act of indecision he ever made. Luck was on our side. At the time, our skipper didn't realize it, but Neal taught him never to give up. It would become such an irony.

# Chapter 8: Iris Harbor

Like fallen columns, rolled charts lay piled on a table built into the back of the wheelhouse. From an overhead lamp, the anemic red light dusted a map on the table. Hunched over its information, Monroe took his finger and slowly traced it across the topography of a coastline.

Pressing his face into the rubber cowling of the radar, knowing he was too far away to get a reflection of the land, he tested the motions and emotions of ineptness. When he lifted his face, the green light from the screen stuck to his features. Both engine oil pressure and temperature indicators showed Neal's repair job worked. He had yet to thank Neal, would never thank Neal, but would remember it forever. "There's no chart for Iris Harbor," he said. "I've got a chart that takes us near but nothing to get us inside."

The chillers remained moody. Since leaving the dock, the temperature in the tanks had risen a degree or two, killing any belief in the powers of positive thinking. You could read the masks of despair as they flicked across Monroe's face. As the red prow of the *Ambrosia* glided through the dark waters and starless night, his imagination fixated on the hurly-burly madhouse of probabilities. Across the hours, the temperature settled on a confident three-degree increase, making in the mind's eye the night darker and the salmon spoiling.

You could only hear his voice, but Skeads said casually, "We're charting nothing new ... engine failing and nothing but headaches. It's called work. We're finding no new water."

"I don't know what more can go wrong," replied Monroe. He pushed his fingers through his hair.

Skeads, filing his nails, said, "We could be swimming. As long as you breathe, it can get worse."

Monroe put his face back into the cowling of the radar, "I smell like I peed in my armpits."

"Possibility. Yeah ... I can see it, real possible you overlooked it until now. Look at it this way Skip," continued Skeads, and you could tell he was enjoying a moment of dark humor conjured from his skeptical assessments of life: "All we're delivering is high-end cracker-spread for some highbrows lounging in some linen-sporting restaurant. It helps them feel successful. Hell to pay, we'll all be dead someday anyway. There's somebody someplace who is really suffering. Some mother is watching her child starve or prostituting herself while we dump in our pants over dead fish. Look at the bright side of this, there's a good chance you might be famous after this trip. Hell, that's all we want is fame and money, circus and bread. Hell, from the Bering Sea to Hawaii ... you can be some kind of a commercial hero-suit, a king of kitty chow. You might be able to get your picture on the label. Become some kind of a hotshot in some kind of a seminar selling how you turned lemons into lemonade. Hell, while your blessed mother is hanging wet laundry over the fence, she'll carry around in her apron a can of cat food to show her neighbors your cute mug cheek-to-whisker with an adorable little purring predator." This may have been the longest soliloquy I recall from Skeads. His skinny face twisting into a frown, our deck boss added, his voice tuned to a vow, "We'll get this load of dead fish to market one way or the other. Then we'll get up the next morning and carry on. In the long run, it don't mean nothing, nothing at all."

Monroe, staring out the window and back to the dials, the man in charge nodded in agreement.

The hours passed slowly as we proceeded toward Iris Harbor. Monroe studied the reflections appearing across the radar screen, checking our position from the Loran signals. The day lumbered through the morning, sifting through a gray afternoon into where the dusk died in the arms of night. We pulled watches and cooked meals and life went on. Neal catnapped, attending his routine of checking the refrigeration system and living in the engine room. By midnight, Monroe took a deep breath for the first time in hours and said, "Land. We've land coming up on the screen."

Across the pale green screen, nothing had shown for hours since heading east for our new destination; a point almost neglected on the charts, at best an uncertain revenant. As the cursor swept over the surface, this first reflection appeared like an iridescent filament floating on the improbable, the glowing scratch fading in pursuit of another arc.

The *Ambrosia* would enter at night. A few more hours passed. Monroe took binoculars, slid down a window, and began to look for breaks and reliefs that might separate themselves from the darkness. More timed passed.

If darkness could have outlines, the lines ricocheting through the binocular's prisms revealed enough anemic substance to give our skipper guidance. Having no choice, he was gambling and, without the chart, he had no idea if rocks waited just beneath our course. He watched the fathometer whose red light-digitals clicked towards shallower grounds.

Like a low hanging star a billion years away, a pinhole of light winked and disappeared. As if playing peekaboo, it hid coyly, to wink again. Relinquishing this caginess, within half an hour it beckoned in a steady twinkle. As the *Ambrosia* grew closer to land, with each swing of the cursor at the unknown terrain, the radar outlined on its screen a sketch of land. We moved toward the mouth of the bay as if it waved us in with an invisible hand. Forms emerged from the night summoning us into this frontier, and our work lights caught a dogleg outcropping of rock, dense black against the night, a few weather-worn trees, and a committee of scrubby bushes, cowering in our work light's reach.

A small village for a few people who worked an outpost of enterprise, Iris Bay wrenched a few months of business from an otherwise uncommercial opportunity. Its mouth, the entrance, offered confusion. Our work lights caught dreamy forms of fog hovering in slow, swirling pretenses defying the light wind burring the grain of otherwise smooth water, creating a place twisting real into surreal. Combined with Monroe's fatigue and stress and the hostile ambiguities of the *Ambrosia*, the navigation demanded emotional and intellectual precision inside the shifting perceptions of the mind and senses. We needed to get into the bay without running aground.

"I'll bet there's not even a navigation buoy," Monroe whispered, finally pushing the chart away. He had opened the window, allowing a surge of biting air intense with salt and land to fill the wheelhouse. He pressed binoculars to his face, their prisms sorting the promises of a distant winking light.

Monroe slowed the engines, cutting back our speed; the *Ambrosia* approached the mouth of the bay, and her lights picked up a lone make-shift marker, an inflatable buoy the size of a beach ball. The safety of the hull and a third of a million dollars of salmon rested on something the size of a child's toy. How it anchored itself to the bottom was unknown, perhaps a rusty old engine salvaged from some expired legion of industry. As we muddled toward this solitary association, the fathometer showed less and less water beneath our hull, and our skipper could not help but consider he was fated to run us aground. The *Ambrosia* pushed forward.

We moved through what seemed an abnormality in time and space, slipping past the small buoy, toward an obscure distance punctuating to an elusive vanishing point of light from an uncertain cannery dock. Nothing seemed real except ruin and a brilliant pinpoint of brightness, a shimmering earth-bound star.

We slowed just above a drift and Monroe called the cannery, and the voice at the other end of this flat earth pierced the ether and gave directions free of the slightest hint of stress, "Simply stay in the gut and proceed toward our lights. You're doing bully."

The *Ambrosia* pushed forward.

It was all so easy. Just make the dogleg into the mouth of the bay and stay in the middle, in the gut of what seemed now a summons. The "bully" voice on the other end of the radio transmission would skiff-out and pilot us in.

Sweat rolled off of Monroe. In his gut, he continued to believe all this would end in failure, but he kept inching forward toward the harsh options. It would be on board the *Ambrosia* that parts of the crew and parts of the steel and parts of the moment would fuse into parts of him. He would not appreciate this fusion of zemblanity and serendipity until decades later, when the aging spirit dwells on its reflections.

The fathometer in a duple beat, pulsed from twenty feet to ten, to five, then to three feet of water, creating a razor-thin separation between the hull and the bottom that only nightmares express vividly. Skippers dream of rocks the size of a fortress ripping into a fuel tank. But they wake up from those dreams. Monroe was awake, and this was not a dream.

With only enough throttle to control the current, he said, "Check our stern, and see if we're kicking up any bottom."

Skeads checked, shining a flashlight on the water churning brown from the prop. We were near going aground.

Monroe asked himself, but we could hear him, "I wonder if these guys even know our draft? How much water do we have in this place? I'm not even sure we can get into this hole and tie to the dock. We might not have enough water under us." He pulled the throttles back to idle. Grabbing the handset of the radio and nearly swallowing it, ignoring any call sign, he blurted, "Have we enough water for a sixteen-foot draft? We got three feet of water under us. Is that the way it should be?"

Cheerful, tinny, crackling, the voice replied. "Right you are. I can see your lights just dandy. I'm on the skiff to assist you to the dock. Stand fast, please ... till we meet. Bully."

"Where are we on the face of the earth ... who's the 'bully' guy?" Monroe asked.

Skeads replied, "You're on that place that charges the admission price for skippering." In Monroe's view, he had progressed from losing any profit in the salmon, to running the *Ambrosia* aground, rupturing a fuel tank and polluting the small bay with fifteen thousand gallons of number two diesel.

Distance seemed in our face, rendered flat and without perspective, isolated pools of pastiche light surfacing from Iris Bay until our work lights caught something the size of a pencil dot. This dot, bouncing toward our lights turned into a skiff careening without fear through the water. Its pilot, with most of his face covered in a windbreaker and a night watch cap, hunkered down near its transom. Our "bully" pilot, sure to himself, advanced.

The skiff bounced and bucked until, finally, it pulled up to within ten feet of us.

Monroe pushed his face through the open window and into the night, yelling at the man in the skiff, "Have we enough water?"

"Not to worry," replied the man as if on an afternoon stroll, "we're at low tide. Follow me, please," and rearing around his aluminum skiff, like a pixie riding the back of a shark, without an

101

ounce of fear, he waved us on, gunning the kicker and stabbing the bow into the night with the skiff heaving and ripping through one of the mysterious pieces of fog. The three feet of water beneath our keel remained a fact.

As we neared the dock, our beams leered into what looked as if the back lot of movie set, perhaps some old John Huston film chucker-blocked with the sets of a northern equivalent of the movie, *The Treasure of the Sierra Madre.* Parts and pieces of old machinery like little old men and women peered out in neatly organized rows, their collective ability exhausted, fatigued old props and ghosts still waiting for another chance, but hauled off stage to the edge of a woods and beyond the present action. The relic of a Model A, hiding in tall grass, hanging on like an old man on a park bench, rested on its fenders, its engine long ago salvaged for another ambition. Maybe its relative anchored the beach ball buoy we had glided by into the mouth of the bay. Another relic, an old two cylinder diesel, crouched conjugally joined to its spouse of a generator, both rusting away together in the night. Decades of seasons had visited this waypoint called Iris Harbor. An irony I only see now, we were living the life that Hustons of the world created in movies.

The various washes of light smoothed harsh lines of the dock, painting this picture in misty sfumato that the right painter turns into art. The wharf and cannery were built into a cliff of rocks rising into a forest behind it; the long pilings to which we secured, allowed for the great flood and ebb of the big tides of the region. From the dock, the cannery rose a story and a half, with a dormer for an office protruding from the roof sporting a few antennas. The building showed careful maintenance with equipment in its place, its siding fresh with paint, and that some invisible hand had respected it. Later, we found out that this cannery was owned by the buyer in Vancouver, an older man named Phillips.

They had flown in at night on a seaplane. A greeting committee of three men, uniformed in spotless white coveralls with "Phillips" logos in bright red majuscules stitched across their backs, stood on the dock. As Monroe guided the *Ambrosia* to the pilings, the oldest one climbed down the ladder, and as soon as our rig's rail neared the pilings, he stepped on it, his hand releasing the rung of the ladder, and leaping on our deck like an old cat, he hiked toward the holding tanks.

The second of the group, our skiff pilot, stripped off his windbreaker and night watch cap—though it was cold enough that our breath boiled from our mouths. He seemed at home in a polo shirt, light denim, and work boots. It may have been three in the morning. He breezed across the deck. He seemed out of place, not a man of the north, but more like an insurance salesman with a round face, a rounded tummy, and office hands. Yet, he appeared most comfortable in this oasis, a man of spherical appearance in control of a jagged place.

Falin suddenly appeared, clean-shaven, dressed like he had just left the pages of an outdoor magazine with his sunglasses resting on his beautiful head of hair.

The pilot, filled with cheerful energy asked Falin, "You must be Monroe? My name is Manfred, and I'm sure we can help you." "Jolly goods" and "quite rights" spliced through our pilot's jargon.

"I hope so," replied Monroe, standing a few feet away, his eyes red-rimmed and suffering from the stress and situational humiliation.

Skeads caught a tool bag and then handed it back when the mechanic stepped aboard. This man dressed in spotless white coveralls and tooled cowboy boots was lanky like Skeads but fresh shaven, his hands clean as a pianist's.

The older man's left hand was missing an index finger, burn-scars covered the back of his hands, and a patch of old burned cheek

103

as pale as drug store candle shared his face. Clean shaven, his pale gray eyes trapped behind horn-rimmed glasses rested on a broken nose. Although short in height, the man was thick as an old rugby player.

The others paid deference, calling him "Mr. Phillips." I had yet to make the connection of the other younger Phillips from No Cannery Bay. From my view, British was all over him, and for some reason, I could picture him in a herringbone worsted with a pipe stuck in his mouth, an English don mustered in and through and out of World War II.

Peering into the tank, Phillips reached up to his elbow into the tank pulling a fish from the cold brine. He smelled the fish, inspected its eyes, opened the gill plates and took time studying them while stroking his hand along the length of the fish as if he might be comforting it. An ivory handled filleting knife appeared in his hand, and the blade glided across the fish belly and opened it like a purse. He pulled out a lobe of roe, washed it off in the tank brine, cut a paper-thin slice, and ate it slowly. In a few strokes of the knife, he filleted the salmon. He cut a thin slice of the meat, squeezing it, throwing it away, then cut another piece that he ate slowly. He repeated this process, chewing another piece while staring into the tank. He gave his only smile. Without emotion or raising his voice, he said, "The product still has our quality. Luck's on our side."

Monroe stood back for some reason. Neal and Skeads followed Falin as he showed both Phillips and the mechanic the refrigeration system, and while yakking about the problem with the pigment in the filters. He played the game perfectly, using "we have tried this" and "we have done that." Both the men listened to Falin until Phillips saw our strange engineer standing in long-johns, fishing boots, with his glasses duct-taped to the bridge of his nose. "Who are you?" asked Phillips. At first, Neal seemed stymied. Like he failed to understand the question or added more complexities than the issue

104

demanded.

"I'm not sure," Neal replied.

The older man studied Neal more closely.

Skeads said, "Neal knows this boat better than any of us. He's the man to talk to."

Phillips asked, "So what do you think ... Neal?"

Neal blinked a couple of time and replied, "Well, the vibrations in the pump have changed since I've been listening ... over the last couple of weeks it sounds different ... maybe higher. I'm not sure." Neal, his eyes puffy, beard and hair exploding around his face, started his analysis, finishing a good five minutes later.

The burned-cheeked man and the mechanic nodded, and poker-faced, listened.

"What's your background in all this?" asked the mechanic. He pocketed his hands, his cowboy boots looking ready for a line dance.

"What do you mean?"

Skeads said, "He worked on nuclear submarines."

Phillips asked Neal, "So what's your guess about the brown pigment?"

Neal screwed up his face and clicked off a few blinks and facial twitches. "I think it might be rust. The system has been infected with rust somehow, maybe before installation, and some kind of friction's pulling it off so fine that its character is concealed. It's abrading the system, maybe slowly burning it up."

"Have you ever worked on a system like this?" asked the mechanic.

"No," replied Neal.

You could see Falin's confident expression slip off his face. His body shifting, he stared at Phillips, and his usual hail-fellow demeanor moved into neutral.

"Have you any training in this?"

"Some."

"How'd you figure it out?"

"I listen."

The mechanic nodded in agreement to Phillips.

"Well, for what it's worth, we agree," replied the older man with burned cheek. "She wasn't lying to you. You may as well shut the system down. It's junk."

When they entered the galley, Neal took the mechanic to the engine room, and they stayed long enough for Falin to prepare breakfast.

When they returned to the galley, the mechanic said, "The engines are fine. We can replace the push rod in Vancouver. For now, it's good to go."

"Who did the repairs?" asked Phillips, his burned and waxy cheek a branding.

Monroe pointed at Neal blinking through his glasses.

"You know anything about those engines?"

"A little."

"So, how'd you figure it out?"

Neal hesitated, his lips slipped around inside the parameters of his beard, "I took what I knew and put it together with the manual."

"Yes. I see. You're an ... interesting ... " replied Phillips. He turned to his cannery manager and said, "Load the tanks up with the ice and get this rig on the road. The tide's turning."

"Bully job," the cannery manager said to Neal.

The group abruptly rose and started to leave. Falin held open the hatch for them shaking their hands and thanking them, taking the mechanic's bag of tools. He had both the mechanic and manager laughing as they climbed the ladder to the cannery.

# Chapter 9: Phillips Cannery

Grand enough to accommodate container ships, a tidal estuary forged a gigantic vein in the earth that seemed to bleed with bizarre blood. Huge vessels, floating behemoths, rumbled past our diminutive boat, their mass looming over the *Ambrosia*. Crewmen, dwarfed to ants by the colossal size of their ships, stood on their bridges and gazed across decks capable of bearing our rig with plenty of room to spare. Against the current, their horsepower pushed with growling reverberations pulsing from inside their steel hulls, with props boiling water behind them, with their bulbous prows plowing outbound to disappear into a wilderness sea and towards foreign ports. Once entering the grand expanse, they too became Lilliputians.

On the *Ambrosia,* we felt like a curiosity using the flooding tide to bobble our way towards speculation. We had only a vague idea for the place we searched. First light seeped into the morning, and in this transition, our exhaustion flowed through us. As we slipped deeper into the river and turned a bend, the largest cannery we had ever seen appeared. Its massive sign, buttressed by steel I-beams and visible from 10,000 feet, stated with black letters against a spotless white background, "Phillips, since 1950." Covering an area the size of a football field, the steel-sided, white cannery building stood two stories high. Standing on deck waiting to throw line, we knew that compared to canneries in our town, we had entered the big leagues.

Having to fight the terrific current, pulling into the slip was like threading a needle's eye with five hundred tons of steel. Monroe gave our beam to the current, set the engines to idle, drifted, and then reversed the thrust, the props dragging the rig stern into the slip. As our *Ambrosia* caught the shadow of the dock and willingly nestled her 500 tons into the slip, a team of workers in white coveralls and hard hats stood by to receive our lines.

On the dock stood the two men, Mr. Phillips and his son, the buyer at No Cannery Bay with the suitcase of money. Self-evident, the scarred face Mr. Phillips was the founder of the logos embossed on the backs of his many employees, covering the steel holding tanks the size of houses, emblazoning across trucks and forklifts and cranes.

Securing the lines and cutting the engines, the *Ambrosia* rested with its load of salmon. Monroe climbed a ladder to the dock, leaving the management of unloading to Skeads.

Standing amidst the handiwork of his achievements, the scar-faced man seemed indifferent, perhaps inured. "You made it," said the older Phillips, "You remember my son?"

They shook hands, and the younger Phillips left and climbed on deck to find Falin. The social pieces fell together.

"Yes, sir. At least we made it this far."

"Risk makes life more interesting." Phillips smiled, the burned skin capable of only suggestions of a smile and measured humor.

"Planning and hard work are good partners. But without luck...." Without finishing the sentence, he looked down on the deck and waited for a technician who had dissected half a dozen salmon. This man peered up to the dock, giving a thumbs-up.

"See what I mean? We calculated. We rolled the dice. We hit the numbers. Our Lady Luck accepted our bet and will pay us ...

"The unimaginative risk money in Las Vegas for this same emotion." He studied Monroe, "By the way ... on your engine ... I want Neal to work with our mechanic."

"Mmm-hmm. Yeah, Neal's probably sleeping beside it. He won't leave the *Ambrosia*. It's his soulmate. He says he can hear the

109

rig talk to him. Hell, I'm beginning to think the rig does." Monroe shrugged, his eyes finding a cigarette butt on the dock.

Phillips picked up on this observation and picked up the butt. "I've been trying for years to get the staff to fieldstrip those damn things. We'll figure it out someday." He returned to the subject. "Yes. Years ago, I lived for an aircraft, and it became so real to me that I would talk to it. I still see now..." He sighed. "You've got a ... special man in him, in this Neal. Being strange is less important when you have talent. The only ability I ever had was that I can see the talent in others. I grab them up like some men grab trophies.

"We live this life...." Phillips left the thought unfinished. He waved his hand over the dock, the employees, the river traffic, "This river starts with a trickle ... less than that ... a raindrop. Life started with less. And they say there are no miracles." His voice lowered. "We're doing fine. For me, even if we had failed, it's worth the risk." Thin lines of wear etched his features, his eyes a gauzy-yellow, rimmed by a thin sheen of red. "What would we do without risk, without work? To be part of its mystery? What mischief replaces it? Hell, how much tragedy is created by its lack? How many wars avoided by its blessings? Someday, I'll not have risk and work. What's the mischief then?" He shook his head, uncomfortable with the direction of the conversation. "I ramble on too much. You're lucky to be young. I envy you. I remember...." His voice trailed off.

Walking away, he said, "You'll do well as long you don't quit. I envy you."

Monroe would never forget those parting words.

\* \* \*

Work, place, and time combined, and the fish became money. Skeads, Falin, and I removed the hatches and Neal set the pumps to

110

drain the tanks of their brine. The work resonated through the whine of hydraulics, of churning gears, the yelling workers, and like some sci-fi half-beast half-man the dock crane approached and shifted its head over our deck and began pulling from the hold brailers filled with salmon. Somewhere, a joyful Mammon grinned. Within the engine room of the *Ambrosia*, Neal and the mechanic—those tooled cowboy boots off and work boots on—pulled the engine apart and repaired it. *Ambrosia* purred from the attention, her paint glowing with her narcissistic red.

Parts found places. Falin made fast friends with the younger Phillips, and they went off to talk marketing. Monroe talked to management, beginning to experience another aspect of skippering. A new perspective appeared, and different people started to see him as they saw themselves performing shared administrative details; unaware, Monroe's suit started to chase him. Skeads stayed on the deck, keeping an eye on the unloading of the salmon, checking the weights of the brailers. Though opposites, Skeads and Monroe worked well together and it would be a relationship they maintained and enjoyed into the future. Our deck boss seemed content to be rid of Falin as he watched him leave with the younger Phillips. He said to me with an indifferent temper, "They're perfect birds of a feather. They'll preen together." He enjoyed an occasional play on words. I began to see how much he disliked Falin but never imagined its ends. Late in the evening, Falin joined the work.

The day accelerated, and with floodlights tricking the night into false noon, evening's approach hyped into the witching hours. Time flies when making money. Slipping with fluid precision into the work and time, another crew entered with their white coveralls embossed with "Phillips" across their backs. Replacing his comrade, a new operator slipped into the chair. The Phillips cannery operated like a machine of human parts, and by dawn, the floodlights took a deep sigh, dimmed, and retired. Then sounds found a respite. The river reappeared, and the behemoth ships changed from nightcrawlers to steel hulls churning their way out of this gut of water. As dawn appeared, an unseen curtain closed on this work, closed on the workers, and the composition evaporated, only our crew and the *Ambrosia* remained. For some reason, we forgot our fatigue. Neal was right, she had stuck with us.

On the dock, Mr. Phillips and the mechanic with the tooled cowboy boots stood together. They climbed down the dock ladder and greeted us.

Falin and I finished securing the deck. Mr. Phillips gave Monroe several cases of canned gourmet salmon as a gift. "They're destined for markets in France. The roe goes to the Japanese Christmas market. They use salmon eggs for gifts. It's been very profitable for us. It's all sold. Cash in the bank. By the way," the scare-faced man paused for a minute, fixing on Monroe, "I want Neal. He did an exceptional job with that engine and nailed the refrigeration. He's too smart to be a fisherman. He laughed at his comment. With a little help and tutoring, I suspect he will fit here. But I thought I'd at least ask you first. It's not above me to steal talent. He laughed again. I like intelligent people around me." The man enjoyed negotiating.

Phillip's bluntness unbalanced Monroe. "Well ... well ... he can make his own decisions." I could tell that the old man's power nonplussed our skipper. Also, I don't know how to describe how both envy and disbelief both flush and reveal the treasured façade we maintain of ourselves, where the shames and vanities can no longer hide behind our masks: Falin's, while standing in this small drama, revealed what only a painter's canvas captures. He, too, for different reasons, looked stumped.

Skeads found Neal re-taping his broken glasses sitting in the galley. "Get on deck. Kid, you've got a job offer. Don't be stupid. Take it. The man wants you. Take the deal."

In front of Phillips, Neal found himself standing in his long johns and boots, rubbing eye sockets stuck behind his wacko glasses. Heroes seldom appear heroic.

Phillips gave him a short pitch of his intention: "Come try us. If it doesn't work out, I'll personally see that you get back." Falin stepped back, slack-jawed.

Neal's response hinted of omens and of unstated and unfilled prophesies. "No. I can't. I promised the *Ambrosia* I'd stay until we get back, until it's finished. I've promised her."

Phillips studied Neal whose eyes fixed with not a blink in them. The older man glanced away toward the river, his expression turned and shifted to a melancholy, framed less as a disappointment than failure. I can't describe the subtlety. "Yes, I can understand that. Yes, I know what you mean. Yes. I should have seen that in your nature. It's not about the money. I felt like that once. But you've enough crew with experience. It's not life and death. It's not a war. I think you can help us here and maybe we can help you in some way. Reconsider."

Neal adjusted his glasses, firmly pressing them on his nose. They cockeyed across his nose but his eyes filled with conviction. "No, sir. I can't."

"Youth," the older man said. "I was young once. Yes, maybe when you get finished with what you must do." Phillips sighed. "I had friends in the submarines." His filleting knife appeared in his hand, and he handed it to Neal. I hadn't noticed it before, but an artisan had carved the bone-handle into the body of a fish and the head of a man.

"Here, take this. I need to give it to you. Someone gave it to me. It's not really mine to keep. You might keep our operation in mind. Better yet, you might bring it back."

113

"Neal, take the damn job. Get out of here," said Skeads. His voice tense, our deck boss stared at an event that to the rest of us seemed random luck. His face, his usual stoic attitude unsettled, lost its balance, and his expression turned to a plea, twisting to unintentional anguish. "Hell to pay. I'll help you pack. Get out."

Falin watched all that transpired and remained speechless. His jawed tightened, and with no sunglasses covering them—his eyes always seemed a little too close to one another—our magazine man studied this unexpected graciousness, or perhaps, plea.

"I think we can get your *Ambrosia* back on our own," said Monroe.

The mechanic said to Neal, "You're natural at this stuff. Hell, we'll get you fixed up with cowboy boots and some glasses that fit. This operation's helped me."

Neal, shaking head, stared at the deck. "That's not the point. You're missing the point."

Skeads didn't miss any points. I suspect now that both he and Phillips sensed those aspects that rumble under the otherwise overlooked surfaces of life. The old man pitched once more. "I wish you would reconsider, as an older man to a younger. I think you belong here. Reconsider."

Decades later, when I recall this moment, I can't remember if *Ambrosia's* soulmate and engineer even looked at the knife or said a word of gratitude. But he kept it. It may have been one of the kindest gestures he had ever received. Alternatively, it may have been fate if such coincidences exist.

In less than a month, his life had changed from a homeless wanderer to being recruited by one of the most successful businessmen in the industry. But Neal shook his head, and without further words, opened the hatch, disappeared into the aft house, and went to crank up the engines. The *Ambrosia* yearned for open waters.

# Chapter 10: Neal

After several days of open water, less than twelve hours separated the *Ambrosia* from town. With Monroe in the wheelhouse, another night closed over us and a calm sea followed our path. Fresh from a shower, Skeads' wet hair framed his boney face like strands of pale old yarn. He slid behind the galley table, laid his tusk cribbage board down, shuffled his cards, dealt two hands and played against himself. He ignored me. It was Neal's turn to cook, but we wanted to eat without having to suffer from his culinary malevolence. I had prepared three pans of meatloaf mixed with Italian sausage and wrapped in bacon. They slow-cooked and filled the galley with their soul of pork, salt, excessive fat, and comfort. Red bliss potatoes waited to be mashed with diced red onions and butter. The cabbage salad waited in the wings for a compliment of a mayo-vinaigrette, and our hunger sat at the table licking its chops. A cold beer would have been nice.

After several hours in the engine room, Neal joined us and sat at the table reading his book of prime numbers. During our leisure time, Skeads and I practiced avoiding Neal's uttering, but in the galley's confines, we couldn't ignore his chant-like muttering. His restive face hovered over the pages. He rocked back and forth, and the words "yes, inevitable, yes" emerged loud enough to jump, squirm and fidget into our otherwise shared silence. Taking space and shape, these gremlins scurried around the surface of the galley table, bumping into the tusk and across my dinner preparations.

Neal blurted to Skeads, "Are you winning?"

Without looking up from his cards, he replied, "You never lose when playing against yourself."

For several minutes, we listened to Neal and his chanting. His face twitched. Skeads looked up from his game, his eyes the palest of blue and his skin one shade above typing paper. "Are you okay, Neal?" The *Ambrosia* rolled lazily throwing off by a few degrees any illusions of a level surface.

Looking up from his book of math, Neal again asked Skeads, "If you know a wrong is going to happen do you have a duty to prevent it?"

"What?" asked Skeads. "So, you're still there?"

"No. No. Nothing like that, nothing like that. *Ambrosia's* made her peace. We've answered her demands. She's going to do the next crew fine." He muttered to himself and then said, "Yes, Yes, something like that. But there is a serious fault. She sees it. She sees it and tells me."

"Are you all right?" asked Skeads. He rearranged a few cards in his hand, saying without looking up, "Neal, are you okay?"

I kept my back to them because I wanted to avoid Neal's strangeness, a strangeness that seemed this evening closer to madness. I turned away from my meatloaves and potatoes and opened the refrigerator.

"If you know that an engine is going to fail ... with certainty. With certainty, do you have an obligation to prevent it?"

"All engines fail soon enough," said Skeads. "All you can do is try. What's the problem?"

"If you can see horror coming, are you responsible for preventing it even though it hasn't happened?" Neal's voice had turned raspy as if he might have been shouting for hours over the rattle of the engines.

Skeads put down his cards and listened to him as if they might be playing cribbage together. A minute passed while he studied

117

Neal, and then weighing each word like a card in a losing hand, he softened his voice to where I could barely hear him above the engines.

The strange conversation caught Skeads' skepticism off-guard. "I knew we might get here. I can't answer that question. I'm not into this kind of talk. I avoid that stuff....

"We're both outsiders ... you and me. But it doesn't really mean anything. You can't let the past or the future strangle you. You can't control the future. It doesn't exist. All we can do is the present. Do the best you can. We're meant to fail and then survive. Failure and pain ... that's the way it is ... leastways for guys like you and me. Stay out of the future. Put your head under a pillow and sleep. Get some rest. Think real hard about your friend."

Even from a distance of forty years, before that future in the galley unfolded, I remember this strange conversation, so unusual for men who work in a brutal place. Standing there in the galley, watching the players compose themselves within this picture, I still see our deck boss's ghostly face, twisted and gargoyled, as if peering down from some gothic-portico-mantle. Skeads, while preparing carefully for the future he denied would come, was a man who hated the past he was captured by and which he withheld from us. And then there was that damn strange-carved board over the galley table, and with the knot carved into an eye and painted by some unknown woodcarver, the eye staring and observing Neal as much as any of us.

Neal ignored what Skeads said, and asked, "If you can prevent an engine from failing, why not a murder when you can see it coming?" He glanced everywhere, and his eyelids clicked behind his duct-taped glasses, the surreal question fouling the galley, killing attempts at a decent meal.

Skeads shook his head, and his stringy hair boogied a little

118

around the sides of his skull. Studying his cards, he picked up a peg, only to replace it in the same position. Unnerved, his eyes shifting between us, he replied, "Only a fool believes in the future. It only exists when it's the past, and then it's too late. It's a forgery inside our heads we fill with fairytales. The suits believe in the future, but it only feeds their needs. Most of them would rather deal with the future than the here and now. Keep an eye on the day. With some luck, you can stay ahead of the ... joke."

"That's not what she's saying. She asks to prevent it," replied Neal.

"She?"

"*Ambrosia*." As another wave slipped under our hull, taking its time, shifting from port to starboard, the boat swayed once more.

"Eat some supper and get some sleep. Rest helps." Skeads returned to his cribbage, but after a minute he looked up and saw Neal, his head nodding, still looking at him with his lips in silent chant.

"I'm sorry Neal. But I'm the wrong guy. It's all nothing to me. I can't even stop it inside myself. Give a man a chance between buying a new truck or doing something decent, and he'll pick the truck, praise bigheartedness, and then ignore the damage. Christ on a crutch, the atrocities committed in the name of good would gag a maggot. We keep the killing, as long as we keep ourselves at a safe distance that fits into nice little values. The big shots preach, and we listen. We believe their nobility just as long we never smell the stink and see maggots. Stay away from feeding maggots." Skeads laughed without joy, and with his teeth stained so brown and his skin so bloodless, his laugh seemed rotten, the laugh of a corpse. "Get through the day. Today is certain. Fix today. You've done good with the refrigeration and engine. Be content with that. Rest and dance with your friend when we hit town."

119

Falin appeared fresh from the shower. He wore pressed Levi's and a clean cowboy shirt with button downs, but no sunglasses. With a fluffy towel, he dried his hair and ran a comb through it. I could only think how sorely he might miss it when his hairline—like mine—retreated and its abundance began to mass around a shower drain. I could see him with a comb-over. For this trip, I was tired of living with him and his confident attitude. But I envied him for some crazy reason. He believed life unfolded without having to pay for bad decisions, selfish desires, and goals. I was jealous that girls found him attractive. He had a great truck. Maybe, I began to dislike him because I shared the same desires, desires no thicker than a dollar bill or the paint on his red truck. I hated seeing myself too clearly.

Falin asked Skeads, "You winning?"

Glancing at Falin, Skeads' skinny lips twitched waiting to respond, "You never win when playing against yourself."

Neal looked up from his book, noticing the two different answers Skeads had given to the same question. He said, "A 'never' equals 'not A'. You can't have it both ways."

Falin stopped at Neal's answer, shrugged, and kept talking. "I picked up some hot information about old man Phillips." He had said nothing about his night out with the son of Mr. Phillips. He slid into the bench of the galley and looked around the table waiting for a response. Neal ignored him, Skeads waited silently.

"Seems that Mr. Burnt-face Phillips flew those fighter planes in the sky over England. World War II. Got shot up three times and survived. He's the real deal. Larry told me ... there's a guy who knows how to party. But Phillips after the war moved to Canada and started that whole business out of a 32-foot day-boat. He's got money in shipyards, gold mines, motels, owns four banks and big property in Barbados. The cannery is a ground floor of an empire,

120

but it's his first love." He looked around the table for the effect of his inside knowledge. Skeads acted indifferently, and I, impressed. Neal, staring out from his duct-taped glasses, rocked back and forth.

"I'd like to be like that someday. That's what I call success. Phillips is an important business contact." Falin switched subjects. He looked around at us, "Man, I'm ready to see Sabrina. I miss her." He sang some jingle and rolled his shoulders in a two-step. "What smells so good? You're not cheffing are you Neal? Hey, you knocked 'em dead at Phillips." His joy and buoyancy beamed from his delicate features. Let there be no doubt; he was a good looking guy, particularly in his mind. But his deep blue eyes crowded just a little too close to the beautiful bridge of his unbroken nose.

Neal addressed Skeads. It sounded almost a plea. "She's telling me. She knows. She's told me something I don't want to hear. But I must listen to her unless I break my word."

Neal asked Falin, a question that had been circling for hours, "Why'd you hit me and break my glasses?" There seemed no rancor in the question, more like a plain and straightforward query.

Skeads folded his cards. Staring at the table, he said, "Get out of here Falin. Go comb your hair." I felt the same way but lacked the courage to back the statement up. When recalling this event, I now regret that maybe, if I had backed-up Skeads, between the two of us we might have changed events waiting to occur. Neal's words with a life of their own, tiptoed across the table, over the tusk, and to Skeads. Our engineer, a conduit, passed on what the *Ambrosia* passed to him.

Neal said to Falin: "She's indifferent to the absurd, but she knows great harm. That's the formula. You're going to be the skipper."

Falin smiled. He accepted this information with pride. "I didn't think you had any respect for me. I appreciate that."

At the time, we all failed to see that our crazy engineer foretold the future, for he saw time without distinctions, as a process, as future joined to the present and melding into the past. He was right; it was all connected.

"You're going to hurt people and kill someone." Neal never shifted his eyes from Falin.

Falin seemed not a lick off his game. "I appreciate what you said, but you're not looking good. Take Skeads' advice and stick your head under a pillow. Dream about your basketball chick? This trip's almost done. You'll find another rig."

Skeads said quietly, "Neal ... Falin's not the skipper. You need a rest. Maybe some help. It won't mean nothing a hundred years from now who's skippering what. Let it go. Get some rest."

"Sure enough, get some rest so you can polish up that cannery chick in that dead-man sleep you do," added Falin.

"It's more than that," replied Neal.

Without raising his voice, Skeads seethed, "Falin, I don't like you." He fumbled for a cigarette. "I've killed better men than you. And now it kills me. I got nothing...."

Neal rocked and chanted in disjointed words and phrases, glancing between Skeads and me. With his eyes clicking behind broken glasses, he asked, "Does the expression for hull speed exist outside of water and hulls? Which came first? Before any hulls and water would the formula still exist waiting to exist?"

He begged Skeads, "Does an expression for us exist before we are born? If no one is here to see, does our formula still exist? Are we all just waiting to fulfill ... a formula? Do we exist waiting to exist? In the same way that a formula for hull speed waits for water?

Is birth our ... our singularity? What is death?"

Neal chanted on, talking to himself and making no sense to any of us. He peered into the pages of his book, his finger tracing the lines.

Skeads tried to help. "Neal. You're way over my head. But you need sleep. Eat something and get some sleep."

"I'm destined to die. It's in the proofs." Neal tapped the open page of his book. "She tells me. It's in this book...." Neal turned and stared and blinked at Falin standing above him. "She's figured it out. I don't want to do it, but she told me to prevent ... that's why she made sure Mr. Phillips gave me the ... the totem."

I avoided the moment, thinking it would go away by avoiding it.

Neal said, "But I had to stay because she wants me here to protect her from ... from what she has told me. She doesn't want to be part of it." His voice trickled off, and he lowered his eyes to the table. His forearms rested in a perimeter around the book.

With unusual conviction, I mashed the potatoes. I turned off the oven, and I could hear over my shoulder Falin say almost apologetically, "Neal you need to find something else to do. This kind of life doesn't work for you."

I looked over my shoulder as if my shoulder might hide me, trying to ignore a galley shrinking with every word.

Staring down at Neal, Falin stood up and ran his comb through his thick hair. "Maybe that cannery chick can settle some sense into you. God knows she's put out enough while you've been mumbling around here for the last month. If you know so much about numbers and manuals, what formula am I? What does your *Ambrosia* say about me?"

"Singularity," Neal replied without hesitation. He added, "Mr.

Phillips understands. He gave me Dagon."

Neal studied Falin like a cipher in his book. "She shuns what you require. Avoids. But you'll make her. If somebody doesn't stop you, you'll use her to kill."

We had no idea if he was talking about the *Ambrosia*, the cannery girl, himself, or all of us. We had no idea he was foretelling a future only he could see. He turned a few pages in his math book where a formula or expression was underlined in pencil and a penciled star in the border. He ran his finger back and forth across it.

Eyes may be the window to the soul, but the face frames the enigma. I watched Skeads' face wither to grief and disgust, the two emotions battling across his pale and bloodless features.

Falin leaned over the table, his white teeth sparkling, and said, "What are you talking about? The rig or some rosy story of your cannery girl. Kid, you don't make any sense. Never have. I'll give you the engine room. But, you're not sharp enough to see you can't polish a turd."

Neal said, "My duty."

The gift, the filleting knife with the bone handle, carved into a head of a man and the body of a fish, appeared in Neal's hand, and the surgical blade went straight for Falin's throat.

With a potato masher paused in mid-mash, I stood dumbfounded by the attempted throat-cutting, and before Neal could make the blade strike twice, Skeads gripped his wrist and pushed him to the floor. The ivory cribbage board and cards came alive, leaping from the table and across the floor. The book didn't budge, like it was nailed to the table. The *Ambrosia* trimmed steady as an anvil. I'll never be sure, but that carved eye in the board stared at all of us, then twinkled.

It would become quite an irony that Skeads saved Falin's life.

# Chapter 11: Margins

Five seconds separated the beginning from the end. Three heartbeats. The muscle on the side of the Falin's neck was opened no differently than the belly of a gutted salmon. Sliced. Without thinking, with one hand holding the potato masher, stymied by the distortions of the unexpected violence, I handed Falin a dish towel, and he pressed it to his neck. He seemed amazed more than injured or scared, and taking a breath, he commented casually, "I didn't think the pussy had it in him."

Skeads had twisted the knife away from Neal. As if he had planned for this violence, without raising his voice, he told me to get Neal out of the galley. Our strange engineer's attack finished, he collapsed, and I restrained him with little effort. I held him in a loose headlock.

The engines slowed to idle, and from the wheelhouse, Monroe clambered two stairs at a time down the ladder to the galley. One of his feet slipped on Falin's blood and smeared it into a red frown. Completely off guard, our skipper glanced at it as if it might be a scar across the linoleum. Depending on the perspective, the smear of blood across *Ambrosia's* galley deck could have been as easily smiling up at him as frowning. Seeing the knife, the blood, and the tusk and cards scattered across the galley floor, he asked, "What's this? What's all this?"

At first, when Monroe glanced at me with my loose headlock around Neal, it appeared we were fighting, but then he saw Falin pressing the towel to the side of his neck, with the bone-handled filleting knife resting on the green linoleum. The knife's destiny fulfilled, its unique carved human head lay gazing across the green floor.

Neal chanted, "Did I stop it? Did I stop him?"

In a resigned, tired voice—to whom I don't know—Skeads stated, "Can't you see what will happen?" I have no idea what he meant by this.

Monroe repeated, "What the hell is going on here?"

A testament to his admirable physical courage, Falin had recovered a composure that he had never lost. "Man, you're going to jail." With that statement, I began to see what Skeads meant. But Falin ignored the idea that he might be bleeding out. In disgust, holding the towel to his neck, he kicked Neal and then hit him in the face, sending our engineer's glasses—that had miraculously stuck to his face—to the floor. I saw the blow coming, but I failed to shield him.

Oblivious to the punch, Neal asked once more. "Did I get it?"

Even then, I thought how strange he referred to Falin as an "it."

Monroe and Skeads pulled the wounded man away pushing him into the galley bench.

"Let me look at it," Skeads said, pulling aside the towel. The knife had cut into the muscle but had missed the artery. "You'll live to see another day ... leastways from this."

Falin proved a tough guy, showing little fear or pain. He played the moment with an adroit drama and consummate craft, working this event intuitively to his advantage, straddling the cleft between victim and hypocrite.

"I'll see him in jail. He tried to kill me. You all saw it." Falin possessed, or maybe a better description might be, was possessed by inexhaustible confidence. Whatever truth is, he knew it.

Something of the moment occurred, one of those overlooked, unexpected exchanges, which when recalled later in life, proved

126

significant and I still remember it: Falin said to Skeads, "I didn't know the little shit had it in him. Thanks for saving my life. I owe you." The thanks would be accurate—to a limited analysis. Skeads took a pressure bandage from the first aid kit and secured it to the wound, saying, "Falin, you do find meaning in life, and mostly when you're its center." Our deck boss added, "I couldn't care less about saving your skin."

Skeads' reply went ignored or unheard, and like a scene in a cowboy movie, when the wounded hero steps-up to the front screen, Falin replied, "Doesn't matter. He's going to jail as soon as we hit the dock. This needs justice."

Monroe said to me, "Get Neal into his bunk, and tie him to it if you have to."

Skeads, his face pale, empty, twisted into the words, "I'm sorry Neal. Way back I should've stopped it." To no one in particular, perhaps to the *Ambrosia*, he added, "For sure, it's done."

Neal, chanting in a strange language, his eyes fixed, a different world now owned our engineer. As I pushed and half carried Neal towards his bunk, he said, "I tried. I know she saw it. Her eye...."

I'm sure Monroe was considering whether this maiden trip omened any future for him as a skipper, for in one trip he'd come close to running a boat aground, had come close to losing an engine to a madman who then saved the engine, and had come within a few hours of losing several million dollars' worth of retail-price salmon. Now, he had come within an inch from witnessing a murder. From his perspective, it may have been prudent and sane to start looking for a dishwashing job. A flummoxed Monroe said, "What's next?"

The answer from Skeads struck the table like a hatchet, "Throw him overboard. We can put him in a crab pot. He won't suffer much, not that it matters." In the galley, his calm appraisal, echoed, both

127

convincing and insane. His face looked no different than when playing his cards.

"Jesus, don't lose a grip on this. I need you," was Monroe's gut response.

Skeads replied, "Grip has nothing to do with it. We're in the middle of no place, floating on five hundred fathoms of water. Right now, right here, we are the grip. Put him in a crab pot and throw him over the rail. In the long run, it may be for the better."

In this irrational moment, the only irrational moment I ever saw in him, nonetheless; the way this event unraveled, an event whose consequences would require a lot of time to fulfill destiny, his solution might have proved no worse, and perhaps, the best of terrible options.

Skeads retrieved his bloodstained cards off the floor, as well the pegs that had followed the tusk. On his pants, he cleaned them no differently than he would the blood of a salmon.

"That's fine by me," replied Falin, "We can say he fell over by accident. Hell, he's crazy enough to where we could say he jumped overboard. It's not the first time. He's insane. We're probably doing him a favor."

Monroe, stunned, stood silent for a moment with his eyes fixed on the walrus tusk. He gained control and said, "Nobody's going no place. I'm tying this rig to the dock with the guys I left with."

Falin replied, "The guy's a certified loony. We have no idea what nut house he escaped from. He might still come after us. We could say he attacked me and then jumped overboard."

Skeads wiped the blood off the tusk with the discarded towel. "Falin, this is one of the few times I agree with you. Neal is nuts ... but we're all crazy. We just hide it better."

Skeads peered under the table for another card, found it, placing it in his deck. "But you got it all wrong. I'm not throwing Neal overboard. I'm throwing you. Justice is luck ... it's all about who's holding the cards." His laugh rasping the air, he added, "Hell to pay, if I can't live with it, I'll be right behind you. In the long run, we're no different from those seagulls you shoot. In the end, we're all target practice.

Falin's face looked slapped, sullied of any pretentions. He appeared more shocked by Skeads' judgment than from the wound. "Neal did this to himself. I never forced him to cut me."

"Bull. When you sucker punched him ... if he had a knife then ...You were just smart enough to catch him sleeping. You've been provoking him. And we put up with it. Don't ask me why. If you'd kept your mouth shut ... you deserved what happened. You can't see the difference. But it don't matter.

"Here's what all of us are going to do. We keep this on the boat. It was just a fight, and there's no need to call the cops. You slipped in the shower. That's the way it's going to be. If not, I'll open you up or die trying. It don't matter no more. I've had just about enough of this life." He pulled out his survival knife.

Monroe pleaded, "Skeads. Help me out. Put the knife down. Stand down. Help me out here. I need your help. You're doing no good by this."

Falin's eyes, both steady and defiant, said, "You won't do it. Even if you could get away with it. You wouldn't kill an unarmed man."

Without a doubt, Monroe and I believed Skeads when he said, "Don't bet on it. I couldn't care less. It's taken me years to figure out—it's fools like you who are dangerous." The carved eye of the *Ambrosia* stared from its plank and leisurely blinked for the second time.

Falin said, "I'm not the one who's crazy. He's the nut case. He's talking to the walls and hearing the boat talk. He broke the law."

"Law? You're right on all of it but it don't mean nothing." Skeads turned to Monroe, "What's worse, throwing overboard this monkey, or...?

Monroe replied, "Falin didn't try to cut his throat."

Skeads said, "He was provoked. I'm saying the law will never see what's right. They'll see the law."

"Skeads, if I have to stop you myself, I'll try as best I can. You'll have to cut me. You need to back down." The *Ambrosia* rolled, lingering on the list.

"Your god made the ways we die, not me." Skeads' pale, thin skin tightened over his face, but he never raised his voice. "He made us, His deformed children, His sorry tools, His bungling creation. What kinda monster...."

"Why?" replied Falin, "I've done nothing to you. I thought me and you were on the same side."

"You make it easy to hate humans. I hate life ... but lack the guts to end it." Skeads put his knife away.

Falin looked at Skeads, "You hate life? That's not my problem. What's that got to do with this?"

"Because this life is here, right now, and we're going to screw it up."

Even years later, I'm not sure if Skeads made any sense. His unknown past connected to this moment. I slid over to the meatloaf, sliced it, and put more butter on the potatoes, generally making a fool of myself, avoiding the situation. "Maybe we should eat something. The meal's ready, and we shouldn't let it go to waste."

My pathetic suggestion went ignored.

Skeads said, "So here's the deal. Neal walks. I get him out of town, and I'll get him to Phillips."

Falin replied, "No way. He tried to kill me."

"I'm not bargaining."

The standoff lasted about a breath. Another bloodletting loitered in the spaces separating the three men. The engines below, in neutral, purred like heartbeats waiting for another moment of violence. The sign swayed on its hinges and seizing the galley lights the eye blinking uninhibitedly. The *Ambrosia* rolled in a gentle trough.

Falin studied Skeads, "All right. Maybe I did play him too hard. I thought he could take it. I'll look the other way on this. You keep him away from me, so I don't hurt him, and we'll call it an accident. We're only a few more hours from town anyway. You've got my word." Falin acted the picture of sincerity. With the lights separating his handsome features, the thick collar of the bandage seemed like a platform juxtaposing his head from his body. Skeads had played his game.

Monroe asked, "Have we got your word on this?"

"Without a doubt," said Falin.

Skeads said, "Mark my words Falin ... they'll be a settlement if you cross me. Leave Neal alone."

The game played by Falin and Skeads folded, but this conflict would dictate their futures and twist rabidly around one another. But now, the compromise seemed secure, and we started to feel we could breathe and perhaps eat dinner.

* * *

When we pulled into town a collection of different people

131

gathered on the dock. Along with the fox woman and the cannery girl, the troopers waited. The only answer I could think of was Falin had somehow called his uncle at the cannery.

His pressure bandage secured around his neck, Falin, without throwing a line, leaped off the *Ambrosia*. Grabbing the ladder, he shouted more at those standing on the dock than to us, "You can't ask for my word when I was bleeding to death. It's what I had to do. We can't have guys like him running wild. He tried to kill me. It's not about me. That madman could hurt anybody."

As the troopers handcuffed him, Neal offered no resistance. He never looked back.

Work filled the day. At first light the next morning, Skeads and I went to the jail to visit our engineer.

As Skeads and I approached the door of the trooper station, Neal's cannery friend was leaving. She may have been camping out all night to see him. She was still wearing that field jacket and stocking cap like she'd just left a barracks. As if carved from a beach rock, her round face held no emotion, and without a tear in her eye, her eyes pierced through us finding more significance in what was behind us and ahead of her.

She let us discover for ourselves. I believe she wanted us to experience it for ourselves, a form of native stoicism. We were too late. During the night Neal had hanged himself.

I don't recall if anyone claimed his body. I know that Skeads, Monroe, and I accepted the event with no comment between us.

Neal had guessed right, or maybe, he did see into the future. Management fired Monroe and hired Falin as the next skipper of the *Ambrosia*. Monroe thought his future finished.

Damned if Falin wasn't a terrific skipper. Very capable. The *Ambrosia,* she treated him well. Women liked him.

132

For several years, Skeads never mentioned Neal or much about Falin for that matter. We were all strong, silent types then.

# Part III: Skeads and The Fishing Vessel, *Sunburst*

# Chapter 12: Skeads and Billins

A bottle of 86-proof sour mash stood on a salvaged, green, Formica table top. This mesa made a convenient resting place for a stack of back issues of the local paper, a leather pouch of tobacco and a rolling machine. A mug of hot coffee, a Siren of sorts, sang for the companionship of a couple of ounces of the glorious amber. On the top shelf of a bookcase, Skeads had crafted a sanded, sealed driftwood rest with the walrus tusk settled comfortably into it, awaiting a game. Over the years, since before both the *Faith* and the *Ambrosia*, he had added a few more etchings to its ivory surface, and now he figured he wanted to add the herring boat he and Monroe had invested in. Indeed, as these memories composed themselves and waited for their entrance onto the ivory stage, the provincial artist in him would continue to etch the events of his private history. On the lower shelves, Shakespeares, Dostoevskys, Mowats, and Chandlers enjoyed their companionship, hail fellows well met.

Outside the window of his small Airstream trailer, a benign early morning and last gasp of winter painted an impressionistic illusion of a northern fairyland composed of snow adorned bushes and trees glistening among the frozen grays and mud. A blue moon dangled in the night sky like a nightwalker's eye, projecting its bright white light into the straggly stands of trees sentried in dark columns lining the rutty entrance to his home. Skeads sat at his table feeling the chill seeping through the window pane and touching his nearest hand and cheek gently, leaving the other half of him sensing the warmth of the kerosene heater. Across the table, where another chair rested in the silence, a chessboard hosted a bloodless battlefield waiting for a suspended attack from a white rook and knight poised to determine the fate of the black king.

Living Spartan, he had tuned the trailer with the small kerosene heater, a Coleman two burner camp stove, and a small refrigerator that during the winter months he never needed. No TV or radio. A single bed lay against another wall. Out here, he lived a solitary life that suited him, a content man but for the elusive sleep.

In his quiet space, he watched hazy steam from his coffee drift upwards and then disappear. He gripped the handle of the bottle and poured the first shot of the morning.

His trailer, a small model, had been abandoned by one of Monroe's crewmen, and between the two of them, they had hauled it over to the lake property Skeads had purchased a few years back. His skipper showed-up one day with the telephone truck and installer, and Monroe, perhaps the only person he would call a friend, had obliged him to put in a phone.

Skeads looked forward to browsing through the thick stack of last month's thin bi-weekly newspapers, to read leisurely through the town's recent history—old news now—and then to head for town and see what might be happening by chance at Polly's. He needed to talk with Monroe, his business partner.

Skeads had just finished a brutal fishing season. The intensity of the experience lingered to unwind slowly, disassembling, often involuntarily cascading from his unconscious to swim without discipline in the lakes of his mind. At night, in a warm bed with a few shots, his memories unconsciously released and broke into their roles, the individual scenes recurring like black-and-white photographs, as fixed and as persistent as flesh-and-bone reality. The local paper provided a prop for his eyes to focus on, at this point more a diversion.

The herring run appeared as nothing more than a high expectation. The boats and fishermen faithfully assembled according to the season, but only a few foolish fish showed.

Skeads had hoped to pay for the boat and the gear that Monroe owned as much as he, but the facts of the season proved he had scrounged only enough off the fishing grounds to pay for his food and fuel.

Unable to sleep, he arose early and tried to fill the morning darkness with this newsprint stretched out before him, but his mind's eye could only see his borrowed leaky tent. He saw the constant wind cut across the water rich with odors of sea and salt, its beach paved with black and gray smooth stones and laced with black seaweed. A drizzle created an unforgiving mist with the drippings, tasting like steel. Morons called it Spring. His crewman, not a moron, gave up and went home. He held the man blameless. The wind, more a warrior-raider, churned the shoreline the fishermen worked, and they watched this indifferent gusty force rage. Sea fowl hunkered behind wind shadows. Skeads sometimes wondered if he had died and waited for Charon to row him to his eternal home, a lake not of fire, but roiled slush. His tent leaked with a vengeance. For what? For the money, he thought, or perhaps the fear of the unintended consequences of quitting.

However, while sitting at his table, he knew in some time and place that this last month would turn into the bar-room-embellished-adventure, memorialized, sanitized and romanticized, and then be carefully honored on some shelf of the memory. As he took his first sip of coffee and mash, as the strange, incomparable sweet-edgy flavor filled his mouth, the last month began to seem more like a dark comedy. The herring season was behind him now, a contained semi-history, being tucked away in the cubbyholes of remembrance, and when sitting surrounded by the comfort—and perhaps illusory safety of the warmth—he resolved he would fish herring the next season. Next year would be profitable; this season had been merely a recreation education, an adventure, an ascension of a continuous curve. A glimmer of hope still dwelled somewhere in him.

138

For conjoined in this apparent abscess of nature, there could be found a unity, a crispness, an intensity unequaled any place else in his life, a grand indifference where seagulls and puffins and otter foraged in chatter and squawks and squeaks, raising their young, abandoning their dead, feeding on a common sea that both provided and took their lives. Together they endured, a shadow-nobility; they ascended by the mystery of the will to live. Skeads shared in this exquisite malevolence.

* * *

Flipping through the pages of the paper, his eyes lingered on a brief article, maybe two inches long. The lower left corner of the third page reported an accidental death had occurred on a boat while tied to the dock. The name of the boat was the *Ambrosia*. It didn't surprise him. He immediately recalled the tragic human confluence joining Neal and Falin. Regardless, in this new tragedy, the name of the deceased had been withheld pending the notification of relatives. In the brief who, what, where, when and how of the article, a diver had been killed under the boat while cutting off a line tangled around the output staff. The twin engines had been accidentally started and incomprehensively put in gear. The article failed to report why this happened, the "why" capable of howling. Though Skeads may not have muttered anything either to himself or out loud, though the article may have stopped his reflections on the herring season, and though he may have accepted this kind of occurrence as if it were a consequence of a dangerous life, his focus changed when he read more.

He searched farther into the issues until he saw the obituary of the diver who had been cut to pieces by the props. He knew Dan Billins, a drifter like so many who lived up north, like many pushed and pulled by someplace down below and through the wandering process find themselves surrounded by destination.

Stumbling into town with nothing much more than what Billins could carry on his back and the weariness of what he escaped from down below, the man came to rest. For this hammer-hard town felt right to him, that particular moment of the found locus, when you feel you belong and can rest. And he was correct. The town hosted him well.

This young man settled in. A crew cut distinguished his handsome face, and a bullet-scarred cheek rescued any prettiness from his clear blue eyes and perfect skin. Two missing fingertips disfigured his left hand. He met a pleasant, half-native cannery girl, married, and fathered a child with round and ruddy countenance. The child was the perfect picture of hope with dark eyes from his mother and skin that seemed to blossom from a pale rose. They, as a family, stood out in no unique way, having no inclination to stand out as they seemed to have found contentment in a place, in themselves, and in a settlement most people in the Lower 48 would have seen as a harsh-blown and frigid non-place. Whatever demons or disappointments they might have brought with them, whether malaise or wrath, all the baggage shifted, drifted, and found a peace; they found in their companionship a gentle enclave they never took for granted.

Two years ago, Skeads came home to find his water pipes frozen solid from the well pump to his trailer. That evening, the idea of crawling around on the edge of the night with a propane torch and heat gun was out of his comfort zone. He had spent the day working on gear, and another two hours crawling around on his back would not be Plan B unless it had to be.

A stranger had stuck a flyer on his truck offering, among other services, to thaw frozen pipes for half-off. At eight o'clock at night, he figured no one would answer, but he took a hail-Mary calling the number. A woman's voice answered and said without the need to raise her voice, "Billins, it's for you."

When she put down the receiver, it clunked a little, capturing the background noise of a child goo-gooing, and of all things, a Baroque piece. In a few seconds, a voice with a hint of Minnesotan accent answered, replying without hesitation that he would be right over as if crawling under a stranger's trailer on a freezing night required less effort than finishing up the evening dishes.

Skeads, skeptical, figured he might see the man by ten the next morning, but within twenty minutes a truck pulling a tow-behind portable welder appeared with headlight beams bouncing around in the darkness, each pothole putting in silhouette spruce or scrub bushes along the scruffy road leading toward the trailer. A young man jumped out dressed in clean, tan, insulated coveralls with a handful of tarps and portable lights to spread around on the ground under the trailer and around the water pump. It took a while, but after dragging the welding leads to several different areas beneath the two-foot abyss of the undercarriage, the frozen copper pipes began to allow water to pass. By ten, the laid-back, patient man named Billins was smoothly coiling the leads, wiping off each as he replaced them on their hangers under the covered bed of this truck.

For Skeads, something else of note happened, a thing that would join their paths in an ordinary business transaction, an occurrence shifting into one of those surprising pleasant memories that enter your life, the moment of an exception singled out into the amiable unforgettable. When the young man handed him the bill, he seemed embarrassed. Skeads looked at the handwritten receipt, frowned and nodded his head like he might be looking at a hand of cards poorly played.

"I've been up here awhile. How long you been up here?" Skeads asked, only then noticing Billins two snipped fingers.

"Awhile now," replied Billins.

"Well, I'm not trying to tell you how to run your business, but

141

man, you can't make a living up here charging prices like this ... not on a night like this." Skeads' hand involuntarily left his pocket and stirred around the freezing night air as if this gesture gave leverage to all he had learned about business in the north. His gesture disappeared into the night without a whimper and returned to his pocket.

"Look," Skeads said, "twenty-five bucks, not nearly enough. Don't hardly pay for fuel. Not up here in this freezer."

Billins shook his head and looked him in the eyes saying, "Nah. Not a chance. I said half-off. That's my price tonight. That's what's in the flyer."

Skeads countered, "Man, that's hardheaded to the point of stupid. Fifty ain't enough. But let me pay at least that." He pulled out a fold of bills.

"But that's not the point," Billins said, "I stand by the flyer. I'm a man of honor." To Skeads, at first frigid blush, this statement seemed so corny, so bald-faced innocent, and at best, so naïve, he laughed in the kid's face until he noticed the scar. The youth was serious as a death's head, the picture of a kid trying to prove a point if to no one else but himself.

Billins affirmed, "Nope. Twenty-five. Half off. That's what I said I'd do it for. It's either that or nothing. I'll catch you next time. We're not talking about money that's going to change the world. I'm doing fine up here. My baby's got shoes. My gal's happy. We're in a good place. You know, you might consider that charging anything on a night like this is more pathetic than good business. I've had a few spades-full of pathetic and want no more part. Hell, I'm buying some diving gear. You keep me in mind for that."

The breeze had dropped off but still hard as an anvil, the mean temperature squeezing ice on the invisible lake until you could hear it crack. Skeads watched the youth look into the winter night that in believers could forge doubts about the soundness of hope and divine purpose, but he saw in this youth something quite astonishing, mongrel and gunshot, not quite the roadmap of a man's face yet, but filled with sincerity, a genuine humility almost embarrassing.

Billins patted the hood of his truck, grinned and judged himself, "I'm doing great. My gal will have a hot toddy waiting for me. For sure. You give her a call now ... let her know I'm pointed home."

Without further comment, Skeads handed cash to the man who had thawed the pipes he lazed-out.

With his insulated coveralls as clean as when he started the job, Billins put the cash into an envelope, tucked it inside his coveralls, climbed into the cab with its heater blasting warm, and backed the truck and tow carefully down the rutty path. Skeads watched the headlights cleave their beam through the darkness, fade, and leave the spruce and scrub and himself alone, listening to the ice crack on the invisible lake.

During that winter Skeads ran into the young man several more times, and in passing conversations, he learned only that Billins the welder issued from a past he didn't talk about. A mystery. The cannery had thrown him some work, and eventually, his work ethic resulted in more jobs, and he was indeed doing fine.

One afternoon, with the youthful pride of accomplishment, Billins handed Skeads a few business cards with the logo of a polar bear wearing diving gear and driving a welding truck. To make things right, at the end of crab season, Skeads brought the family a box of crabs. He met Billin's wife, Gina, at the door and she was stunning, Anglo-tall, with winter-night dark eyes shying even a narcissistic man. Her skin was clean and a lighter shade than her native ancestors. A countenance, the north and the quiet of an island village, complimented her. Several times, she invited Skeads to

143

dinner, but he never got around to attending.

However, that was a long time ago now. Sitting in his trailer, drinking booze and coffee, reading the past newspaper, Skeads watched the morning arrive considering in his mind's eye a Billins dead. The simple starting of an engine, where it roared in the way only 1000 horses of torque can, and in a brief lethal moment the twin propellers chopped the life out of the young man.

Skeads finished the article, took his sip of lukewarm coffee, the liquor settling his mind with acceptance. Sitting by the window, with the room's cold and warm bifurcation, he watched the last of winter's abuse of spring, listened to ice on the lake crack, and in his mind heard the inscrutable weep.

He would drive to Polly's and find the gossip.

# Chapter 13: Polly's

Entering Polly's, Skeads still thought about Billins. He would visit Gina but dreaded it.

The smoky, dark bar hosted a collection of uninhibited drinkers. All of them ready, willing and able to drink and eat within those tobacco-veneered four walls. For a true bred-to-the-bone dive, it was a place that also boasted an unheralded achievement. This humble establishment served excellent food, truly fresh seafood that had never sacrificed its juices to a freezer.

Skeads walked into this windowless refuge. Natural light entered only when the door opened. Behind him, the sunlight cast a rectangle that squeezed around him to collapse across a cancerous carpet. To find the paisley design required a study and effort, perhaps rubbing a boot over the nap to excite enough of the exhausted pattern to reveal the designer's vision.

Photons scattered pell-mell into the light-eating shadows. The intruding sunlight, realizing its hopeless position, disappeared as the spirits of drinkers-past closed the door. Anemic flames from weak votive candles on the tables wiggled in the darkness. On stools at the bar, a line of drinkers in heavy work clothes assembled, one of whom was curious enough to investigate what caused all the disturbance of the darkness. Moving his shaggy head to its gimbaled limits, he gave a studied and serene look. A rocks glass rose to his lips and moistened them, leaving a glistening silver trace on his whiskered face.

Skeads' eyes adjusted. He studied an area where the plastic, checkered table covers added their meager input to the shifty ambiance. Through the haze of cigarette smoke, he saw Monroe and Mallary seated, and walked carefully between the tables towards them. Pulling out a chair that showed years of indifference, he turned it around so that his arms could lie on top of the backrest, then sat down and waited. He knew he would get pounded. He ordered a plate of fried scallops.

Monroe sat wordlessly, but his eyes spoke essays. Mallary launched first with his unique diction. "Well, lookie here, the big time fisherman returned from the great north." He leaned over the table for dramatic effect; a baby-face smile stuck on his attitude. "Made a killing big-shooter? Hey, how about that tent, eh? There be a lesson to learn in planning that one, eh?"

Encased within spotless insulated coveralls, Monroe had established himself as a skipper and looked the part. He seemed successful with his city boy manners and an east coast university education. Not adorning the typical beard, he was clean-shaven and had a demeanor more like a businessman, and over the past few years, he had learned how to skipper a rig. Skeads' thin lips parted just enough to show tobacco-stained teeth and a chipped tooth beginning to turn black. That was his smile.

The waitress, poker-faced, her hair pulled back to a ponytail, wearing a sweatshirt and denim, drifted over to him, and dropped on the table a bottle of beer and a shot of sour mash. She stuck a hand on her ample hip and said in southern silk, "Ain't this special, the cowboy returns. I heard you were a real John Wayne." She pushed a few hairs away from her blue eyes and pretty face, blinked twice, and gently nudged him with her hip.

"Put it on the money tab ... the scallops too," Skeads replied, nodding at Monroe.

He took a deep breath and said, "You wait till next year. There's money in that fishery. And when I left, I burned what you all called a tent."

146

"So, when you coming back to work?" asked Monroe. He knew the answer but wanted Skeads to grovel through a few more pieces of the failed season.

"How about I never left except in name. Would you believe that?" replied Skeads. He took a sip of whiskey. "I figure in a couple of days."

Monroe, unable to hold back laughing, said, "Hey, it's good training. There's no real hurry, but after lunch would work better. We got plenty of gear to repair. Plus, we got halibut season in a couple of weeks." He referred to the next season opening.

Mallary, unable to keep quiet, added, "Why, if the urge is great, you can leave some of that filthy lucre you filched from the fishes so we might imbibe on your largess. We have repaired stacks of gear. Mucho-mucho, senor. Feel free to head on down to the gear right now. Though, if you care to check it, we've fulfilled most of your fair share of these labors of love."

Skeads downed the shot and cleaned off with a sip of beer.

"I don't have your money for the gear," he said to Monroe.

Mallary chimed, "Of course not. Why stop living like the other leeches living off the back of free-enterprisers? You've lived the life of charity ... why stop milking an honest man's need ... to nourish his wife ... like an eagle provides his young ones ... on the mere inconvenience of your holiday ... your retreat in the wild pursuit of the easy money found in Poseidon's northern paradise? We're all a forgiving family ... Are we not?" His smiled lacked two bicuspids.

Mallary, the cheeks of his baby face now glowing a wrinkly pink, leaned farther over the table, far enough so his edgeless, round mien appeared camera-ready for a jar baby food jazzed up for centenarians. "Like Poseidon says, 'No fishies? No catchy? No lovey.' Ah-ha Skeadsman, that's why it's called 'fishy-fishy' and not

147

'catchy-catchy.'"

Monroe remained neutral and shrugged his shoulders. "Skeads, you made it back safe and sound. That's all that matters ... really." He burst out laughing and waved for another round of drinks, adding, "I heard the weather was cold and not nicey-nicey?"

Mallary drained his beer bottle.

Monroe said, "No need to reach for your roll; it's on me." He smiled from ear-to-ear. Then he leaned back in his chair, "Besides, it's a fact, the crew has already done most of your share of the gear work? But don't feel guilty about it."

"That's what I'd expect a suit like you to say." Skeads wiggled his finger for another round before Monroe's order had arrived.

They sat at the table and talked with the wreckage of lunch plates waiting for the waitress to pick up. Skeads recounted the season saying he had been happy with the way his rig—actually his and Monroe's—worked. Adding, he might shape the nets a little differently, but he was ready to do it again. Monroe talked about the coming season and what work needed to be done. During another round, Polly's invisible hand began clearing the lunch crowd of fishermen, cannery workers, and a few local businessmen.

Spending the afternoon working on gear looked less critical. The waitress came over and wanted to clear the tab. She had also worked the breakfast shift. Skeads paid the bill, claiming it was an interest payment on the money he owed Monroe. Monroe checked to see if the tip was big enough and ended up throwing extra cash on the table, saying he had 'served the public' while at the university— the hidden snob in him never used the word "college"—the experience teaching him it was the most thankless job he ever worked.

"I'll need to take care of a little business. If I start tomorrow...."

said Skeads.

"No problem," said Monroe.

What Skeads said next wasn't an afterthought, but a blunt question. "What happened on the *Ambrosia*?" He meant the accident he had read about in the paper. "What happened to Billins?"

For both Mallary and Monroe, it was a tragedy without a personality, one of those luckless occurrences read from the distance of newsprint. Monroe said, "I never met the guy ... seen him around town and the cannery. Heard he had a wife." To them, this butchery lacked any intimacy because Billins was merely a name.

Skeads and Monroe knew the *Ambrosia* well. A few years ago, the rig had been theirs to grapple. Whatever happened on that rig was less a known quantity than a random act of nature which subjected everyone. The *Ambrosia* always seemed like a floating enigma wrapped in a bewildering personality. However, Falin, the skipper, had established himself as a capable, successful and respected. He was making the big money and generous with it. Billins died that day, joining the ranks of the other hundred and fifty thousand who died that same day across the face of the earth. The next few days would swallow the event.

Small towns stir their mysteries and gossip, the issues expanding and contracting according to the curiosity of the community and how well the players are known. By the time the harbormaster, the cops, and the emergency people arrived at the *Ambrosia*, it appeared a mere misunderstanding had become a tragic accident. It was as if Billins had jumped over the side of the boat without telling anyone and then Falin, unaware, started the engines. The incident entered into the town lore.

# Chapter 14: A return to the F/V, *Ambrosia*

Skeads believed the *Ambrosia* owned the most beautiful lines of all the workboats in the fishery. When he left her, other than his duffle bags, from her steel and form, he took nothing but regret, bile, and shame. Falin beat him. Time had subdued the fantasies, if that's what they were, of revenge. The *Ambrosia* had taken Neal and now Billins. To Skeads, the two events created another boiling cauldron filled with violations of the balance he hoped for in life.

Time had been kind to both Monroe and Falin. Falin took over the *Ambrosia,* proving himself successful both as a skipper and excellent businessman. In the subsequent three years of fishing seasons, he had rolled his success into both wealth and canny investments. Monroe was no different. When he had been essentially fired from the *Ambrosia,* believing his career finished in the fishery, he assumed he would return to the lower forty-eight and start teaching. However, it was not to be—mainly due to Skeads. In the fleet, his deck boss possessed respect and connections, and he used one of them judiciously. He approached a man called "Chief," who had a 56-foot rig made of fiberglass, not a prestigious material to craft a boat, but it came with licenses, crab pots, and an opportunity. Before Monroe knew it, he was buying his rig, the *Sunburst*, and with owner-financing from Chief, he became the owner and skipper in one nifty move. Both Monroe and Skeads worked it with great success, and in gratitude, at the beginning of the second year, Monroe forced ten percent ownership on his friend and deck boss.

Luck blessed their first year. The fish jumped into *Sunburst's* gear, and both fin and crab gave themselves asking nothing in return. Monroe made money. Oodles of it. During the halibut season, to him an unfamiliar fishery, the catch was so great, he paid for the boat and gear. He won Nature's lottery. Monroe discovered the three aspects that determine success: calculated risk, hard work, and luck. The scar-faced Phillips was right.

Luck, too, kissed Falin. The first crab season he fished as a skipper, thinking courageously out of the box, he dropped his gear near a small rocky island that other skippers had assumed inhospitable for crabs. On the rocky bottom of the surrounding grounds, he found soft pockets of sand, dropped his pots in clusters rather than customary rows, and struck it rich. He instantly became what was known as a high liner, and needless to say, the glamour boy took to success like a bird to wing.

But this day, Skeads inspected the *Ambrosia*, walking back to the stern imagining Billins with his body caught between the turning and slicing twin props. What that moment must have felt like, the terror before shock pacifies the mind, before the surreal and the malice demands resignation, and when that moment beckoned and the young man saw the present collide with the future. Skeads could picture his decimated parts sprawled on the deck, like a man hit by a rocket grenade, and perhaps enough left of him for one last thought of his wife and their child.

Skeads wanted to talk to Falin and hear the story from the man's pretty lips. His intuition told him more aspects existed in the tragedy than a failure to communicate.

He drove to the cannery where Falin and his uncle met and walked up a flight of steel stairs into an office of a couple of metal desks, a few chairs and a room appearing about as comfortable as a toilet without a seat.

Falin and the cannery manager convened at opposite sides of a neat desk. Ignoring his apprehensions and his vague questions, burying his social animosities, Skeads entered the place of business and negotiation. As the door opened, Falin who enjoyed sharing his

151

sense of success and good nature, glanced back over his shoulder and saw the deck boss. Instantly smiling, he welcomed him.

"Hey, Dude. How've you been? Long time, no see." He stood up to welcome Skeads. "I wondered how you did with the herring. Heard it was tough. You know my uncle? 'Course you do. How's life been treatin' you?" With guarded eyes, the uncle peered through senatorial glasses. He sported a trimmed haircut attempting to cover his bald spot, but this rise to the situation failed, with skin glistening through thin strands of gray hair. On a cushioned seat, shifting in his khakis, he crossed his arms and wordlessly waited with lips pursed off-center from the implicit vertical line of his thin nose.

Skeads respected Falin's ability, indeed gift, to live in the present. Falin knew what Skeads thought of him, that he held him responsible for Neal's death, but the successful skipper could compartmentalize, ably ignoring the visceral sentiments bouncing between them.

Skeads replied, "Doing good. There's some money to be made in herring. Next year ... maybe." Awkwardness filled the room, the unease when everyone knows they 're lying, but still trying to connect the strings of the social song-and-dance. He avoided chitchat, and asked, "But I knew Billins pretty good, and I'm trying to find out what happened. You know how it is? I know it's maybe all settled, and better left quiet, but I need the help a little. To settle the thing for me."

The manager shifted in his seat, crossed his legs, and refolded his arms. Falin's face relaxed into a shifting cloud of concern, the ghost of a sincere sympathy emitting from his persona. "Yeah. It was terrible. I still dream about it. Terrible. I can understand your concern." Convinced of its authenticity, his sincerity calmed his face. "Look, I got a little more business here. I'll meet you down at the boat in a couple of hours. Say three? We can talk then. Catch up

152

on lost time. We need to do that."

"Yes, catch up. At three," echoed Skeads. Having never sat down, he tried to turn around and leave, but the manager rose quickly to join his standing nephew, his comb-over fluttering in response. The uncle remained silent, frowning a little more, and together, in an uncomfortable unison, they shook hands, all friends well-met.

As Skeads climbed down the stairs to the cannery floor, he wiped his hand off on his denim jacket.

* * *

Skeads' watch read three. The sun hidden behind the clouds wanted to set early. From the dock, from the perspective of low tide, he could look down onto the deck of the *Ambrosia.* Like a lawsuit waiting to happen, a spindly metal ladder suspended down the face of the dock and without incident, Skeads cleared each rung, stepped on the railing, jumped on the deck, and walked toward the aft house. The deck was clean of seaweed, bait jars, crab shells, the usual detritus unattended by a lazy or unmanaged crew. Two crewmen worked on lines, and he knew one of the men, Cody, who ignored him. He could see Falin radiating his big smile in the wheelhouse. He loathed the sucker and having to talk to him infected the lesion more.

Entering the house, the boat smelled of pine oil; he noticed the galley orderly and polished spotless. A notepad rested on the table with written work instructions for the crew. Missing was the handcrafted board with the carved *Ambrosia* into the grain and the shifty paranormal eye; all of this gone as if it had never existed. Even the eye-hooks had been removed from the ceiling. Skeads had hoped to see failure rather than order, to find the evidence of a rig being gutted to keep costs down and profits up. The *Ambrosia* looked disgustingly pampered.

153

As if reading Skead's mind, Falin called down from the wheelhouse, "Hey, we're taking care of your baby. See anything different?"

Climbing the stairs to the wheelhouse, Skeads could see the man peering down at him, his radiant face an intuitive familiarity. "Good to see you. I thought you might've forgotten. Can I make some coffee?"

"No, I won't be here long. I see the old carved board is gone."

"Yup, it's gone to my new house. Remember that weird carved eye? It's over my fireplace."

"What? Just the eye?"

"Nah man. You gotta be joking? The whole board's hanging over the fireplace mantel. The board and that insane eye. You should come by and take a look at it. Even in the house, that crazy knothole follows you around. I tell you what ... the house turned out well. Had a couple of local guys build it. Did a great job. I gave them a bonus. Got a sound system that the chicks love." He winked. "When you going to build on your land?"

"Yeah, I passed by your place a couple of times. I could stop by one of these days. I might build a small cabin on my place, but trailer's enough." For the third time that day, they shook hands. For Skeads the convention was meaningless, a wordless-dance on a smarmy floor that Falin sauntered on as easily as Skeads schlepped. "What kind of salmon season do you expect?"

"We'll tender salmon through the summer. Like when you and I worked together. I deliver to Phillips. You remember him? Can't forget him." Falin paused for a second, looking at the chart table. Then his conversation groped around in the past. "Wasn't that a trip from hell? What was that crazy's name? The guy who hung himself? Ned or Nat? What was his name?"

"Neal. His name was Neal. I never caught his last name. It's not much important now. In a way."

"Neal. That's right ... Neal. Man ... was he a piece of work or what? Who could forget him?"

Skeads nodded, "For sure. Who could forget him? But I never saw him as crazy. Different, maybe."

"Yeah, that's a better way of looking at it. I should have been easier on him. Another one of my regrets." Falin frowned and shook his head.

Skeads wanted to say more but left the small talk do the work. He waited while Falin talked about a new truck, about crab gear he would add to the next season and described the sound system for the new house. "The women love it," he repeated, smiling and winking.

"Yeah, I can understand that." For a fleeting second, Skeads wanted to ask him about the silver fox fur woman, but he wanted far less to hear the answer. Strangely, without any apparent triggers, a scene in his life, a long-lost memory, intruded. He recalled when very young, almost before memories appear, and some man his mother knew took him to a traveling carnival, one of those summer events appearing around the Fourth of July with a parade, and rides, cotton candy and where everyone in town showed. At a sideshow, a petting zoo, he touched a snake. Other kids in a nearby group kept a distance and feared the slandered creature.

"What's that you say?" Skeads asked. "The gals like the crab gear more than a house with a sound system?"

"No-no. The sound system. You still got that sense of humor ... don't you?" Falin said, a laugh hissing from his belly

"Well, the gals have to love something." Skeads paused, allowing a little time to drift. "You know ... I read in the paper about this guy Billins. Just this morning. I knew him a little. Did a little

155

business with him. Helped me at my trailer once. If it's not too much ... talking about it, I mean ... What happened?"

He remembered seeing nothing to fear in the snake, even as a young kid the being seemed so clean, efficient and elemental. He watched the snake, with its pure nature, its pure instinct squeezing out the underlying fear from inside the kids, but the quiet reptile offered its head to him, and he felt the sensation of an obscure dark world.

The air in the wheelhouse seemed to thicken around Falin. His usual confident mien slipped off his face, only to find a likeness waiting for a recomposition. He found it—remorse. "What happened? Yeah. Worse thing I ever saw." He paused, his face open to Skeads', the picture of regret. "I was the one who started the engine. It's killing me." With eyes rummaging for a place to rest, he beseeched Skeads. "I'd give anything to take it back. It's been terrible on Gina. It's my fault, and I will have to live with it. The buck stops with me."

"Gina?"

"Yeah. Gina Billins. Don't you know her?"

Skeads replied, "Somewhat. Gina Billins. Yes. Dan's wife ... widow."

"Right. His ... wife. I'd seen her around town before all this happened. Beautiful gal. Both inside and out. She and the kid's without anyone now. Great, great chick. I had boat insurance that's gonna help her out a little if the insurance company doesn't run. You know how it is. You never know...."

"Yeah, you never know." Skeads waited.

Falin leaned against the consul, his watery stare finding no place to rest until his gaze wandered out the windows. Skeads sat vigil in the starboard captain's chair listening and studying the face in front

156

of him, a look filled with consideration and concern, a humbled face entirely convinced of its humility, the grief skewing his face with licks of angst.

Falin's face quivered. "Look, there were no caution signs up, on the engine, on the console here." He pointed to the ignition switch near the rudder control and engine dials. "Billins never put them up. He never put a dive-watch up. Nothing. You know when you're diving you're supposed to put up warnings."

As the definition of a minute changed, growing longer than he wanted, Skeads waited. "Well, it's a major screw-up. But I've had a few of those myself." This observation withered to a period.

"Yeah. We're all in the same game. You know how it goes. As they say, don't jump into the game if you're not into the game." Looking out the window, Falin cut a suitable profile of sorrow, enough to convince both himself and perhaps a gullible saint. His eyes turned away from his inquisitor into a cloudy sky and then back to the chart table. Skeads intuitively followed the course to this waypoint, until his pale eyes fixed on "it." On the chart table, a dollar bill had been rolled into a nice, tight tube and put in front of him for their casual appointment.

Falin noticed that Skeads noticed. The skipper of the *Ambrosia* picked up the tube, smiled, and said, "Would you like a taste?"

Skeads shook his head, his mangy hair appearing to rattle. "I've enough bad habits." Reaching into his jacket, he removed his half-full pint and a wooden box of hand-rolled cigarettes. He took a sip, studying the bottle like it might be a skull. "I'm always confused if the bottle is half full or half empty. Your head can wear out the idea of halfness. Neal used to say that in an elegant world, halfness might be infinite." Across Skeads' thin lips, a smile traced an arc, flattened, and vanished. Falin failed to notice the deck boss offered no sour mash.

157

Cocaine had become the latest instant gratification of the new-rich, and in the lower forty-eight, had starred as a nightclub social lubricant hallowed for its chic-but-casual persona, the new adoration to instant gratification. Skeads thoughts returned to the petting zoo. The man he came with mined coal and spent his life in the mountain pits. The young boy remembered reaching out with his palm and the snake curiously offering its spoon-head and twin black nostrils to his fingertips. The reptile pulled back, hesitated, fixing him in its mesmeric eyes, to again approach his fingers, allowing, consenting, accepting his youthful candor, and, in that touch, Skeads remembered his first primeval trace, the sense of the unique, the abyss separating him from the other kids holding back. He would be different.

"This is perfect stuff. No habits. Increases energy both in body and mind. You'd be surprised who in town likes this stuff. It makes you feel strong. Chicks love it." Another wink.

"Strong? I could've used some 'strong' with herring this season."

"Man, you ought to try it. It'll surprise you."

"Yes. Yeah, I'm sure it's full of surprises. But it doesn't take a lot to surprise me." He studied Falin's face, a visage that in a few minutes had fully recovered from its unbound and broad wrestle with grief and its secular confession of remorse.

Skeads stood up and said, "Well, maybe it was fate. You know … like Neal, or Ned, or Nat. Whatever his name was. Maybe the answer is not for us to know. Hell-to-pay, maybe there is no answer, and we're just too scared to admit it."

"There's no confusion about this." Falin nodded and referred to the rolled dollar bill.

"I don't mean that. I mean about fate. How our lives turn out, roll out, unfold ... unravel."

Falin looked at him, shaking his head in agreement. "Yeah man, there's forces ... luck ... whatever you want to call it ... out there." Once more, the distance outside the window summoned his attention.

"Out there. Forces and luck? I like that. Serendipity, or Zemblanity." Skeads stood up. For him, the conversational loose ends tied themselves.

Falin said, "Yeah-man. Look, whenever I'm in town I got a Friday night poker-party. A good place to meet some shakers and movers in town. Even Monroe shows up once in a while. I'd like to see you out there." He waited, paced himself for a minute watching Skeads, adding, "You know we've had some bad blood between us. It was probably my fault. I was a jerk. We need to let that go. Like you used to say, it don't do any good. Yeah, well, I've moved on."

Nodding in agreement, Skeads took a deep breath and exhaled slowly. "Possible. Probable. I can see myself showing up one day. Stranger things have happened. I might talk to Monroe about it one of these days. Everything's as probable as it is possible."

In his mind's eye, he saw the snake, the lingering, intuitive intelligence, a knowledge above reason, the all-seeing eyes, and for the rest of his life those eyes predestined on him. "It's time for me to head out."

"Well, I hope I could help you."

"Yes. Yeah. Help," Skeads replied. As he climbed down the stairs, he turned and asked Falin, "Why did you put the engines in gear if you were still tied to the dock? Wasn't there another crewman onboard knowing about Billins under the boat?"

Falin deer-eyed Skeads, the unexpected question gagged any subterfuge, and gut reaction turned his face to a gargoyle's. He

159

choked out an answer, "I don't know. I don't know. Christ All Mighty, you don't think I don't ... It was terrible. The worst day of my life." He looked at Skeads waiting for sympathy, for an absolution.

Tired of Falin, Skeads sent flat words over his shoulder, "No it wasn't ... not for you. It was the worse day of Billins' life. And maybe yes, maybe no, maybe the worst day of Gina's life."

Stepping out to the deck, lighting his cigarette, giving Cody a nod on his way to the dock, Skeads murmured, "An unknowable day of the finite halves. Neal would find that interesting."

# Chapter 15: The Seal

I only thought about this incident years later, after I had read Skeads' notebooks, and when I started to write this account of him. How strange the memory collects its bric-a-brac, where this discarded stuff sleeps in the unconscious, waits decades to blossom, to then open like a lily or rise from a slimy bottom festering like a corpse. Now that I've many years behind me and only a few in front, this long-forgotten moment seems worth mentioning. Indifferent to time and place, even a small recollection desires meaning.

One afternoon not too long ago, I visited a Goodwill store. I still shop there for clothes and "finds." It's a place similar to a collection of attics waiting to be wandered, and I've always been voyeuristically curious about what others discard. The floor sported chipped linoleum and rows of shirts and pants on tired hangers, and I found an abandoned roll-on suitcase thinking I might buy it, and at the back of the store, near the salvaged cooking utensils, an excellent toaster oven for five bucks.

A couple of weary bookshelves stood like antique walls whose purpose had been long lost. Most of the books had spent their better days resting on more intimate shelves, but as I browsed through them, a coffee table book stood out. Sun had faded the tatty dust cover of a book about the North, but it still held a gentle picture of a seal, its sad brown eyes looking straight at me. When I opened it, light dust fell from it, almost like dandruff, and a deep musty odor lifted from its pages, as if no one had opened it in years, perhaps decades. On the inside of the cover page, "Andy" had inscribed in the faded blue tracing of a ballpoint pen: To Claire, Forever, Andy.

The pictures inside told about seals and where they live throughout the world. I flipped through the glossy photographs of seals, and suddenly one of the pictures of a spotted one forced me to linger. Ice surrounded the seal, its irregular spots swarming its face, with those brown eyes staring at me, intelligent, almost human, and there a connection to life occurred. I returned the book to the shelf and left behind the roll-on I didn't need. I don't know why I didn't buy the book, and I regretted not buying the toaster oven.

A few days later, on a Sunday morning, while lazing in bed, a memory drifted in along with the dawn light squeezing in between the slatted blinds. Then out of nowhere, I remembered a morning forty years ago, on the *Ambrosia.* A now forgotten season, I don't recall the date or even the precise bay, both were unimportant. In that lost time, an unimportant but strange incident, found significance only while writing this recollection.

With the remainder of the crew bunked down, Skeads and I, with not a care in the world shared a quiet morning in the wheelhouse. Beneath a gray overcast, we hid in a strange little bay sheltered from a furious storm outside our anchorage. Skeads and I lounged in the wheelhouse. Tumbling and rolling down to the bay, an occasional adiabatic ball of wind hurly-burlied, kicking up snow off a steep wintery mountainside. We could see the evidence of this inscrutable body hit the water, and while gusting across the surface tensions, it traced with invisible hands, lines of lacy foamy ribbons. Drinking bitter coffee, the wheelhouse kept us warm and safe.

Skeads hand-rolled cigarettes. I had a book in my lap. I know I've mentioned this before, but hands are miracles. If the evolutionary time-tape were re-wound and played again, I still question if our hands after 500 million years of evolution would appear as they are now. Michelangelo never missed this miracle, over and over sketching them in metal-point detail, hands that play a violin or piano sonata, or paint a Matisse or Cezanne, or squeeze a weapon's trigger or pull purrs from a cat, or sighs from a lovers embrace, or comfort a child trapped in its midnight nightmare, or roll several cigarettes.

162

We would catch octopus in the crab pots, and sometimes use them for bait, or throw them in the bait freezer. On anchor days, Skeads might dangle a limp carcass over the rail to see what it attracted. This particular morning, a family of otters gathered near the boat, showing their pups how to feed on the octopus and its dangling legs. Full of energy and life, they pirouetted through the cold water and floated on their backs dancing and splashing, sunbathing beneath a sunless sky. The creatures entertained one another in a harsh locus. But these brown eyed critters possessed in spades that joy of life we humans only occasionally experience. A jubilant family, oblivious to their harsh life, they clearly shared in each other's innocence.

I'd never seen otters grouped into what looked like a family, and I asked Skeads, "Do they keep a family?"

Skeads looked up from his cigarette rolling. "Maybe."

"Do they herd-up like seals?"

"I don't know."

After about ten minutes the otters alerted, ruffled the water and disappeared beneath it. Near the boat, the head of a dog appeared, or what I thought was a dog.

"That's not a dog swimming around the boat?" I asked, leaning over the console of the wheelhouse, peering through the windows and into the frigid water.

"No. It's a seal. Some kind of a spotted seal ... never seen them around this part of the Chain. Could be a fluke."

That's when I noticed a birth defect ravaging and contorting his face, permanently exposing half his teeth in a malevolent distortion across its face. "What's it doing here?"

"Who knows? Might'a ran one day when it was a pup and

163

started to move. Maybe this bay's a waypoint along to wherever it will come to a stop. Maybe it will never stop ... until it finally stops."

"You think it's all alone?"

"Maybe. Maybe not. Perhaps it was shunned? Maybe its rejected it for some reason, drove it off, and it started to wander ... to this place." While inspecting one of his cigarettes, he added, "Maybe it got sick of where it was at. Hell, maybe it's come as far as it can, and lost or forgot the way back. Or doesn't give a damn."

Skeads put on a flannel shirt and went on deck to smoke a cigarette. When he approached the rail, the seal backed away keeping his eyes on him. It slipped beneath the surface of the water and then reappeared. They spent minutes considering one another.

The seal circled the boat slowly and then returned to Skeads, its brown eyes and deformed features fixed on him, resting in the water, not unlike a stray street dog crouched in an alley; both of them indifferent to the cold wind cutting ribbons on the surface tension of the bay. I read a book.

After about an hour, Skeads returned with his hands and face blue from the cold. He ignored the condition.

I asked, "What's it going to do? Live in this bay forever? All by itself? Will others try to kill it?"

"I don't know. If it tries to join them ... maybe. Maybe it was rejected by its own. Maybe his mother pushed him away, figuring it'd be better off wandering than be some kind of a birth freak. It ain't from here, but it is now."

As we sat in the wheelhouse, the seal reappeared, stared at Skeads for the longest time, and then turned away and slipped off.

That was all. Nothing happened. No conflict, no climax, just resolution. Skeads said no more about it. And I thought nothing

164

more of that morning until forty years later after flipping through a book that I returned to the Goodwill bookshelf. As I recall the seal never returned. In a way, this recollection was still unfinished.

* * *

Another time, in a completely unrelated moment, Skeads smoked a cigarette and offhand mentioned his mother. I have no idea what triggered it, but he mentioned his mother, and that they lived outside of the town. One day she told him he must leave. She gave him some cash and said, "You need to leave now. Get away from all this and never come back." He never said if she was crying or anything. Just what she said.

I asked him where he was born? He answered, ignoring the question, "She lived a different life, and when I started to understand why the men visited, she begged me to leave and never return ... couldn't really blame her."

Skeads never mentioned his mother again. It seemed too private to ask him about his father. Years later, when I came into the possession of Skeads' journals, in all their detailed pages and metal-point sketches, he never wrote of his family.

# Chapter 16: Gina

The sun wished to set, but it was too early. A wall of dark clouds pushed a drizzle drifting across the harbor and through the cold air. Indifferent to returning to his trailer, Skeads drained the pint, returned to the liquor store, and bought another. A case of half gallons bivouacked at his trailer.

He waited in his truck cab for some thought to find his mind. Rolling down the window an inch to release the smoke, he touched the flame of the Zippo to a cigarette. The raindrops stuck to the windshield, and he looked out between them across the parking lot to the pharmacy and a nearby pitiful public square where a drunk on a bench waited for nothing in the rain. Opening the pint, each sip stung, warmed, then lingered in his mouth, waiting for some providence, waiting for some intervention that might lubricate the brain tracks enough for one original thought to occur—at least an original thought for him. Finally, a sip found a notion, a notion of visiting and paying his respects to Gina Billins. Now was the time. Billins' trailer, her trailer now, was a few miles from town. Retrieving the key from the floor mat, he cranked up the truck.

By turning right off the paved airport road, he entered a dirt secondary ascending a wooded hill. This incoherent path ambled between two-acre lots, through spruce trees starving for warmth, past trails and smaller let-ins jutting into land tracts spotted with trailers, finished houses of rough cut lumber, hand-built homes, half-constructed homes with steep roofs and batten-board siding waiting for the green wood to dry and settle enough to finish the inside. A unique community of dwellings built on a cash ethos rather than a lending pathos. No building codes out here, as this topography cobbled into a rural and singular community that the bankers avoided as much as the occupiers avoided the bankers.

Skeads had not visited Billin's trailer for at least six months. Driving down the entrance laid with crush-and-run, he could see Billins had started to build a life with borders. A barn of rough-cut spruce was large enough to park a welding truck, equipment, and a well-designed workshop. Several hand-built windows let into its sides, and a smokestack for the wood stove extended up the outside wall, anchored with thick wires against any wind, and safely clearing the steep roof. The beginning of a house foundation lay near the trailer; treated wood posts anchored into cement caissons and ran wild waiting to be cut to elevation, band boards, and floor joists. The work showed all the evidence of a tool-head, carpenter-head, hands-on guy. When he saw this place, Skeads thought about building a small cabin on the lake, but the inspiration only survived to his next sip.

A Toyota Land Cruiser rested in front of the porch. He took another sip of the whiskey, waited for a moment. Curtains opened a little, and he saw the image of Gina pressed against the pane. Slowly replacing the cap on the bottle, he had no liking to talk to a window or a widow. From where he was born, a hole of a place from which he had escaped, his mind's eye still watched the widows walk alone through the coal mine town. He climbed down out of the truck and climbed up the stairs of the porch.

Flared stairs ascended to the porch where newel posts, handrails, banisters, and balusters enclosed the deck. A nice piece of work. The porch stretched much of the length of the trailer.

All the boards and wood had been treated with linseed oil and screwed together rather than nailed. An outdoor grill made of handset slag stone stood away from the metal of the trailer.

Not knowing what to expect, wishing to avoid this meeting, he had no desire for this visit and questioned why he went through the motions. But before he could rap on the metal door it opened, and

167

she appeared with the child looking up at him, a beautiful child with Billins' facial features and brown-black eyes souled with shy curiosity. The child's skin matched Gina's, smooth and clean without blemishes, with a pale, dark wash shimmering beneath the surface. Both she and the child smelled of soap.

She recognized him immediately and seemed pleased. With the child's gaze never leaving Skeads, the boy's tiny arms wrapped around his mother's denimed leg. Her lips quivered into a smile, and her eyes softened. Skeads' shyness couldn't hold her eyes, and he noticed her feet covered in heavy knitted socks. He noticed the midnight ravens gazing out from eyes.

"I just wanted to give you my ..." He hunted for the right word, one that would make rubbish of her grief. He gave up and stood there. He shook his head, and his unwashed hair dangled, and his shoulders shrugged.

"Come in. I can do coffee." She spoke using soft consonants. With no drama, she looked at Skeads, and he had to carefully listen to her for she spoke only above a whisper.

"Not necessary. I can't stay anyway ... work to do," he replied, stepping into the trailer.

"Dan liked your company. He respected you. Come in. Please."

He entered the small living room, stood on a mat, took his boots off, and felt embarrassed about his unwashed socks and feet. He always showered on the boat. He wanted to light up a cigarette but knew neither Billins nor Gina smoked.

"I have a pint out in the car. Let me get it." He knew she was a teetotaler. "I wouldn't mind a touch in the coffee."

"Billins has some ... what you like."

Black and white photos of their life and what they found

interesting hung on the walls: winter snow, a picture of a mysterious paw print, trees in winter relief, a smiling Billings with baby and wife and an old model Toyota Land Cruiser, the details they found of value. A coffee table took up part of the room, but the floor space owned too little to be called a living room. For Skeads, the room reflected prudence, thorough and complete, dwelled with simplicity. Hand-carved wood rested around here and there, and on closer study, these objects turned into impressionistic miniatures of a walrus, of an eagle in flight, of driftwood shaped and sanded into a caribou hoof, a cat's paw, a larger piece capturing inflight seagulls cut of burl and landing on a weathered plank. One picture of their family snapped in Lady's Cove, a place farther out the road, where a small lodge and restaurant squeaked out a living. The young married couple ate at an outside table, surrounded by two feet of snow and their laughter. Her coffee and his beer were stuck into the snow and ice on the table. Skeads saw a picture of his trailer with the Adirondack chair facing the lake. As a thank you gift, Billins made the chair for him when they formed a partnership buying additional welding and diving equipment. Skeads remembered his business partner describing the chair as a place for him to park his butt when drinking and looking at the stars on a cold-ass night.

Billins laughed as easily as Skeads failed to laugh. He spent many silent minutes looking at the area carpet and then noticed it was handmade. Skeads wondered if Billins had lived for another thirty years how all this expression of their life lived together would resolve. On a shelf rested books for a correspondence art course. Another book lay on the floor: *Civilization* by Kenneth Clark.

"We took that picture when you were out crab fishing." She pointed at the picture of the chair.

She brought out the coffee and a bottle of whiskey. They were both stoic people of few words, people who had not learned small talk, and he could hear a truck bounce around on the road outside.

169

She asked if he would like to listen to the radio. Billins had put in a sophisticated antenna that worked well.

"How you handling ... this?"

"I'm ... Aleut," she said.

"Can I help you?"

"No, everything is fine. Wheeler feels terrible. He cries. He's been very nice to Paul and me." She looked at the small child.

"Wheeler?"

"Yes. Mr. Falin wants me to call him Wheeler."

"Ah ... yeah. That makes sense. That's what the 'w' stands for ... J.W. Falin."

Unable to wait any longer between the interludes of small talk, Skeads asked, "Did anyone ... Falin ... anyone tell you how it happened?"

"Bad things happen all the time. There may be no reason."

"He's a careful man. He watches ... details."

She did not respond to his observations as if Billins' work ethic was incidental to death.

The child sat beside her, never taking his eyes off Skeads, studying him like he was an alien. He had no desire to pick up the boy.

With words, soft and without edged consonants, "Billins wanted to take us on a trip across the states. Visit San Francisco. He liked museums. I've never seen a museum. He wanted to take us to a symphony and the Grand Canyon. We had things to do. And the house." She looked at the kid, and Skeads avoided looking at her, relieved whenever her eyes ignored him.

He finished his coffee and whiskey. For Skeads, they had exhausted their only common thread. There was no reason to prod the subject longer.

"Thanks for the coffee." He needed to leave and felt released when slipping on his boots. Gina handed him a travel brochure from San Francisco. Skeads had been to San Francisco and found it confusing and noisier than deck equipment. People were abrupt and indifferent.

He opened the door and passed through it quickly, but Gina pressed into his hand a small totem of carved bone and the picture of the Adirondack chair. No bigger than a baby's finger, the totem depicted a hunter. "They found it on Billins," she said.

The sun rushed towards night, and the air had turned colder. He avoided looking back. Walking down the stairs, as Gina closed the door, he could hear the ravens in her voice saying, "I appreciate you coming by."

# Chapter 17: A Midnight Monkey

His watch-face stared back at him. Four hours of sleep. He brewed coffee. The chess board waited for him to play, but he could only think about the previous day, his brief visits with Falin and Gina, her child and the ghost of Billins. From the percolator, he poured half a cup and then filled the rest of the void with whiskey. He took out a slice of white bread, spread peanut butter and strawberry jam on it, and wrapped it around a banana. He couldn't shut his memory off. But at two in the morning, when the ravens started to caw, the most intense and persistent couriers returned with a vengeance.

Though it was cold, he cracked the door to the trailer, and began to roll cigarettes first by hand, and then with a machine given by Monroe. Rolling three by hand, he switched to the roller, comparing the two. Putting a cigarette between his lips, he opened the Zippo, and the kiss of its flame created embers at its end.

In his early morning mind, the embers of the memory of the burning hooch and the dancing monkey ascended from glowing ashes. It may have been a village pet, blinded by the heat, no eyes, lips burned away from teeth creating a silent ivory gate for the village phoenix.

Skeads thought.

He saw himself as an experiment. Perhaps all humans were experiments. Scientists used monkeys and mice, but the ravens used him. Fate used humans. Wouldn't it be ironic if Aristotle got it wrong? That man was not the rational animal, the paragon of animals, but the merely the proof the serpent knew more than all of us? Did Neal see life this way?

The monkey burst silently from the smoking embers, its arms

akimbo, a dancing smoking doll, a carbon anodized harlequin, smoldering, trying to howl, its mouth cooked into a silent "om." How the creature danced this far seemed a miracle.

How ironic these miracles. You can learn to accept absurd circumstances and call them life, a place several circles below melancholia. Not despair. Call it doom. Not the death mask, he had accepted that on the *Faith*, but the doom forged in the hope of nihilistic plainchants or the voices of Mallary's frozen demons and angels, those trapped chorales mute in the sanctuary of the earth, from those two-in-the morning sleepless vigils when the ravens resurrect and caw out the futility and absurdity of life. And, yet, the will to live, to live, to live.

Like tectonic plates in the bowels of the brain, the forces only grate and shift, struggling and clashing against one another, ravens gnawing at each other's throats for yet another night—to collapse in an exhausted enigma. Mallary believed in gargoyles. Booze nursed the edges.

They could smell the village, the abandoned cooking fires bequeathing their smoky oils and fish sauce, leaving their bouquet in the surrounding jungle, across the abandoned rice paddy, across the sound-sucking silences of a free-fire zone. Those innocuous descriptions that innocuous suits use to collate carnage from a village of grass. Suits that dine in restaurants at night: A cooked monkey, maybe medium rare, rare enough to still breathe, serving the will to live is never found on the plate of the day.

People in grass houses shouldn't throw stones.

People in grass houses shouldn't stow thrones.

Don't throw stones at glass thrones.

Glass houses shouldn't stow thrones.

They waited for a while in the tree line surrounding the paddy, listening, smelling, dissecting the village on the far side of the clearing. The exhilarated hunt. Deserted, no pigs, though they could hear one or two rutting and snorting themselves deeper into their jungled liberty. No chickens. Cracked paddies surrounded by brick-hard berms. The dry season desiccated rice to stubble like blond hair rising from the skull of ancient earth.

Circuitous logic fueled on the hubris of education without wisdom, a wisdom feeding on the flesh of its own virtues, of virtues of their confidence, all to torch a bunch of grass hooches in the middle of the stone age. But he knew, he knew, he knew... he was no better.

Skeads never dreamed of circumstances, but as time trickled on, he remembered: A mental triptych by the damned painted with blood and flesh and screams for the damned. Gina's kid, the occurrence inspiring tonight's featured central panel returning for another command performance. His lamentation he must relive until he died. No night time absolutions here.

How long had this village raised chickens and pigs, grown rice, bedding at dusk and rising at dawn? Birthed and raised their children? No electricity? No radio? Post stone age? Culture weaved of grass. One of the portraits of the triptych of circumstances. He never thought about this doom until the ravens arrived at two in the morning, when it oozed and boozed out of his own time regained.

Oh, what a time. The greatest show on earth. While he could still believe. When the narcissism of democracy demanded burning grass to the ground. Ideals sculpted of hubris and faith and political certainties, until time zigzagged through the heart of darkness and the night bleeds, to where you blaze at two in the nihilist morning, befriended by your self-medication and an occasional midnight visit to Angela's.

The hooches liked it. Once kissed by the Zippo, hot embers are fate.

Halfway through the torching of the village, the monkey ... the child ... the monkey ... "It's a kid," said one of them as the form wiggled from the embers. A child fearing strangers more than fire, burned beyond gender, beyond the future. Skeads released the safety and killed the smoldering collateral damage for the thousandth-night vigil.

He pulled down the walrus tusk cribbage board, studied the etchings, took out a piece of paper and began to doodle an idea for another sketch. He knew the ivory waited for more stories. He lit another cigarette, put together another coffee. His disfigured tattoo: "Death before" a patchy burned skin lay on the table.

Never burn grass houses for glass thrones.

Why on Earth ...

Images swirled in his mind: on the road a small patch of coreopsis blazing yellow lightning, a starry-starry night that only a madman could paint, a ladybug whose hard wings thundered with dots darker than his blackest nightmare, the joy of a babies smile, the smeared mouth of a monkey's horror ...

Tomorrow he would work.

Yes. Yes. Yes. Why ... on Earth?

For Skeads, the miracle was less found in life than the will to live.

# Chapter 18: Sadlerman

Gray and suspended in small raindrops, early dawn waited for Skeads' to switch on the windshield wipers and whisk away their temporary residency. It occurred to him that Officer Bill Sadlerman might know a little about the Billins' accident. On his way to Polly's, he decided to pay the man a visit.

Sadlerman had been sent to an outpost of civilization, had been remitted to the town to "cool off." FBI trained, and Los Angeles police force employed, his life had been threatened by gangs, and he had been sent to the Aleutian Chain for his safety. He quit drinking, his wife left him, and he found the Aleutian town comfortable. Skeads shared one out of three. He first met Sadlerman drinking coffee at Polly's one night, and in a momentary and unusual expression of social grace, he offered to take the stranger salmon fishing.

He entered the austere office, and the same counter separated the same three desks and same metal chairs that had once processed Neal into his last and final room. Ready to leave, the nighttime desk officer, an elderly woman with a puritanical bun, instinctively lowered her head to better peer over her square black-framed glasses. She looked ready to star as a TV judge. Like an empress, she sang, "Sgt. Sadlerman, you have someone to see you."

Hiding a smile, Sadlerman replied, "Hey Greta, can you fetch-up some coffee before you leave?"

"Poo," she replied, and wrapped in a parka and crowning her bun with a red thick stocking cap, she la-di-dahed out the door leaving in her wake neither a smile nor an adieu.

"Gooood morning, Mr. Skeads. Coffee?" Sadlerman smiled. Skeads tried to.

The officer stood shorter than Skeads by at least half a head, but the man was muscular, with thick hands, thick shoulders, and a broken-nose apportioned by gentle blue eyes. Crewcut and blond, he didn't take himself seriously but took his job very seriously. He considered himself lucky; his work liked him.

Skeads' smile thinned, and he gave the man a nod; he liked his humor.

"That night-desk officer has the humor of a caribou."

Both men exchanged social chitchat for a few minutes, then Skeads drop-kicked his first question, "Did you know a fella by the name of Billins?"

Sadlerman became very professional. His blue eyes sobered, and his persona changed from light and airy to professional. "Boy, you know how to start the morning off with a gut shot." He let the inquisition settle a little, "It depends what you mean by 'know.'"

Skeads thought for a minute, looking at the officer looking back at him. They knew the conversation had turned professional. "Had you ever met him around town? Ever talked to him? Had any reason to know him?"

"I hope you're not thinking of putting a set of jumper cables on me? Look ... I know where this is going, and I can't help much. Even if I did know I might not tell you. You tell me. How did you know that I was down there ... that I had to make the report?"

"I didn't, until now. I just found out about it yesterday. Billins was a good man. I'd like to put the pieces together ... just for my own ... self. Can you help me or can't you? I could maybe use your help."

Sadlerman motioned him over to his desk, pulled up a chair, and pointed his broken nose towards it. "Well ... how do you really feel about it? If you need to be abrupt, don't worry about it. I don't know what side of the bunk you woke up on but try the other one. Hell, consider buying a new bed."

Skeads laughed a little and sat down, pulled out a cigarette, put it between his lips and didn't light it. Sadlerman didn't smoke, was a recovering drunk, and he could smell the alcohol on Skeads' breath and the tobacco smoke plastered on his body. Stale air brewed in the room. A commercial radio sat silently on the counter, but the police citizen's band occasionally crackled with static.

"I've got to cover the desk for another hour until the morning clerk comes in. Coffee?" He leaned back into his chair and took a deep, slow, breath, never taking his eyes of Skeads.

Nor did Skeads take his eyes off Sadlerman. When the disgusting coffee arrived, Skeads pulled out a pint and poured a dollop. The officer pretended to see nothing.

He asked the officer, "So you knew Billins?"

"I'd only seen him around town. Never had any problems with him. With his short haircut and all, I figured him to be ex-military. But I never had any reason to know him or not to know him. I did notice he wasn't much of a drinker or smoker. Saw him with a real pretty gal at Polly's one night. I noticed he was drinking a soda, like his gal. After the ... accident, I found out she was his wife. Nice woman."

"Accident?"

"Coffee?" replied the officer.

The officer listened to Skeads' quiet, precise question. A little impatient, Sadlerman said, "Look, my being there first was as complete an accident as anyone might expect. Plus or minus one damn minute, I might have missed the whole thing and never been involved ... in the accident. Some guy by the name of Cody flagged me down while I was driving in front of the cannery, him crying there'd been an accident. Now that's three coincidences you got

178

right there ... Billins, the crying kid, and me driving by ... you might call it uncanny.

"I got out of my cruiser, and Falin and Cody already had Billins on the dock. Or what was left of him. It looked like he'd been through a meat grinder. By the time the medics got down there, there was nothing to do but put the pieces in a bag."

"Was there anybody else around? Any other witnesses? It seems impossible ..."

Sadlerman interrupted him, "There you go again. I can tell you got a case of the butt, but Skeads, buddy, I'm not new to this rodeo. When I came on the scene, the first thing I did was start observing. It's my job. The cannery was empty of any crew. I looked up at the second story office windows. Saw nothing. Nobody was staring down or nothing. When the medics arrived, a manager came down from the office when they heard the ruckus ...

"When I arrived, there was Falin, Cody, and me. They didn't even have time to make a call. Falin was soaking wet. He dived under the boat to pull Billins out and lugged him onto the dock ... by himself. Damn near heroic."

"It just doesn't make ..."

"You're right. It doesn't make sense. It does seem improbable, but for the next two weeks, I checked around. Nothing. It was like what's never supposed to happen, never happened. You know better than most that shit happens. Every day. All the time."

"What about his work truck? Where were the safety buoys? No safety watch?"

"I even checked to see if there was any blood on them. They hadn't been taken out of the truck. It was like Billins had done a prelim dive to see what he was getting into. Maybe then he would put out the safety gear."

179

"My gut tells me this stinks. So, some sucker goes out there and dives under a rig, starts cutting out the line around the shaft, and doesn't warn anybody? Bull."

"You know. I have the same feeling, but I have to work with facts. I've seen too many cops get their instincts wound-up and then find facts to prove their instincts. That's not how I work. Coffee?"

Sipping coffee that grimaced his face, Skeads shifted in his seat. "I knew Billins. He was anything but stupid or ignorant. The guy used to put booties over his work boots before climbing into his truck. Even a moron up here in this mud-hole takes precautions under a boat."

Sadlerman frowned, scratched his flattop and leaned back. "You're right, it insults the intelligence and common sense. But something stupid happens a thousand times a day. I've got to deal with what I saw when I got there. I'm not an instinct man. I'm not going to find stuff to prove a hunch. With facts, you can make the world flat. I'm a cop. That's not how justice works for me.

"... Now listen to me ... when I saw Falin, he was in shock. He looked completely out of it. I still don't think he knew Billins was under the boat ... thought he was in the cannery. Cody was speechless. Hell, to begin with, that boy's not the freshest oyster on the plate. I questioned them half a dozen times. Together and separate. Their story of what happened never wavered an eyelash."

Skeads shook his head, his shaggy hair shifted.

Sadlerman smiled. Like Falin, his teeth shined. "When you going to get a haircut and start looking like a soldier? Coffee?"

"When hell freezes over. Yah. " The deck boss filled his mouth with coffee. "That's the sorriest coffee I've had in months. I hope you don't give this stuff to your overnight guests. They might hang themselves."

180

The officer leaned forward and placed his arms on the desk, "Sure I do. They never want to stay another night after drinking this battery acid. Look, Skeads, I like you. You're a good guy. Without a doubt, Falin's an interesting character. I've seen him around town, and he's a piece of work. I'm not sure what he's up to. But he hasn't even a traffic ticket. By the way ... you do."

Somehow a fly appeared, the little blue-headed miracle surviving a frigid birth, buzzing around and becoming a third party in the small room. After a few minutes of circular explorations, it assumed a place on Sadlerman's coffee mug.

Skeads lifted himself off the creaky chair. Looking at the fly and then at Sadlerman, he said, "Interesting. I haven't been in the place since Neal hung himself."

"Who's Neal?"

Skeads replied, "Just another guy."

\* \* \*

Grit and dirt fouled piles of snow covering the pavement of the parking lot. Several muddy trucks stood driverless waiting for their owners to give them life and a purpose to the next phase of the day. Skeads sat in his truck for a few minutes; it had been a restless night and a bad start for the morning.

When Skeads entered Polly's, an unfamiliar sound greeted him: "boink-boink-boink." He waited for his eyes to adjust to the dark interior. A few catatonic icons sat at the bar either nursing their first drink of the day or hold-overs from the previous night's purgatorio. Seated at a table, sipping a cup of coffee and reading a newspaper, a shadow similar to Monroe's hovered in the meager light of the struggling atmosphere.

As he approached, Monroe shifted his concentration from the paper and smiled up at his deck boss. "Punctual. You had breakfast

181

yet?"

"Yup. I ate at the trailer."

"What? Booze and coffee?"

"That and a sandwich."

"I don't know how you do it."

"What? Eat a sandwich for breakfast?"

Monroe accepted the honesty. "Right. So, we got plenty of work to get ready for halibut season. We'll slay halibut."

Skeads waved for coffee from the waitress. She winked at him and brought a mug and fresh pot. She leaned her full body near him, placed the mug on a checkered plastic table cloth, poured the coffee, and pulled a strand his stringy hair. "Cowboy, you need a haircut. I can cut your hair, but you need a wash-up first."

Ignoring the one-sided repartee, listening to the incessant "boink-boink-boink, he thanked her for the coffee."

Monroe returned to his paper until Skeads asked, "What's that sound? Not natural."

"Mallary's. It's some kind of new electronic game he's playing on a television screen. Pong Man, Mule Man, or something like that. It makes that noise. "

"Interesting. That means when I come in here in the morning, I got to listen to that? All we need is a pinball machine in here. "How can anyone think with that going on? Not natural."

"For you to ask about what's natural seems unnatural."

"You know, that machine could use a pair of wire cutters or a baseball bat."

Without looking up from his paper, Monroe nodded his head in agreement.

Skeads went to inspect the source of the noise and found Mallary hunched over the screen. "Hey, you," he said softly, "you want to turn down the sound?"

Without looking up, Mallary whispered, "Sound? What sound?" His baby face, a shadow, hang-dogged over the green glow of the screen. "Why, why it's the Skeadsman himself ... in living pale and white. Sit puppy and behold. Pull up a seat and join me in my new found addiction ... indeed ... possessor. I'll introduce you to the wonders of this psychotic-ambivalence. It's more than a game, it's ... it's companionship in the arms of oblivion. No. Nay. I am inaccurate. It's a parallel universe. Without saying a word, phrase, allegory, it teaches you that all starts on the outside of being, and all slowly works one munch at a time in what seems like eternal circles until you find ... singularity.

Skeads watched what looked like a tiny yellow circle with a wedge cut into a mouth munching through a maze of dots and channels. "Boink-boink-boink."

"Let me find and finish the meaning of the universe. I'm losing and still hooked. It makes no sense. Look at that cute little head eat the screen. Don't stop me." His blood-shot blue eyes riveted the screen. "I'll join you in thirty-two seconds, an eternity. Damn, the eternity."

Skeads retreated to the table and sat down. "I thought Mallary was a little smarter than a test tube. I think he's got a nosebleed from it."

Monroe replied, "Get used to it. I've read it's big in the States." Without looking up from his paper, he added, "I heard some guy say that in the States they got on a TV screen where you can drive fast, shoot, and kill people. They call it a game."

"I heard it called 'virtual reality.' A new conception of life," added Mallary, joining their table. More coffee arrived. "As if reality isn't real enough?" The baby-faced man with blood-shot blue eyes took a sip of coffee. "So why is the Skeadsman so distraught this drizzled morn?"

"I'm not angry about anything."

"Touchy-touchy are not we? Yes. No. Maybe? But ... 'Distraught' I said."

The machine again started to boink. Mallary and Monroe waited for an answer.

"I talked to a cop I know. Asked him about what happened to Billins. He wouldn't or couldn't tell me anything I didn't already know."

"And?" they said in unison.

Monroe folded the paper and said. "I know it's a tragedy. I know that he's dead. I know that Falin was the skipper and bears some responsibility. But I didn't know the guy. What's it got to do with me?"

"I knew him," replied Skeads.

"I got it. That's important to me because of you. But there's going to be twenty or thirty guys get killed between here and Dutch this year. You and I will not give it more than ten minutes. We've all known a few guys who ate it. One day we will eat it. What happened to him is out of our control. You need to get on top of it."

Skeads listened, and said, "It's important to know what happened."

"That's a cop's job. We're fishermen. In the long run, it doesn't matter. The earth will not stop spinning one way or the other."

The "boink" machine, now under the control of a new player,

kept munching.

"Can't they hook up some headphones on that stupid machine? Do morons pay to listen to that?"

Mallary swigged some coffee, rutched in his chair, "Skeadsman, the manager put it in yesterday, and it hasn't stopped since. I heard he's ordered another one. Behold the future, and it is us. A delightful muse pointing at meaning in meaninglessness."

"Not sane." Skeads pulled out a cigarette and set the Zippo to it.

"So why you obsessing over this?" asked Mallary.

Skeads said, "Something stinks about it. I talked to the cop this morning about it. The guy's smarter than me, and he's got no answers. Billins' wife seems resigned. Falin ... he's the poster-boy of remorse. There's something not right about it."

Monroe waited silently.

"Who puts a 109-foot rig in gear when it's tied to the dock?"

The waitress poured more coffee. A ghost of steam escaped from the throat of the pot. Monroe looked pensive. "Skeads ... people get killed by stupid mistakes. It may have been bad luck. If you live in a dangerous world, you make dangerous mistakes."

"It's important."

"Maybe yes and maybe no. Maybe you already know and don't want to admit it," said Monroe.

Mallary said quietly, "My Skeadsman can't balance the scales of justice. Ah-ha, those balances scuttling around in endless searches across endless sea beds for the endless beauty of justice. A challenge for a lifetime. For sure, but consider filthy lucre is easier to balance and more fungible than those shuttered scales. Rock-sure, if the goddess wanted a perfect world, would she not grace it so?"

Finishing his coffee and folding his paper, Monroe said, "Here's my rock-sure check. I got a business and a million dollar boat on the way, and we got halibut and salmon and crab that we need to catch to help pay for it. If not, I'm done. You got a herring operation about this time next year. Don't think that's not important. Maybe as important as playing a minor player in injustice. Billins' is dead. Not a player anymore."

The door to the restaurant opened, and a gray morning pushed in what looked like a family of three. The man with a baby face and bloodshot eyes said quietly, "There's more life swimming in oceans than its turgid surface reveals. Our Hollywood hero reaps more profits from extraordinary waters than all the bowels and bounty of Mother Nature."

Falin, Gina, and Billins' child had entered Polly's.

# Chapter 19: When Skeads shopped

Finding a job at a grocery store, Gina burned or sold everything from the past, moving to a small apartment in town. Only later I learned she kept what she called her crafts.

When Skeads shopped at the store, they would exchange brief nods, her eyes following him up the aisles as he placed the groceries into the cart. However, when meeting him at the register, they would exchange only those civilities people use who are islands unto themselves, who shroud unresolved anguish and can fathom no further explanations. Her husband, his business partner and perhaps even friend, had died and they both had accepted that nothing would bring the man back. Skeads, a man acknowledging the where and when of Billin's death, completely lacked the nature to accept its vicious yet ineffable resolves. I believe he was incapable of finding or saying anything of consolation to either Gina or himself:; for him, it had become a void that turns to a cut, a cut that opens a gash, and a gash that cures on gangrene. While Gina experienced a resigned sorrow, Skeads' ravens marshaled fury.

Skeads would occasionally see Gina with Falin—at the theatre or even outside the church, the good-looking guy poised with sunglasses playing the family man. But she seemed to keep a reserve, her face without emotion, not much different than when Skeads had visited her at the trailer. Half of her was missing, and she found the other half in the kid's hand and smiling only at him.

\* \* \*

The various fishing openings that year arrived with discipline and order. Skeads worked with his unique focus and dedication. Work for him, not unlike booze, lubricated, smoothing the angry, rough surfaces. He respected Monroe and worked hard for him:

187

showing early, leaving late, offering leadership through quiet example, and often deciding to sleep on the boat to get an early start.

Whenever possible, Monroe and Skeads preferred inexperienced crewmen, favoring to train new guys in their method and tradecraft. A kid working at one of the canneries showed work ethic. His most distinctive physical feature was that he was trying and failing at sprouting soft wisps of red beard. Working at the cannery, the kid was agile and displayed a knack for operating the crane, the forklift, and showed no hesitation for finding work rather than waiting for the work to find him. Talking to the cannery manager, Monroe took him out for one trip, watched him suffer sea sickness and not lie down, and noticed that in the kid's spare time he practiced the necessary knots and learned a few recipes to share in the cooking. The boy listened. They hired him. However, the young man never talked about his past, and they discovered why. He was underage. The boy called himself Maverick. His given name was Reginald.

Monroe was correct in forecasting the future of that year. They not only slayed the halibut but also the salmon, and they would slay king crab. They started to make real money, money that didn't just buy an extra case of bourbon, but money, when used prudently, could change their lives. With a heated market, the canneries started to compete with one another, and the prices of the product rose until they smelled like roses.

The last patches of snow disappeared, the sun came up earlier, days grew stronger and stayed longer, and the rocky earth warmed enough to stir the skulking flora to burst green from its false grave. Half-way through the salmon season, Monroe talked Skeads into running the *Sunburst*. His deck boss and partner had more than enough skill from the years he had worked up north, and Monroe understood Skeads very well might know more than himself. Monroe never feared to hire men who had more talent than himself. Meanwhile, he returned to the shipyard down in the States to help build the new boat.

When onboard the *Sunburst*, Skeads would bring out his walrus tusk and Maverick would watch as his mentor played against himself, moving the pegs, shuffling the cards, cryptically commenting, "You can never win when playing against yourself ... but then again, at least, someone wins." Skeads would retire his game and study the etchings on the white bone: the walrus rising up from the beach; a seiner pulling a net; a composition of cirrus and cumulus clouds. He had a small sketch pad, something that he could lay in his hard hands, and with a stubby pencil, he sketched what might someday be etched into the bone. To find shades, he would wet his tobacco soiled fingertip and smudge a little here and a little there, look at it, and then turn a page and begin another miniature of the same likeness, of the same theme—a miniature of Billins, Gina, and their child. The tusk told stories across the back of its ivory.

But one final improbability—though by far not the least— regarded Cody. This crewman of the *Ambrosia* appeared as if an unexpected pearl from an oyster to see if a position was open on the *Sunburst*. For the summer, Falin had turned over the *Ambrosia* to another skipper, and as events turned out, Cody was trying to find a distance from Falin. Skeads hired him on the spot. He hired Cody with a vengeance, with the same vengeance when years before he had jumped off the *Ambrosia*.

# Chapter 20: Skeads pays a visit

When Skeads entered Polly's, the late-night band music and general hubbub drinking people create pushed both against the walls as much as against his eardrums. Aside from the music and revelers, the place seemed as consistent as a straight line. He searched the bar for a familiar face.

At first, he missed it, the clear voice of a country rock tenor, the soft rural lyrics drifting throughout the restaurant, with the other band members backgrounding the lead voice and guitarist, allowing him to take the front of the stage. Usually indifferent to bands, Skeads found the source of the voice. With an acoustic guitar hanging across the lead singer's chest and his hands nimbly hitting chords and licks, Falin reigned the stage, sunglasses poised across his face, playing the role of a lead crooner.

Skeads returned to his search of the bar, finding Mallary's weathered visage hovering in a back corner. As he drew closer, the man in the darkness read a tattered paper with his craggy eyes. Cigarette smoke loaded the air within the walls of the place, and the band began playing a line dance. The tiny dance floor filled the chiaroscuro with faces and moving bodies. Motionless, the baby-faced man rotated his blue eyes in their crinkled sockets and waited for Skeads to say something.

"Why you not playing that boink-game you like?" asked Skeads.

"You mean the very one that enslaves the innocent? Ah-ha, but I can see now you rest on the laurels of a big shot skipper. Those lofty altitudes will convince you that hubris and omniscience are second only to the addictive filthy lucre you high and mighty types filch from nature. You bought a suit yet? But, I digress ..."

Skeads interrupted. "You want a job for crab season?"

"... and to answer your first question ... and good evening to you ... when I started to dream it, when the little critter started to invade my dreams, eat at my brain, to snip and nibble away at ... at who I am ... I quit. A withdrawal of horror. Horror. What I mistook for a good friend, turned fiend. That nibbling head possessed my soul. Worse. My dreams. Nevermore ... I tell you and all, nevermore. But ... not to change the dismal subject ... have we not the time to survey the terrain of our festive establishment? And to your second question, yes."

Mallary returned his eyes to the paper, and the band played another song.

Skeads answered, "Yeah. Falin can sing and play the guitar."

"Yes indeed. Damn well too. Dammit." Mallary shrugged his shoulders. "God gives both to the deserved and undeserved."

Skeads ordered a beer and a shot and took a stool that creaked in response to his weight. "You weave a long-winded answer to a simple question. What more am I supposed to see?"

"Do what you do naturally. Fulfill your pale eyes with the wonderments of the human comedy."

Falin filled the front of the stage and sang a ballad like he had been singing for years. Remarkably natural, he ruled a bar stool that had been brought up with a lone spotlight haloing him while his tenor voice hit pitch-perfect notes, and the lovelorn phrases flowed from between his lips as he versed a story of the lost love, of the pretty woman who walks on by, of the "moment of crushing loss and emotional abyss." The sunglasses glowed, reflecting meek candlelight into the darkness of the room. The patrons of the night grew silent and listened while he hit riffs on the proverbial gently weeping guitar. The man rained words lilting on the refrains

191

expressed in a minor key. His face twisted in love-lost agony, and, well into the song, with not a trace of guile, the crystalline trail of a tear slipped from behind one of the glowing black lenses. He was terrific.

With applause, youthful men and women wearing evening attire of flannel shirts, denim, and work boots, returned to the dance floor. Others joined in, laughing, talking, their animated faces dancing over the small table tops.

"So, he's a movie star," said Skeads.

Yes. Yes, he is. Give the talents their due, my Skeadsman. But our place reveals more if you peek deep."

Skeads' eyes roamed across this nighttime raucous until he saw Mallary's point of interest. Emerging from the milieu at a table stretching out with immense nonchalance, lounged a clean-shaven man dressed in a long black leather coat with a bolero hat raked over an eye.

"You mean the hat boy? What's that suit mean to me?"

"A hat extraordinaire my slender friend ... watch the bolero hat ... watch him ... join with one of those hand-rolled smokes and enjoy while the drama ascends from our slanderous carpet. Note how his highball glass holds the light from the table lamp. Note the composition of the scene, its liquid contents simmer in a frozen, iridescent suspension. Why, it's clarity. It's story suspended. Where's a Rembrandt when you need him?"

Skeads had already pulled out his leather pouch and papers, a process of meditation; he tapped the tobacco into the paper bed formed by his fingers, rolling around the shredded leaves, his thumbs working the mound gently until smooth throughout the length of the paper. He delicately licked it, putting it between his stained teeth. He opened his Zippo and turned an end to an ember. He smoked, drank, and studied the scene.

A man in work attire approached Hat Boy, who then stood up and sauntered, pulling this man with an invisible tagline into the deeper shadows of the restaurant; this nighthawk hero glanced around, and the duo slipped into the restroom. They returned within a minute. The man in the black leather coat and bolero hat mastered a ritual; this service occurred with several other revelers over the next half-an-hour. Skeads rolled another cigarette and ordered another shot.

Wetting the tip of his gnarly finger, Mallary turned another page pointing at its surface, "You read the article about the salmon sports fisherman? Brown bear protecting its cub nipped the head from his shoulders. The blessed irony that humans pay to experience fishing."

Looking up from his paper, Mallary said, "Hark, Penelope arrives."

"Who's Penelope?" Skeads exhaled smoke.

Polly's door had opened, and Gina entered.

"It matters little ... but sadly, Narcissus seeks her, not Odysseus."

She saw Falin who had taken a seat at Hat Man's table.

"My, my, my, how the plot thickens," said Mallary. "But not to create unnecessary thunder, I've been watching this sporty-dressed suit for the last week. A man of enterprise. He abuses an evening at the loo ... why the man owns the bladder of an adder. Or perhaps he hosts a financial empire in a bathroom stall."

The song ended, and Polly's quieted to a subdued quiver. From his clandestine place in the shadows, Skeads watched Falin and Gina dance the next song. Dressed like she had come from the grocery store, Gina glanced over her shoulder to Skeads, and then never

193

looked back. Falin acted the man of courtesy. The band resumed with a line dance, and Falin wanted to join her. She declined, and with his eyes focused on her, he entered the line by himself. He could bop with the best of them, prancing the intricate steps faultlessly, laughing and showering her the attention that women would adore from an attractive and wealthy man.

Hat Boy took the floor with some gal crowned with a cowboy hat sporting a lizard skin hatband and feathers. He pranced with smooth confidence and in rhythm to the beat of the drums and guitars; the long leather coat collected rays of meek sheen within its folds. The gal returned to the table with him, and he bought a round. Gina refused anything alcoholic, though Falin tried to get her to drink. He tried holding her hand, but she showed no interest.

Skeads had seen enough. He left his drink of sour mash, finished the beer, returned his tobacco pouch to his coat, and said to Mallary, "Save my seat. I need to go to the toilet. I'll be back in less than an hour. Don't drink my shot." He left through the back door.

* * *

That was the night Skeads visited Falin's house. The idea that he visited an empty lakefront house meant nothing to him, but when meeting Falin months before, on the *Ambrosia*, he had suggested he might stop over. This evening would be the first of his two visitations.

He parked his truck a quarter mile from Falin's house, pocketed his flashlight, and with a pry bar and fisherman's gloves, he slipped into the dark tree line paralleling the road to Falin's place. For ten minutes, he waited in the darkness and scrub brush to see if anyone might be in the house. Situated at the end of a roundabout driveway, he slipped quietly through the underbrush to the back of the house where the living room faced the lake. He knew what he searched for but doubted he could find it. Peering through the windows, he studied the living room for movement. Finding the back door, he placed his ear against its surface and listened. In the next move, he made no pretensions of elegance. He covered his hands with the pair of work gloves. If nothing else, he wanted to damage and intimidate. With a subdued pleasure, he jammed the pry bar on the hinge side of the door and ripped them out of the casing. He inspected the entrance for any security device. None existed. The house opened into a clean and organized mudroom with a rack to hang wet clothes, another rack to put boots upside down over heating vents, and a heavy duty washer and dryer. Across from it, another door opened to a kitchen that expanded to a large living room with exposed beams and a cathedral ceiling. One wall consisted of floor-to-ceiling windows overlooking the mirror of the lake; another wall had a stone fireplace and the carved sign of the *Ambrosia* resting on a granite mantel. The beam from the flashlight seized the eye staring out across the living room and into the kitchen and then at Skeads. The eye that had once watched over the *Ambrosia* now regarded a chic-but-casual living room and scanned across to the kitchen alcove to where a box freezer stood.

Falin's bedroom paid tribute to the essence of male modernity. The beam of Skeads' flashlight boogied through the décor of what you might find in an upscale men's magazine, with the usual excesses of a king-sized bed, a beautiful hand-made desk of oak and matching overstuffed chairs upholstered in leather. Twin lamps with rawhide shades stood at attention on either side of the bed. Skeads ignored all the panache and entered the walk-in closet searching for a safe. No safe. The beam scurried across the walls, its yellow orb hopping across the white surface of the sheet-rocked walls and a full-length, wall-mounted mirror to finally lose itself in the bathroom. He entered and checked under the sink, wondering if the interest of his quest even occupied the house. Maybe it hid in the cannery or on the *Ambrosia*. He returned to the kitchen and saw two

195

padlocks securing the stainless steel box freezer. He pulled the freezer away from the wall and, taking the pry bar, broke the hinges and began rummaging through the contents. Packages of game and fish filled it. Pulling out a couple of layers, he found a shopping bag secured with duct tape. Skeads cut open the bag with his survival knife. Out fell bundles of hundred-dollar bills neatly secured in plastic wrap. Not interested in the cash, he broke several bundles open and threw them on the floor. That would make an impression. He doubted this event would be reported to Trooper Sadlerman.

Knowing that this quest was a longshot, he had about given up. As he began to leave, he noticed the carved sign again with the steady eye whose whittled countenance followed him around. The flashlight caught and held the strange iris trapped in the sclera of an eye examining the dark living room. He noticed a flaw. Not in the carving, but when the beam of light scanned under the mantel, it ricocheted off a seam. Unlike the other mortised stones of the wall, this piece friction-fit.

Within a minute he had ripped out the granite mantel, aimed his flashlight into the slot. Five bricks of cocaine indifferently stared back at him. He pulled one, cut it open, and threw it on the bed.

Within an hour he returned through the back door to Polly's. Gina had left. Falin played the guitar and Hat Man worked his trade.

Mallary had faithfully waited and mused on Skeads return, "Ah-ha. Have you returned from the toilet? By-the-bye, on your largess, I've started a tab. Time is money, even for a man of humility such as myself. I assume you've been toileting away? My Skeadsman must have the bladder of an elephant."

Mallary watched Skeads sip his whiskey and light another cigarette. Concentrating on his newspaper, he whispered loud for his new employer and skipper to hear, "Caution, my dear Skeadsman, caution. Let not Billins and Gina crack your heart and stave your

196

brain. In one we are many, and we unknowing write our own myths."

# Chapter 21: Narrator returns

I had been working out west in the Bering Sea for three years, never returning to the states or visiting the town. Finding refuge in brutal work in a brutal place, a place farther into the Bering Sea, I found water, where sacking my moods proved not only possible but probable. With vague objectives, I had effectively dropped off the face of the earth, retreating from the ravens and reefs that too often haunt youth. And it worked.

While working my last rig, as chance would have it, three events aligned. The skipper of the boat on which I worked had a son who had dropped out of college and wanted to return to fishing. I had decided to return to college. Therefore, without shame, in the middle of the season, I could leave the rig and give my position to the skipper's son. Another rig in Dutch Harbor was delivering a load of crabs to town and would give me a lift. Funny, but once I had found a plan, or a plan found me, the jagged parts of life started to fall into place. With any luck, maybe, I could visit Skeads for a few days before either flying down south or finding another free ride on a rig heading to Seattle.

Skeads and I had exchanged several letters, and it was surprising how his letters proved thoughtful, though, when thinking back on it now, except for my prejudices, there was no reason why he should not be meditative and capable of expressing his thoughts in any number of forms. I confirmed this when I was given his journals. However, at the time, I never saw the etched tusk cribbage board as anything but a game. I had heard he was making a small fortune running the *Sunburst*.

During those wandering years, although I had little interest in any future, I had saved my crew shares like a miser, and I had enough savings to return to college and attend like a rich kid. For a while protected away in the Bering Sea, the idea struck to teach at my old high school, a school I had hated. From sheer chance, this fluke formed of its own, and I discovered there's nothing more agreeable than when money, goal, and serendipity coalesce. Irony casts futures, and futures are cast from reasons for being.

We arrived in town at night, and as I thanked the skipper and crew for their hospitality and help, oblivious to the cold, my enthusiasm threw my worn duffle bags—one full of books and the other, work clothes—on to the frozen transit dock. Shouldering them, filled with the energy and joy that blesses youth, finding Skeads became the objective. I wanted to thank him.

* * *

In high school, I was chucked into reading Homer's *Odyssey*. As I sat in the classroom, bored to near death and with eager eyes looking out the window into a world that seemed ready for my unrestrained energies, the teacher was unable to relate the story either to myself or perhaps himself. I had, as yet, no idea that life is an odyssey. We live our own myths.

In a way, I have collected a few people in my life the way some people collect jewelry. Skeads became a diamond. Perhaps, it was the sheer randomness of our first meeting.

On the early days of my odyssey, when I first arrived in town, the *F/V Faith* found me. We, Skeads and I, crossed tracks by total luck. Five minutes one way or the other and we would have never met. This harsh but good fortune provided a destiny loaded with alterations. He gave me a brutal job, and with almost a mathematical certainty my life veered, then forged to an unintentional destination. But, it would take years ignoring this luck of our chance meeting to recognize his importance in my life.

Trudging down cannery row, finding Polly's unchanged as the

stars, I learned I had just missed Mallary. I talked to a stranger who told me where to find the *Sunburst*. I drank a quick celebration. Then I walked.

From the dock, I saw the lights in the cabin of the *Sunburst* and tossing my duffle bags to the snow-covered deck, I climbed down the wobbly ladder and entered the galley no more or less than as an adjunct to the frigid air. Three years of separation stumbled in with me.

The crew lounged in the small galley. The time that had whittled me had carved Skeads. When he looked at me, his character was unchanged, still stoic, but the seasons and his unhealthy habits had raced through him. His thin face had withered more albino, his eyes now malarial orbs, and his tobacco-stained teeth featured an incisor that had uninhibitedly abandoned his mouth; he couldn't have cared less. Not looking the least surprised at my arrival, he said, "It took you a while."

I closed the hatch and half-way smiled while Skeads' eyes surveyed. He smiled, saying, "You've changed."

Perched to Skeads' side, Mallary nodded, a sly smile resting on his lips, his baby blue eyes fixed in their weathered sockets, and with a wink aimed at me, he said, "A wandering fish has come home to roost." Nothing had changed, particularly his random oxymoron and the occasional catachresis.

He played cribbage, his two hands of cards dueling with one another; he occasionally moved the pegs down the columns of holes.

A very young crewman whom I didn't know worked cooking a chicken and red potatoes. A head of cabbage waited to be slawed. I remembered that whenever possible, Monroe and Skeads preferred inexperienced crewmen, favoring to train new guys in their method and tradecraft (like yours truly). I would later learn that the young man never talked about his past, and Skeads discovered why. He was underage. Monroe had obtained a release from his mother (there was no father), and he had a lawyer draw up the paperwork. With sprouting soft wisps of red beard and blue, clear eyes, the boy called himself Maverick. Through this night watch, while Skeads and Mallary and I listened to the weather rattle the rigging, we caught up on lost time, sour mash, and coffee, but our skipper never allowed Maverick to drink booze.

While Monroe was down south preparing the new boat, Skeads had been crab fishing for two months and enjoyed an exceptional season. His strategy for the king crab season had paid off. Right out of Falin's playbook, Skeads decided to fish in the rocks. It was an idea he had been thinking about a long time. The common consensus paradigmed that the omnivore crabs roamed soft bottom, that the creatures foraged, moved and bred avoiding the rocks. But during the salmon season, he experimented with two unmarked pots, prospecting during the midnight hours, studying with the sonar the bottom of an area he thought might have possibilities. In this illicit experiment—for it was totally illegal—Skeads discovered an unusual formation on the bottom: the sonar showed pockets of sandy bottom, and he suspected, regardless of the traditional viewpoints of fishermen, the crabs might coalesce and find forage in the pockets of sand in this region of rocks. In this midnight piracy, he placed his two illicit prospecting pots in pockets of sand between rocks. Letting the pots rest, he drifted in the night for a few hours, and then he pulled them. The pots were full. The money came from thinking outside the rocks.

While we talked, the latch clanked and the metal door to the galley opened, a billow of frigid air pushed the last crewman into the warm air. He wore no coat, no hat, no gloves, nothing to protect him from the winter. Maverick glanced over his shoulder and dropped the chicken. "What the hell happened to you?" He'd never seen a man who had been tortured. Cody stumbled into the galley.

He looked at our group with a face having been used for batting practice. He said to Skeads, "Falin accused me that I broke his trust."

Skeads' eyes lifted and silently rested on Cody. Blinking once, he waited to fully absorb the picture. He looked at Cody's hands and noticed a thumbnail missing, the blood tightening into a purple splotch around this absence. "So, what happened to Billins the day he got chewed up? You were there. You know."

Maverick handed the man a dishtowel and said, "Wow, you really got crushed." The man's eyebrow, cut away from the forehead, drooped over its complimentary eye.

Pointing at his face, the eyebrow, in particular, Cody asked, "What should I do?"

Skeads cursed filthy, "If you're talking about the eyebrow, duct-tape it." Cursing another muttered salvo of filthy words, "Looks to me you or Falin got no idea what trust means. I hate the damn word." I had never seen Skeads this angry.

Cody, nearly frozen, slid into the galley table bench. "I'm in trouble."

Skeads let the observation rest for a minute. "It's Falin and Hat Boy, isn't it?"

Cody remained silent.

Skeads added, "I'm talking to you. Don't play games with me if you want my help. It was bound to happen. Swim in a toilet, sooner-or-later you turned to sewage. Everyone swims in a toilet at least once. It's your turn. Trust me. Whether you're watching or doing, you're just as guilty. Cankers your soul."

After a minute of silence, Cody repeated, "I'm in trouble."

Skeads poured a shot into a glass, took a sip and passed it to the crewman. His face turned calm but his eyes hardened on to the man in front of him. "So, you going to tell me what happened when Billins got turned into fish bait? And don't tell me Falin's not a widow maker. You know. You're part of it, aren't you? You were there that morning. You lied. You're an omission man, just like me. Don't mean to preach, but you can do ugly, or you can watch ugly and say nothing. Not much difference."

Our skipper asked again, "So what happened to Billins?"

Cody showed no interest in the pain. "I'm a fool. I should have never trusted the..."

"Trusted?"

"Falin. He's mad. He's off his rocker. In town, he stopped me. Drove me over to his place for a drink and a doobie, and some guy in the leather coat was waiting. We did some coke. They stomped me. Both of them. They tied me up, coked-up and beat the hell out of me. They laughed."

"That guy in the leather coat ... was he wearing that stupid black hat?"

"Yeah."

"So, he's Falin's 'suit?'"

"Nah man, it's the other way round. He owns Falin. He owns that uncle that runs the cannery. Both operations pass drug money through the businesses. They're making big money. When they take *Ambrosia* to the states for shipyard work, they bring back duffle bags of the stuff. Before they hit a town, a skiff comes out and takes off a bag and disappears into the night.

"That dude with the coat pulled out my thumbnail. Hell, after that I'd tell him anything."

"So, what happened to Billins?" asked Skeads.

"I was doing so good here. They want their lost money. I got ten acres and a house in Idaho ... paid for ... this only happens in the movies. I trusted him. They want my land."

Skeads pulled out a cigarette and put it between his skinny lips, poured Cody another shot. "So Falin and the hat guy... the...."

"They want their money. The street value of the coke. The street value. They gave me three days to pay up. They want my land. I didn't steal nothing, but when that shit pulled my thumbnail out, I said anything to buy time."

"So, what do they mean ... you stole the coke?"

"No. Somebody busted into Falin's house a few months back and took coke and money."

Skeads replied, "So that's what they're saying, that somebody stole their coke? Who says one of them didn't steal it and hustled the situation?"

"I got no idea what's going on. They said cash was missing. That's all I know. Cash and the coke." Cody winced as Maverick with a gauze pad pressed the gash above his eye, squeezing Neosporin into it. The kid appeared to enjoy the activity.

"So, they're saying cash is missing?" Skeads almost started to laugh out loud. "That's a hand to play. I should've enlisted in the drug business if they're the competition. But it's a good hustle for one of them."

Then Skeads revealed a little tidbit that only later I would learn from his journals. He said, "Who hides a shopping bag of hundreds in a padlocked freezer? Down-right hilarious."

He quietly studied Cody's missing nail. "You know that Billins had two missing fingers. Just the first joints. I never asked him how. He never volunteered the answer. What's a thumbnail in the big picture? Maybe a teachable experience, eh? Before Falin turned him into a piece of meat, you know he had a great life with the wife and kid? Did you see Billins' life? You know how his wife described him? A man of many parts. She said that admiringly, meaning he was complex, not thinking about the horrors of what happened to him because of you and Falin."

Cody remained silent, his hand on the snifter, his eyes on its rim.

"You're not like them. Come on now. It's fact-time. Some people call it the truth. So, what happened to Billins?" The question floated on the soft vibrations of the generator engine below. Skeads' pallid face hovered above the tusk. He leaned over it and whispered, "Man, you have to pick a side. Strange how ravens work."

Cody started to chew on his bloused lip, and his eyes cast about looking for any place to rest.

Skeads said, "Don't pretend you don't have a nose when you're swimming in shit. You know the stink. You're not like Hat Boy and Falin. Billins ... what happened to Billins? It's time ... you knew this time would come. The question was always resting here, in this galley, every time we ate together, every time you brushed your teeth looking in the mirror. Always. Don't insult yourself. So, what happened to Billins? You're not like Falin and Hat Boy. What happened the day Billins died, got turned into meat? How Gina lost her husband. How the kid lost his father. Falin chewed him up, right? He killed Billins for Gina. Right? Old as King David. I want to know. I need to know. I have to know because it's eating whatever's left of me. I can't sleep at night. Tell me! I may not have the wisdom, but justice needs to be served.

"Why'd you cover for Falin? Was it the insurance? The insurance would have left him free of negligence. The cops? You had coke onboard? If it looked like Billins' negligence, you guys

205

were covered. Did it come down to something as stupid as money? Was it just money? Or drugs? Or Gina?"

Cody looked like he was closer to responding but still held his tongue.

Skeads added, "It's funny strange, perhaps feral serendipity, how when the human sense of justice is violated, its beak needs to be wet. Hell-to-pay, it's taken us 500 million years to achieve guilt and shame. We'll spend the next 500 million years sidestepping our best accomplishment. Talk to me. Help me out. Where's your shame?"

Cody replied, "The leather-coat-guy wants money. After pulling my nail out, he smiled and said he could cut my balls off just as easily and sink me in the lake. He kept rubbing this skull ring in my face, saying it needed a taste. He's got his teeth filed to points. He's the one in charge. He brags about owning the *Ambrosia*. Falin knows where I live, my town. Falin's more coked up than ever; his buddy bought the house for Falin. It's not just the town; they have the Southeast, the Chain, and half of Anchorage."

Skeads said, "It don't mean nothing now. That card's played. Hat Boy wants power. Hell, Falin only wants attention and toys. Hat Boy wants significance. Shit, you're just their collateral damage. But that's not what this is about. What happened to Billins? What happened that morning?"

"What happened to Falin? Falin was all coked up. He was in his own world. Billins put out his marker buoys. He did a dive to check what he needed to free the prop and shaft of line twisted around it. It was causing some kind of vibration around the prop. I was onboard, and he asked if I could cover him. Had me keep an eye out... I screwed it up."

As Skeads listened to Cody, it wasn't hard for us to see Falin after a hard night of partying, climbing onboard to retrieve more

206

coke. He would be in his own world. Then insanity intervened, and its indifference to life changed unintentional consequences into needless horror. Perhaps, Falin in his altered state and lost in his own world thought he was going fishing? Regardless, he started the engines and put the rig in gear. Five minutes one way or the other, Billins still would have been living, a husband and father.

"I couldn't stop it," said Cody, "and by the time I got to the wheelhouse and pulled it out of gear and shut down the engines ..."

Yes, no, maybe. Under these circumstances, I had no idea what was going down, but I could tell Cody looked racked, quivering, his broken face a mask no longer holding any pretentions.

Then Skeads shot orders at Maverick. "The storm's supposed to slack by first light. You take my truck and our punching bag to the airport. You," he spoke to Cody, "take what you think will last and find Monroe down South. If the storm don't slack, I'll hide you at my place 'til we get you down south. He'll cover you there. I'll send your crew-share to Monroe. If you give Falin and the suit one dime, I'll see you regret it. You've done enough to kill Billins."

The night shifted to plan B. Tucked into a corner of the galley, Maverick, as serious as a crusader to fulfill his duty, rested his reddish-blond curls and peach-fuzz beard on his forearms. Mallary went to bed. Skeads pulled out his sketchpad and began to doodle. I read a book. Cody packed his gear. As the storm broke, Cody thanked Skeads, and on this final parting said he owed him. Our skipper handed him a wad of cash and said he should take care of his mangled eyebrow.

Here again, it took me years to recognize that had my trip into town been waylaid by a mere twenty-four hours, I would have never again seen Skeads or Mallary or the fine rig, *Sunburst,* or the remarkable kid Maverick, who hated being called his given name, Reginald.

207

As to our skippers' prediction - we could hear the storm subside around four in the morning, its venom and spleen drained.

But not for Skeads; his venom and spleen commenced in spades.

# Chapter 22: Skeads, Gina, Polly's

"You want Cody's job? I could use you," said my skipper.

Almost kneejerk, I assumed both Cody's berth and job for the next couple of weeks. We left for the grounds soon after that and discovered Skeads' honey-hole had been laid down by other rigs. Their pots lay all over our gear robbing Skeads of both his originality and illegality. In a way, they now shared in it. We spent four hard days moving the gear nearer to town.

During this time, I tried and failed to find a more definitive reason for Skeads intense interest in Billins' death, to give some deeper distinction to my first impressions. Trying to find reasons proved elusive. He never talked about it. Whenever I might timidly ask about this man Billins, a man and incident I knew little about, Skeads would eye me and say someday he might talk about it, but in the meantime, do my job. Which I did.

While I was out west, Skeads had become a very successful and admired skipper. He seemed content in the present, neither happy nor unhappy, neither angry nor at peace, but the contentment and his management insured this year ended with all his responsibilities in neat boxes and ready for what would follow. Living on the *Sunburst*, at any given time of day or night, across the galley table, I could see Skeads and Mallary discussing the various aspects of the *Sunburst*, talking to one another as their faces hovered over charts. Skeads' hands, which I always thought better suited for a musical instrument, wrapped around the glass of sour mash, pointed a long graceful finger with that perfect oval soiled nail and tapped on a place of importance on a chart. Skeads tutored Mallary in the details of the *Sunburst,* the various charts, the location of stored gear, the vagaries and manuals and personalities of the engines and various systems. The baby-faced man was more than capable of running the rig, having been in both logging and fishing since he was fifteen, this in-built knowledge being bred to his muscle and bone, sinew and synapse. In a corner, Maverick floated around their heads listening to their quiet discussion, the kid less an albatross than an intelligent and inquisitive adjunct. Finished with the life of the fishery, I knew I was only onboard to fill in and spend some time with Skeads.

From the dock, Skeads had already picked out a couple of young kids as potential crewmen, trusting both Mallary and now Maverick, to prepare them for their great opportunity.

Skeads and I talked about my future of returning to college. He gave my plan an additional vote of confidence, adding only that to teach kids I would need to loosen up, saying, "Kids need to laugh." How he came up with that feedback, I have no idea. I could never imagine him having a childhood or laughing that much, but he was right, I would need to enjoy teaching.

"It's important. Kids want to live. You get to share that great adventure," he said. What an overlooked adventure, what a mistreated opportunity. For him, the need for knowledge welled from an unexplainable and unfulfilled yearning, perhaps a void.

We day-fished, coming home in the evenings. Some nights, we would go out and have a few drinks at Polly's, and then walk through the darkness to his truck. He would yank open the truck door, its hinges howling with arthritic complaint, but in one move, he would slip into the cab and roll down the window, throwing his elbow over the side, his cigarette smoldering between his skinny lips. Then remarking on some detail about tomorrow, he drove off to his trailer near the lake. He talked to me as an equal, and he had no idea how much I appreciated his confidence in me, but I never thanked him.

Towards the very end of my stay, one morning I woke late to find Skeads at the galley table studying his palm-size sketchpad. The morning pushed against the portholes turning them gray, and after another cup of coffee and whiskey, he handed me the keys to the truck telling me to buy provisions at the grocery store. I had another coffee and whiskey. What appeared to be an afterthought, he said, "I need to buy another handle of bourbon." This small reconsideration would prove as providential as when we first met. He joined me in the truck. He smoked.

The bench seat in the cab consisted of scrap plywood salvaged from the roadside. It effectively lay across the truck's exhausted and abused cushion preventing the exposed coils from poking through the frazzled fabric and potentially turning us to second rate castrati.

I asked him, "Does the missing tooth hold that cig any better?"

He answered, "You'll win no students that way."

In the footwells, more plywood kept us from falling through rusted floor pans. The heater blasted out hot air. The winter-beaten road abused an already churlish truck suspension. But between what pretended to be a road and what pretended to meet the definition of transportation, both seemed suited for our short journey to what would pretend to be a grocery store. It didn't seem strange that farther down the same road sprawled a big-chain store with a much bigger parking lot. Regardless, Skeads insisted on my driving to the smaller one, the one he shopped at.

Saying nothing, making no small talk, his mind sifted through his private corridors as the dingy scenes colonizing the roadside ditch of the town clicked past: broken beer bottles, a rimless tire, a small roll of waterlogged toilet paper. His eyes absorbed the small buildings along the side of the gravel road. He smoked the cig and sipped from a pint.

As I pulled into the single parking strip, the wheel of the truck hit a slush-filled pothole, the truck growled, and the tire bottomed out. "Ambushes," Skeads said.

Muddied gravel and rocks reflected not enough light to find any color theme above gray. The front sign feigned commerce. An "A" and "N" had given up to time and elements, and long ago flaked off the sign's peeling surface. It read, "GELA'S Grocery Depot." The storefront consisted of anemic bat-and-board siding with hunks of dirty snow piled and forming a battlement of soiled ice.

During those few weeks of my stay, Skeads often murmured inexplicable comments, private to the conversation he held with himself, his eyes staring out the mud-grimed front windshield. The tone of this wistful remark, but like a sigh riding on the back of a breath, "I'm lucky to have found this place ... too bad Billins ... and Neal and all the others ... it's a special place for some of us...." Skeads didn't finish his uncharacteristic and unguarded refrain; he was a man who on the surface seemed to despise the past, but later I would believe he was a man possessed by the past.

With the truck panting, I killed the engine. The vehicle sighed, chortled, and stopped. We had joined a couple of other trucks that had limped in and parked in the front of the store; one with a mangled tailgate and a pitiless bumper wrapped to the frame in strands of stainless steel wire; the other beater, still running but empty of a driver, hung on for dear life with the tailpipe exhaling lethal gases. We belonged hip-to-joint in the parking lot.

We had yet to climb out of the truck. I had not heard Neal mentioned in years, and my skipper's sigh uprooted one of those perversions of the past, where sorrow shames grief. I recalled that morning when Skeads and I stood outside the same police station where Neal had hung himself, and how in fatigues, jungle boots and watch cap his diminutive, haunting girlfriend exited from that pitiful moment and walked by us. From a round, dark innocence, her desolate eyes fixed on Skeads, piercing him. Then, behind him, she

212

stopped and turned around and murmured to Skeads' back, "The raven visited me, and it takes responsibility. Forgive yourself. Neal doesn't blame you." At that moment, we had yet to learn that he had hung himself. To this day, I have no idea how she conjured this vision and conviction, but it stopped him in his tracks. He never looked back. Skeads never asked for absolutions.

While parked in front of Gela's in the truck, I said artlessly, "Neal ... bad luck." Skeads replied, more to himself, "Bitterness and joy, violence and peace, revenge and duty, friendship and revenge and revenge and revenge. Don't let them kid you: revenge will be sweet."

Trying to change the subject as much as psychology, I asked, "Who's Billins?" The question failed again to marshal any comment from Skeads. I would later read in Skeads' journal about Billins. But that day, he continued cryptic, hidden from me. He replied, "We're players to the last breath. Know how to bury the dead."

* * *

I opened the thick metal industrial door to the store, and the place looked worn out from decades of being driven hard and put to bed in a cockroach palace, a business evolution resulting in a couple of open display coolers and several rows of foodstuffs.

Skeads shopped indifferently, and for what consisted of a few bags of groceries, we made our way to the checkout counter and a half-native girl working the register. She recognized Skeads and gave him a shy smile, waiting for him to say something.

Nodding his head, he said, "I heard you moved in town ... lately."

As we unloaded the groceries onto the counter to bag them, she said, "I don't mind it." She was quiet spoken and ignored me. She added, "Our house is paid for, and we have a contract on it." Her rolling consonants made an unusual lilting dialect I had heard before farther out the Chain. Aleut or Inuit. I knew nothing about her life but noticed she spoke in the present.

Skeads introduced her to me. "This is Gina. She likes painting pictures and things to look at from around here." He didn't mention she was Billins' widow.

She replied, smiling at me, but addressing Skeads, "I have something I want to give you. From Billins. From us. From when you visited."

"I'll be in town for a while," he said.

I had no idea what they were talking about or what he meant. At the time, I knew nothing about Gina, and I thought it unusual that our skipper introduced me to her. He was a man who never introduced anyone to anything except work. We packed up the groceries.

Skeads looked at his watch and asked Gina, "Lunch?"

She smiled.

The three of us sat in the truck with the bags of groceries stuffed where they might fit.

As I backed out of the parking lot, she, sitting between us, said to Skeads who stared straight ahead through the dirty windshield, "I saw you at Polly's one night a few months back. You never talked to me." She was not coquettish. It could have been a statement as easily as a question. "I thought maybe you were mad at me."

She sat a little closer to me than felt comfortable to me. She smelled of fresh soap, and I ran over the same pothole I had on entering. The hub lurched on its axle. I felt like a fool, conscious only of myself. It was the beginning of a tortured forty-five-minute lunch in which I would find myself socially inept. Gina said, "Don't

214

feel bad; it's a hole everyone hits."

Ignoring the pothole, Skeads replied to her question, "I noticed. But ... it didn't seem important to say anything. It don't mean nothing."

She interrupted, "Yes, I remember you left early."

"I figured you were with Falin and the leather coat guy. Somebody like me only makes ..." He again replied without finishing, changing the subject by asking, "What's Falin been doing lately? I heard he had a good crab season. He's got a nice house ... an interesting buddy with that leather coat and ... nice hat."

She said, "I don't see him much now. He's in a different place than me. I'm a Catholic girl." Her voice coasted to a silence. She spoke both in the present tense and past tense as if the time and knowledge that separates them was pointless.

I had no idea she was Billins' widow or that Skeads had been a business partner with the man. In the end, it would take a conversation with Mallary and Skeads' own journals to fill in the details of that history. Skeads never said a word to me about how the *Ambrosia* had, in a way, gamed Billins' life.

By then, it was pointless. Skeads was a predator.

# Chapter 23: Skeads, the narrator, and Gina at Polly's

Polly's possessed the split personality of a place both half full and half empty. In the dim lighting, the ever-present cloud of tobacco smoke congregated around the tables, loitered for a few moments, and then somehow shifted upwards to form a thin cloud against the sticky ceiling tiles. We slipped into an empty table covered with a checkered plastic cloth, set with flatware rolled in cheap paper napkins and the ubiquitous hexagonal salt and pepper shakers with screw-on metal caps. The waitress saw Skeads and abandoned setting the table. Perfect white teeth filled her honest smile, and her vast blond bouffant jiggled and glowed in the smoke. A healthy-boned woman, her skin faultless, I could tell she deferred to my skipper.

Gracefully sashaying across the exhausted carpet to stand near him, her round and denimed hip hovered as close as you might stand without transferring body heat. She first ignored Gina and me, asking Skeads in a feigned affectation, "Would you like to order sir? The usual? Cheeseburger ... and of course the way Polly likes it and, sir, fries with a long neck and shot?" He twisted his head on his neck like he might have a crick and nodded. His neck popped.

I ordered a burger, and Gina asked us, "Can I get the scallops?" Of course, we agreed, and as the waitress pulled away from the table, she slipped from an apron pocket a stack of cheap napkins, glancing at Skeads with blue eyes. Hating the attention, he cricked his neck once more, and it popped again.

The tabletop rocked back and forth. One leg rested in a hole across the landscape of the gnarly carpet. Skeads ignored it. In my need to be impressive, in my fantasy as the fixer of table imbalances, I took a paper napkin, folded it, and slipped it under a leg. My pretentions made my stupidity worse. Or maybe, my stupidity made my pretentions worse. I had picked out the wrong leg. Now, the table leaped back and forth.

Gina looked under the table testing it a little. Taking a small wooden wedge from her hooded sweatshirt pocket, she removed my failed paper napkin attempt at my displaying the mastery of the universe and slipped the piece beneath the proper leg. She eyeballed me across the table, and said with an understated smile, "Different leg." Then, for me, the lunch began to find a downhill direction.

When the meals arrived, Skeads ate quickly, stood abruptly from his chair, and even more abruptly said, "I got business in town. Give Gina a lift to the store and take the groceries to the boat." It was an order.

He walked two or three steps and then turned around saying to Gina, "You take care. Let Paul know I was thinking about him. He's a good kid. I know he'll do fine, real fine. You're doing a good job." He added another uncharacteristic but memorable turn, saying, "My mother did as good as her chance. I could have done better by her." Unforgettable, this unsolicited statement bewildered both Gina and me to where we exchanged glances but said nothing. When he left through the door, we didn't discuss it.

Skeads abandoned me with my burger and Gina with her plate of fried scallops. Alone with this woman, I again found myself instinctively trying to be a man I would never be. I had spent my last six years in the fishery, a fierce social wasteland allowing scant opportunity to practice gentility. I had not been around women for a long time and had lost what little social chit-chat I might have ever possessed. I could talk to crewmen easily enough because we shared the fishing life, but I had little to share about experience with women. My attempts at panache clowned into a hopeless charade.

I had noticed Gina only on a superficial level until Skeads suddenly left me. Her face could easily hold the attention of a

217

photographer, one of those National Geographic outdoor exotics of the village girl with long black hair pulled to a ponytail, the dark eyes content and perceptive, but the compositional focus on the shadowy smile rather than a grin. To the urban-eco-reader, this still life might suggest that nature breeds beauty and innocence, a quality we take for granted, and if left alone, life would be perfect. And, of course, in this picture, a background of snowy volcanic mountains smoothed and pacified the viciousness of ice and freezing wind. Her hands were kind and soft and feminine without pretention of polish. She wore a hooded sweatshirt with frayed drawstrings.

I couldn't drive a beat-up truck without hitting a pothole the size of a moon crater or even balance a table. I may as well have been babbling in tongues to her. Her presence frightened me.

While trying to make impressive small talk, primarily about myself, I bit into the hamburger to discover an unintended consequence. With her dark eyes, Gina saw me slowly start pulling from between my lips and the handful of burger a hair—not a short hair—but a long, a very long hair. I started to gag on ketchupped, mayonnaised, and beefed bun. This uninvited strand of hard grew the more I pulled at its length, a length capable of suturing a heart transplant.

Gina watched all this, studying me, saying, "The scallops are good. Thank you. I hear Polly's serves only fresh scallops." She ate her meal, overlooking my embarrassment.

Gina quietly watched as I thought Polly, this woman long dead and gone, meant to humiliate me. A minute before, I had implied I was reasonably wealthy, and I would seek a degree in English, perhaps even art, and start a new life. The single strand of hair had slipped halfway down my throat.

Gagging, I dropped the burger and pulled the hair out of my throat, settling it into a loose coil on the table. With a cautious smile, her dark eyebrows flicked, and Gina said, "You found a hair in your hamburger?"

My masculine pride would not admit I was simply and irrevocably bashful. Better if I could have played the fool marionette trapped in a magic lantern dancing across a shadowed wall of Chez Polly's.

But never mind. Reaching for another napkin, I knocked over my beer. Crashing across the table, the beer trickled into Gina's lap.

Ignoring my embarrassment, she took napkins and started soaking up the spill. I gave up pretentions and took the remainder of my hamburger and soaked up the spill in the plate. Staring at the soggy combination of bun and burger, shrugging my shoulders, I picked up the pepper shaker, shook it gloomily over it and ate in silence, unable to lift my eyes from the plastic checkered tablecloth. If a fool, don't fight it. Perhaps an exercise in humility.

Smiling, she said, "Waste not, want not."

"Franklin?" I replied.

"No one's really sure." She laughed. "You try too hard. You don't really need to."

I knew I would never see her again and gave up pretending we had anything in common. The conversation lulled, and some moron in the back of the restaurant started to play the "boink" game and swear loudly. Nibbling on a scallop, she seemed completely comfortable in her silence sitting across from a lummox.

Polly's was warm, and she had unzipped her sweatshirt. At first, I hadn't noticed, but some sort of a necklace rested around her neck, an object Skeads referred to as "craft stuff." Reflecting the meager lighting, the piece appeared to be, for lack of a better phrase, a sparkly pendant, a necklace formed of fine diaphanous fabric and shards of stone, handwoven into a montage of separate illusions. The

219

more I looked at it, the more the piece blossomed, grew, catching the eye as it caught substance, catching the imagination, and with her negligible movements, the modest shards and weave reflected through an insignificant light some mystery of craft, transformed into a butterfly with wings. Nacre haloed the fore and hind wings, with black veins tatting across their lacy surface; the carved amber thorax and abdomen seemed crowned with a crystalline head with the glittering coils of a silver proboscis and faint antennae. It lived. No bigger than the size of her palm, it floated around her neck, resting across her cheap, worn tee shirt.

"Is that yours?" I asked, nodding at the collage of light and shards. "Did you make that?"

She regarded me, her eyebrows furrowed. My question seemed more an intrusion into her privacy. "Paul and Billins and I walk the beach together, and we find things. We find things on the beach." She spoke in the present.

"How did you make that?"

Her eyes rested on her plate until she said, "Slowly."

I laughed saying, "As ignorant as I am, I can see it would take time."

I knew she found my character banal, dull, without any subtleness, a man with whom she had nothing in common. Skeads and I were never ladies' men.

I asked, "What's it supposed to be? A butterfly? I took an art course in college but dropped out."

She replied, "What's it supposed to be?" With her fork, she cut into the last scallop in half. She pushed half the scallop towards me, and I ate it. She repeated, "What it's supposed to be? Maybe it's a ghost who can't leave yet."

She shrugged her shoulders and zipped up the hoody.

I sighed resigned punctuation, and said, "I'll drive you back to the store. I have work on the boat."

The plates on the table were empty but for the soggy napkins, and I waved the waitress over to pay for the bill, but she said Skeads had already caught it.

"Did he leave a tip?"

The waitress gave a wry smile with a missing bicuspid, "You've got to be kidding."

I left a tip. Gina offered to help, but I declined, saying that the next time she saw Skeads, she might buy him lunch.

In the truck, I stared out the dirty windshield, and when twisting the ignition switch, the beaten beast sounded tired but game for another gallop. I wondered how many it had left. Gina mentioned that she recently moved into an apartment in town and that Angela, the owner of the store, was good to her. She never mentioned that she had lost her husband.

"I have Paul. He's kind."

"Paul?" I asked as if he might be her boyfriend.

"Paul's my son."

I apologized for my social ineptness, "I don't feel too comfortable around women. I seldom know what to say."

She remained silent.

At the store, as she slid out from the truck, she smiled without joy. "You seem very nice. I enjoyed the lunch and talk."

I still thought her very pretty, and I forgot completely to compliment her necklace, a necklace needing no lies for a compliment. When she climbed out of the truck, and with the cranky

221

door still open, she said, "When I look long enough at the beach it shows me what to do. Its parts tell me where to place them. Billins still walks the beach with Paul and me."

With a face ready to fall apart, her voice on the edge of breaking, she said, "Billins use to say it took God 500 million years to make a butterfly." She now spoke in the past.

She closed the door to Skeads' truck and didn't look back. I didn't want to be part of her anguish.

Years later, in an art class, I saw a piece called *Jethro's Daughter*: this ethereal face with its lineless shading and pathos eyes instantly recalled when I first saw and met Gina, and when Skeads placed the two of us together. I thought neither of us would ever meet again. A vain buffoon shares little in common with a vision of Botticelli.

# Chapter 24: Fairy Dust

A mild cold front moved through, and the color of polar ice reflected off the sky. I was content, for that was the emotion of knowing that in a few days I would be moving on to a new adventure. I had found a place in my head, a desire for a future my life had long lacked, a new destination, a glimmer of, if not happiness—whatever that giddy word means—then of contentment, a terrific place for the mind to be, and a relief from the silent twisting in the wind I had believed the cost of living. I decided to eat a gigantic breakfast at Polly's and drink enough to experience an additional liquid morning revelry. The glorious twofer.

While walking past one of the canneries along the gravel road, I saw a state trooper cruiser and a Fish and Game van parked near an access road cutting toward the dock fronting the industrial cubicle of a cannery. The bow of the *Ambrosia* could be seen. The vessel was tied to the dock, and a small group of onlookers stood around. Curiosity demanded a detour.

Among the fishermen and a few cannery workers, stood Trooper Sadlerman and a Fish and Game officer—both of whom I barely knew—whispering and concerned with the ongoing event. On the *Ambrosia*, three Coast Guardsmen had secured her deck with yellow caution tape. Within this border, lay generous amounts of a white powder, some in chunks and still in plastic wrappers. Loose hundred dollar bills scattered across the deck like leaves stripped from trees by a violent storm. The hatch to the aft house was open.

On the dock, bundled up in insulated coveralls, exchanging a quiet and awed conversation, two other men stood nonchalantly around frozen pools of grungy ice. I knew one of them, a refrigeration technician who, several years back, had worked on the chiller system of the *Ambrosia*. Long, loose, red hair still struggled in strings and tangles to escape from whatever existed beneath his stocking cap. He said, "By gory, there's enough candy on the deck to buy a place on the big island, meaning Hawaii," adding with another by gory, "...there's enough cash to take the wife and kids to Disneyland. Hee-el ... for months."

He saw me and nodded. "Hey, where you been keeping yourself? Been years."

All I could do was shrug my shoulders. "Out West. What's going on here?"

"Shit hit the fan man. Don't know if it's related, but a house got burned to the ground last night. The skipper's place. Guy named Falin. Now his rig's floatin' in coke ... looks like fairy dust, don't it ... and cash scattered 'cross the deck. The skiff's missing, Falin himself can't be found. I overheard they just tried calling his house, but funny thing ... if your house burns down with the phone in it, hard to answer-up the sucker." Both of them shuffled their feet and chuckled.

"All hail rock'n'roll. Ain't 'Merca great or what?" added his partner shuffling between the cold and levity and discharging a long glob of tobacco juice to the dock.

Having never talked to him, I had only seen Trooper Sadlerman around town. Evidently, he had inspected the deck, and returning to the dock, he talked quietly to the Fish and Game officer. Suddenly, he dropped the conversation, and I thought he looked directly at me. However, I was not of his interest, for during the short time I stood there, Skeads had appeared behind me. He may have been there all the time, but he glanced at me without reaction, like I wasn't in the game. His face appeared as if concentrating on a hand of cards, or any musing, where the face is blank and void of tell-tale dispositions.

224

The trooper was not a happy camper. He said to Skeads, "You heard what happened?" My skipper listened without an immediate response. He studied, measuring through an enigmatic process both Sadlerman and the Fish and Game officer. He played them. The question formed into a little dialogue bubble dancing between them.

He fired up a hand-roll and inhaled. "Good morning," was his first response.

Sadlerman's face tensed with frustration waiting for anger and a hunt. He appeared to be a disgraced man wishing to attack, his blue eyes and Nordic features high-blood pressured by unsolicited and unwanted circumstances. "Good morning, my ass."

"Maybe ... Good morning your ass. I got no idea. I haven't been on this dock for months. *Sunburst* doesn't deliver here." Skeads exhaled smoke and smiled as best his skinny lips allowed.

"I'm starting to flashback to LA. We got ourselves a big-tent rodeo here. Might need the FBI. I came up here to dodge this crap. I got Coasties seizing a boat. There's a small fortune of coke and cash on deck. You know where he is?"

"Who he?" asked Skeads.

"Hey, come on, help me out here. Falin is he."

"Try the hat boy he runs around with. That's his buddy." My skipper never took his eyes off the officer.

Sadlerman took a deep breath. "Okay. Do you know where that person might be?"

"Go ask Falin. That's his buddy." A light breeze pushed his cigarette smoke away, this miasma rolling over his shoulder and disappearing. "You know I don't travel in that social circle." The words "social circle" echoed into a sarcastic alliteration.

Had it been seventy degrees, our world would have been a

paradise. But with the wind light, the day seemed balanced and perfect for work or mayhem.

The trooper seethed, shifting his jaw in its sockets, he asked, "You wouldn't help me if you knew, would you?"

"If you knew that I knew ... you'd already know I wouldn't. I don't give a damn about Falin." Skeads shrugged his shoulders. "I'm not going to lie to you. I like and respect you too much. I abide by the law. But I don't care where on the face of this heaven-on-earth they are." He waved his cigarette around a little. "I've been out at the trailer 'til I got here and seen your cruiser. I can see that it was a mistake to stop." He smiled, thin, humorless, cold, a nature of stark compositions that life had saddled and branded him. While his hands still seemed ready for art, his face always seemed like a predator ready to swallow his prey whole.

Remaining silent during this exchange, I looked down between my boots to the ice and grimy dirt. Then I saw it. Appearing between my boots, the rich mahogany stained stub of a hand-rolled cigarette loomed, laughing at a thousand ironies, both unmasking Skeads' protests of ignorance and straight to a lie. He had stood on this dock earlier, possibly hours before the drama dancing through this day. Instinctively, my eyes set on my skipper. He waited for me, and I saw the lies in his face. His eyes fixed on the butt and then on me. A wild card jumped into the game he played. Sadlerman and I were other cards in his hand, and I could think of no better hand to play than his. I shuffled a foot and covered the butt, destroying the evidence by grinding my boot into the evidence.

Sadlerman said, "You know his house burned down to the foundation?"

"Who his?" replied Skeads.

"Falin's place."

"Hmmm. Too bad. But then again, people in grass houses shouldn't use matches." Skeads looked at the trooper with not a drop of emotion, his face not unlike the sky above us.

"Well, I gotta get down to the boat," said my skipper, "Hope you unravel this stuff. Who knows, maybe it's all finished but for pissin' on the embers."

"You know I'm going to do my job," said Sadlerman.

"Is that a question? You'd be a duck if you didn't. Good luck."

Sadlerman replied, "I'll be talking to you again. Don't think that because I respect you, you're off the meat hook."

"Be seeing me again? Maybe yes, and maybe no. But I meant what I said about you having good luck. You deserve it."

Skeads then looked at me and said, "I need your help. Had breakfast yet? Polly's?"

We walked in the shadow of the cannery and across the gravel and chuckholes leveled by steel-hard pooled ice. We walked back to his truck. The salty air, and from the cannery, the visceral stink of fish waste waiting for a future in fertilizers, embraced one another.

"You leaving pretty soon? A day or so?"

"Yeah," I said, waiting for him to mention, to maybe explain the cigarette butt. He tossed me the key to the truck. "Use my truck to get around today. I don't need it. I can use one of the cannery's if need be."

I didn't fight the bonus.

When I started the engine, he said with sentiments unusual and out of character, "I enjoyed working with you ... for what's it worth. I'll miss you ... would have been interesting to serve overseas together." He never used the colloquy of "Nam" or even mentioned Vietnam. This was the first and only reference he ever made to me

227

that we both had served in that futility. I let it go without a response. However, now, when reflecting upon it, this response might have been another card in his deck.

Only a short distance into town, first he had me stop at another bar, a rustic place featuring bathrooms with trough urinals salvaged from WWII with dark wood-paneled walls a background for pictures dating back to the thirties of our town. Picture windows fronted the place, letting in plenty of the light otherwise shunned at Polly's. A horseshoe bar was at the back, and we drank a round of cognac and beer. It tasted fresh and alive, stinging and firing both sides of the mouth. It wasn't unlike the cold outside, penetrating and burning, both of the experiences sharing the old saw that too much of a good thing proves lethal.

We had another, and the second tasted better.

Skeads left his barstool and studied a couple pictures of the F/V *Faith* hanging on the wall. He motioned me over and tapping on the glass covering the photo of the graceful creature, he said, "That's where you started. That's where we started." We left the bar.

* * *

We pulled into the town parking lot banked with old snow mixed and embedded with little dead stars of sand and gravel. Skeads seemed neither cheerful nor grim, "Keep the truck 'til first light tomorrow morning. I don't need it. We'll do breakfast tomorrow. Booze and beer at the trailer. Pickled eggs and smoked salmon. I'll put a couple of beers in the lake to chill. Great to be alive."

The curiosity about the cigarette butt incident irritated me, but I said no more. Skeads never volunteered an explanation. For him, the miscalculation drifted into the unimportant past, and, perhaps, the explanation provided an unnecessary excess to him, a useless secular

228

confession slobbered to a couch doctor.

He said, "I got something I want to give you. It means something to me, and I want you to have it as a going away...."

Arthritic hinges squeaked and ground on their joints, and I slammed the door leaving the keys in the ignition. Already out of the truck cab, Skeads stopped walking away, turned around and stared at me. The ice blue sky framed his pale, bloodless features like El Greco captures, those life-tortured characters stymied by a revelation, elongated into an anguished sky, the color-needy eyes fixed in a void, or perhaps, enlightenment. He lighted another hand-roll, cupping it with those piano or violin hands. "Remember," he said, "Don't forget. It might be the last time we ever see each other."

I asked him, "What's going on? Something's going down."

"The frayed ends are tightening themselves up. Don't concern yourself with it. Get on with your life. It's great to be alive. Don't forget that." He inhaled and then said with smoke swirling around his words, "I don't know how, but everything seems to work out. We still survive regardless of what we do to each other. Get on with your life. All this is part of your past now."

He suddenly changed the subject. "You remember Wronski? On the *Faith*?"

I did. The man who had made shore only to be eaten by a bear. The fellow survivor who had visited Skeads while he huddled in a shallow cave with an assembly of feathered scavengers.

Skeads said, "I remember what he said walking out of that cave and into the night ... him saying 'what's left is a piece of cake.' I thought he was talking about himself, but I misunderstood him. He was talking about me.

"I called out to him, 'Where you going? And all he said was, 'I'm already there.'"

As if out of an old Hitchcock movie, a nasty old raven flying on its last feathers landed on the truck, the creature monophonic-cawing into the glacial sky, its crystalline black eyes peered from a cocking ebony head, vetting the truck bed to see if there might be something dead to eat. "Ravens," Skeads replied, "can't live with them, can't live without them. They damn near hunt you down." Fitting thread-to-socket into the nature surrounding him, Skeads gave me a wry smile, and unconsciously displaying his decayed teeth, he said, "Hell to pay."

I shouted back at him, "I thought we are having breakfast?"

He called back over his shoulder, "We did. I drank mine. In the morning we'll finish what we started."

* * *

That next morning, before first light, I rose and made coffee. Mallary and Maverick slept in their bunks. The black face of another retreating cold night pressed against the portholes and peered into the galley. My instinct dreaded stepping outside, knowing the temperatures. A large duct-taped cardboard box with Mallary's name scrawled across it rested on the galley table, so I placed it in his sleeping quarters where he would not miss it.

The wind unnerved the rigging, shaking the lines awake, in a strange comradery arousing them enough to suffer another day. Walking into the cold, when your heart wishes to avoid its venom, tests the miraculous gift of will. The truck needed warming up.

An inch of fresh powdery snow dusted the deck and dock, and it would take a good while to heat the truck, so I started it first and returned to the boat to drink another coffee with a healthy dose of 86-proof sin. Walking back out to the truck through the pre-dawn silences, inhaling the hard frigid air, I listened to my boots crunch across snow and ice. The light wind abused my face, gleefully

230

pushing little needles with a strange fire in my pores and reinforcing my commitment to abandon the place that had been good to me. Over the years, within its disinterested beauty, this edge of the world had eroded away. I had embraced its strange, ambivalent compositions, and in that embrace been exhausted, and in that exhaustion another life found.

The strong heater worked and made pleasant the drive down the dark road highlighted by a few street lights turning mounds of snow simmering. A fellow traveler passed the other way, our beams of light filling the space between our distances and destinations, only then to be observed in the rear view mirror, catching the diminishing red of the tail lights, until they disappeared into our mutually-shared but opposite paths.

Passing by the small town square, I headed out to Skeads' trailer. On the road to his place, Arctic-arrested spruce trees, gaunt survivors of nature, lined the sides of the road and trapped what little light existed into a black-and-shadow landscape.

I had thought, belatedly, about giving some token of thanks to Skeads, maybe a custom hunting knife, or a single malt scotch. For some reason, this thought never materialized. I decided I would send something to him from down in the States, and maybe this morning say a few words of how I would miss him, that I was grateful for the opportunity starting years before on the *Faith*, and that if he wished, he would always be welcome to crash and drink beers at my place.

I had only once been out to Skeads' place, an experience in minimalism, and if possible to live more simply you might have to scrum out of a garbage bag and scrabble on the streets. But I couldn't see Skeads living in any place but here, and after a few miles, a truck-trail nicked an intrusion into the state road, and I turned on to it. The beams of yellow light filled a natural grotto with narrow twin ruts for a path and brush scraping against the rusted

231

panels of the truck. After fifty yards and fifty bumps, the truck-trail opened to a clearing expanding to a dark sky, a view of the frozen lake and my skipper's trailer squatting alone like an aluminum-clad giant beetle. The truck headlights brushed the metal siding with yellow sfumato.

Light from inside the trailer feigned occupation, and unconsciously, I assumed he was brewing coffee with a handle of early morning celebration resting on his table.

I tapped the horn, but it didn't work. On pulling near his trailer, no face appeared within the frame of the porthole window. I figured this was not that unusual for him. No one answered when I knocked on the door. Entering the quiet, warm belly of the trailer, as silent as a boneyard, the kerosene heater stood to watch in the middle, its wick a thin blue diadem flame and a window on the other side cracked a half inch. The bunk made, his books of Shakespeare and Russians lined a wall, with his reading chair expecting occupation, with the coffeemaker poised-ready to plug in, with the junkyard table holding his empty ashtray, his tusk cribbage board and wooden box of pegs waited for company, and beside them his chessboard spread open with the play and motion of a white rook and knight suspended in their hope and pursuit of dethroning a black king. A handle of sour mash stood beside one solitary coffee cup with a pinned note. The note was folded in half, and on its outside, it read: "Plug in the coffee, eggs, and salmon are in the box. Then open the note."

I remember my first instinct was to open the message regardless of his wishes, then I reconsidered, thinking that it might be important to him. So, I played his game. The pickled eggs and salmon and whiskey hit the spot. I opened the note.

It read: "I enjoyed working with you. You did a good job when working with me. I want you to have the tusk to remember me by.

232

Take care, never forget some poor walrus for eternity must rut clams in walrus heaven with only one digger. The North treated us well. You'll find what's left of me down at the lake. After you figure things out, listen to Mallary. Good luck. I think you're making the right decision. Go with your intuition. S."

In reading the note, I missed the phrase, "what's left of me." I poured another coffee and whiskey, not knowing what to think and not trying.

From the trailer, a footpath wandered with a modest purpose to the edge of the lake. Meek dawn lay like a glowing thread on the ineffable edge of the dying night. The wind pushed dust of snow across a small prairie of lake-ice reflecting the shy ecstasy of a tepid moon. In the moon shadow, Skeads relaxed on Billins' chair, leaning back against a spruce. Almost standing vigil, an empty beer can and an empty upright bottle of whiskey contained a couple of cigarette butts. A frozen can of beer waited unopened. An empty coffee cup held his Zippo lighter. His shirt was opened to the night, he was shoeless, he was hatless, his beautiful hands resting together holding an empty pill bottle. His face had always looked coffin ready.

I still wonder why, at the time, I felt nothing. Maybe because the place seemed fulfilled, a circle, the interval perfect, the tonic chord struck. I tried to call the police, but Skeads had cut the phone line. I started to "figure it out," unplugging the coffee maker, turning off the heater, pouring another shot into the last of the coffee, taking a long look around the simple quantities and sums that allocated his life. I took the note and tusk and left.

* * *

On the way into town, I stopped by the police station. Just leaving her night shift, with warm rebreathed air pushing her out of the office, the diminutive night clerk held the door open for me and toothy-smiled. Sadlerman sat behind a desk. His intense eyes lifted

233

from his paper and met mine. Any anger he still indulged from the day before, like a snuffed spirit, vanished from his face.

# Chapter 25: Mallory ties loose ends

I hid on the *Sunburst* until my flight time, thirty-six hours away. Avoiding Polly's, it now dwelled in the past. After Skeads' suicide, I was sick of all of it, finding in disassociation a solitude. It would take years for me to think about my life with the North and Skeads.

Falin had vanished, a disappearance of strange singularity that would baffle law enforcement for decades. Dock and bar room gossip turned Skeads' vengeance into myth.

Over the years, the *Faith,* the *Ambrosia*, and the *Sunburst* would become personalities within me as real as flesh and blood. I remembered the old black and white photos like they might be the breath of the *Faith*, suspensions in time like grave markers holding in a coffin-like old shoe box the boat's soul: those fishermen in wool suits who stood on the dock ruefully eyeing the deck filled with frozen dead; when another generation of fishermen stood over the loyal old wooden rig abandoned by its faithless crew and survived of its own will; when Skeads experienced his delusions or visions of afterlife and lived with seagulls; and when finally bad luck and nature pushed the vessel aground, and Mallary experienced his delusions as it sank with the frozen ghosts of mother and baby weeping and howling.

Mallary and Maverick, though they knew I had found the body, asked not one question of me that might contribute to any myth. For my last hours, the baby-faced man, keeping his own counsel, competently filled the boots of Skeads. He concerned himself with the details of the *Sunburst* and with Monroe's arrival in another week. I guessed Skeads had left instructions in that cardboard box. Sadlerman lost any interest in me that morning when hell broke loose. After the trooper's spiritless interview at the station, I went about my business, and I suspected Mallary knew more than he ever let on.

On the morning of my departure, Mallary drove me to the airport. I climbed into the passenger side of Skeads' old truck and sat on that road-salvaged plywood seat, and that's when Mallary's emotional reservoir, if that's what it was, broke.

A concoction combined in Mallary of a steel-tough fisherman, a man who worked well under fatigue and pressure, and a strange seer of a world filled with spirits and ethereal voices. In a strange religious hybrid, he saw a spirit world confronting commonsense—he, like Blake, never attended church. On the road to the airport, he unleashed the details of the night when Skeads delivered his tribute to Hell.

I climbed unaware into the truck. Between Mallory's thighs stood a fifth of whiskey. He put the truck in gear, lifting the bottle to his lips drinking too much and handing the remainder to me. I suspected this it was not his first dance of the morning.

Amid the clattering between the road, the truck suspension, and what we bounced through, the silent harsh beauty of nature, of snow, of grays, and trees valiantly struggling to live slipped by.

He began: "As certain as the Baby Jesus, something within him stood apart, and it met its dark corpus in a night possessed."

As if he were obligating me to a blood oath, he hissed, "You keep this to yourself. Seal it in your soul like the most grave-dwelling man to the earth itself. Understand this: Our noble friend would have it this way."

For me, two emotions quarreled. One argued, "Escape and evade!" The other whispered, "What happened that night?" With Mallary smoldering on some form of paranormal brimstone, I didn't need to ask.

The inside of the truck stank of whiskey, and I took another

236

swallow from the bottle. Mallary, his voice low and sincere, continued, "The forces converged at Angela's Massage, the living room warm with scents of candles, the girls, the complimentary drinks. It was empty but for Skeads, his distressed spirit, the ladies, and me. Night haunted our skipper's troubled soul. I went upstairs with my companion, and we returned to have another drink. A slow night. As I chatted up my gal, I noticed into the night our skipper had retreated with no farewell. Usually, he would sit and talk a little with his Brooke, his favorite gal. But she sat alone at a table, making strange little gasping sounds—her hands like sparrows fluttering over a lunch bag. I thought she might be crying.

"But spread before her lay courageous stacks of hundred dollar bills defying the poverty found in life. The heavens, or at least the bag, burst manna from Mammon.

"... a paper bag with enough of the ill-fated lucre to start a new life. Her teary eyes beseeched like winged angels throwing down their spears and showering heaven with their tears. Gasping, she said to my companion beside me, "We have no excuses now. We will own a beauty shop."

"Who, where?" I asked her.

"Skeads," she murmured, "He said to me when he left, 'Don't forget ... Life is good ... A miracle. Believe in it if you can.' I must thank him."

And then Mallary continued in words only he could muster in his strange tongue, "On hearing this from Brooke. My drink unfinished, I left to find our skipper. The night teemed with cold shadows formed by the peering light from eyes of forlorn houses. In rotting air, silent, beyond silence, this breath of night hard on my face, I passed the church. I passed that sacred ground beneath the Russian dome and heard the ghosts' songs of anguish, lamentations. I saw ghosts and demons unseen, I breathed air filled with the breath

237

of dead flesh, and I heard a wailing chorus. The ethereal garden bloomed with fiery vapors casting evil through the darkness. I heard the winter weeping. I saw our precious ghost, the Skeadsman himself, kneeling in prayer, kneeling with Grief itself persecuting our skipper, who prayed against an unyielding sacred door, and our ghost beseeching amidst boiling shadows of sorrow, of madness, of Grace's fury. I feared to stop, to give help, to pray with our ghost, to touch my Skeadsman on the shoulder and pray with him. I found the malevolence too dark and too terrifying, and I, too, feared for my soul. Air-dancing demons swarmed with snakes, and winged beasts ... and ... and mutilated puppies, and babies danced with flaming monkeys starved to rattling bones and ravens speaking in tongues, and with thick ethers cauldroned in sin simmering, simmering, simmering across this earth. I saw the noble *Faith* and saw and heard the baby howl and the mother weep eternally.

"....and so, I escaped, ran away. In the night, where we now sit, I groveled past this very truck while parked. I abandoned our skipper. I loved him, but I turned away ... I thought myself his friend ... failed ... I failed ... shame, shame, eternal shame on my eternal soul."

I side-glanced at Mallary, with his hands gripped on the steering wheel, he stared through the filthy windshield and peered into the road flanked with hills landscaped in white and gleaming fresh snow I would never see again except in my mind. I saw Mallary carrying his rock up a mountain without a summit, those weathered baby blue eyes twisted, his crazy talk spilling from his lips to a nonbeliever, his confession a delusional night-drama. In his harsh self-judgment, he said, "I abandoned my friend. Do you understand?"

I didn't at the time and avoided answering his question.

Mallary continued his confession: "But it was before Skeads revealed his plan ... He told me to give you his notebooks and this ..." He slid a paper bag and notebooks across to me until he could

238

push them no farther without shoving me through the door and into the road.

I wanted nothing to do with the notebooks or a paper bag or him.

"Open it," he said.

"Not interested. Don't need it."

"What's that got to do with it?"

When I failed to act, Mallary opened the bag. It contained enough cash to finance a college education and far more: two pounds of hundred-dollar bills bundled in cellophane wrappers.

I took the high road saying that I wanted nothing to do with "that kind of money."

Mallary replied. "Piss and vomit. So, you wish to reject his endowment? Eh? And what will be gained by this gesture? Under our Beneficent Lord's Grace, you stand on the shores of another half-century of life. You think the suits wisdom this manna with more justice and prudence? You think the money in your pocket is more virtuous? You know not its wellsprings, its blood-cost." Mallary's candor ranted. "Don't be stupid. Employ this largess wisely. Let the suits sort their own thunder. This is our skipper's last thunder."

We pulled into the entrance of the airport, and Mallary left the truck in idle, opening my backpack and stuffing it with the bag and notebooks. "Deny not Skeads his last bequests. If burdened too great, better to feed the poor than bequeathing the filthy lucre to the suits. Learn to give it away." His wacko-words and babyface and beady blue eyes finished any argument in me. I kept the money and have regretted far greater transgressions in life.

"You know a fireman found Hat Boy near the burning house,

hanged head-down on a tree like a Roman crucifixion, gagged on Ben Franklins, skull-ring-tortured, mutilated, covered in his white-vile candy, his leather hat stabbed hilt-depth to his head by the bone-handled knife of Dagon. I tell you, as a man who sees ghosts that are as real as you or me, the prudent murderer digs his own grave first. If you believe in prayer, pray for our skipper. They found the eye of the *Ambrosia* in a nest of embers, un-singed, impervious to the fire, staring into the morning."

I nodded my head, pretending to agree, and quickly slid out of the truck, overjoyed to exit and wealthier than when entering it. I didn't ask about Falin or his disappearance, wishing to avoid any more conversation. And as if nothing had happened, I said, "Thanks. Maybe we'll meet again? Like in Seattle."

"Yes, no, maybe ... Don't forget: learn to pray; learn to pray without ceasing."

I nodded again in agreement, almost forgetting to give him a letter, an apologia of sorts. "Could you see that Gina gets this?"

Mallary laughed, his worn baby eyes losing their intensity, "Aha, serendipity ... the pleasant kind." He pulled from his insulated overalls a small wood-canker salvaged from some weather-abused spruce. It was inked in tight black lines, a miniature portrait of Skeads, and signed by Gina.

"She thinks of you and Skeads. She adds her address by-the-bye. Goodbye. Fisherman. Comrade. I pray for you." He retrieved the whiskey bottle.

# Epilogue: Skeads - a small resolution

Monroe and I had not seen one another for more than three decades. Occasionally, we talked on the phone, and he would invite me back to the Island town, but I always declined, wishing to visit the past my way. Monroe was visiting Seattle on business, and we finally met for a couple of drinks at the Public Market near First and Pike. He suggested we check out the Place Pigalle, once a dump of a beer bar.

I crossed the narrow street separating the Sanitary Market from the Public. A few cawing seagulls, almost tame, waddled around dumpsters; the scents of salt and sea and garbage blended thick into the pleasant but chilly hubbub of the city. I watched for a moment the antics of fishmongers tossing fish to one another and how the crowd surrounding them applauded. Over the years, the market had found a new youth and turned from the working class into narcissistic theatre for California expats, tourists, and wannabe gourmands. Regardless, it remained a terrific place. Monroe waited for me with his hands stuck into a crisp denim hunting jacket that had yet to see a hunt. As we entered the restaurant, a northwest wind blew gray-black cloud cover toward Puget Sound.

With white tablecloths and a top-shelf bar, the restaurant was now French both in character and food. The bartender greeted us looking like she expected something more famous to happen to her in the future. Large windows opened to a panoramic view of the Elliot Bay and Sound, and the twenty-table restaurant smelled of fresh bread and garlic instead of the cigarettes and stale beer of the times past. Years before, Pigalle had sported a pool table, in a dim corner an eclectic jukebox headlining everything from Mario Lanza to Patsy Cline, and a drug dealer in the bathroom peddling half a dozen off-market escapes. At our age, our more mature constitutions

241

no longer prevailed over stale beer or drugs, though we still missed the spirit of the old days.

We sat at the small bar. I had asked for a Rainier or Oly, but it was available only in the bottle. We ordered boutique beers and cognac shots. With curious eyes and startlingly manicured nails lacquered with what seemed stars-and-lightening, the bartender shot us a double-take. Monroe waited patiently until the set-ups arrived and he handed the bartender a twenty and almost humbly said, "That's for you. We like the view. We're reminiscing. Could you run us a tab?" I'd forgotten that Monroe worked his way through college waiting tables and always showed deference to servers.

He asked her, "Years ago this place was different. Do you remember when this place did jazz and blues on weekend nights?"

She said no, that she might not have been born.

He said, "Add another twenty percent to the gratuity. But keep an eye on us, please." What he had said didn't seem the least bit rude, and the bartender transformed into a model of concern.

Monroe turned around and looked out windows facing a distant landscape of mountain and sea too often taken for granted. A barricade of clouds clustered in the distance, above the Olympic Rim, and in another few hours the sky would turn a darker gray and start to drizzle. From across the world, ships stacked with containers lay at anchor. In the foreground, the Alaskan Way Viaduct hemorrhaged a vein of traffic, and the rooftops of warehouses, garden condominiums, and office buildings contrasted the grand expanse of the Sound reaching for its horizon. Looking across Elliot Bay to Alki Point, if you knew the history, you could see the ghost of the old Luna Park.

"To the view," he toasted. Like kids, we killed the drinks. We enjoyed seeing one another.

The years had treated him gently. He was a second generation Irish American, with the Spanish Armada bred somewhere into his gene pool. His complexion had shades of the Mediterranean in it, with dark eyes more Castilian than the Celtic passion beating in his chest.

"You still reading your Robert Service and Farley Mowat?" he asked.

"Not for years. I've moved on to Shakespeare and Melville. It's tougher to teach. When no one's looking I still find a rusty copy or two of their tree-hugging stuff."

"How's Gina and Paul?" He ordered another round.

"Both are doing well. Gina has quite a workshop and a small art studio. She's an artist. Very successful ... for an artist. Paul, of all things, teaches college-level math in a high school. He's a crackerjack carpenter and furniture maker and works in her shop during the summer. They're very close. She's a good wife to me and a mother to him. I'm lucky in marriage.

"Whatever happened to Mallary and Maverick? I never stayed in touch with them."

"Maverick turned into a strong skipper. Somehow, he combined the best of Skeads and, not to boast, myself. A good marriage, nice kids.

"Mallary ran the *Sunburst* for a couple of years. Skeads had a will. Left him the lake property. Somewhere along the line, Mallary had mysteriously saved a good chunk of change and moved back to Oregon and started a tent church. I heard him once. He doesn't make any sense, but he does good service for the community. Helps the unfortunates."

"And how's *Ambrosia* doing?"

"She's still out there working the trade. Still very attractive," he replied, "I should have bought her when I had the chance. Her personality disorders have been finally managed. That's when you and I first met."

"True enough," I replied.

"What a trip to break in on." Monroe looked at the tables filling with suits.

"Good practice," I said.

"To be sure," he said. "I figured that trip my first and last as a skipper. My career finished before it was started. Skeads, Falin, Neal, and you. What a deck to draw to."

"Yeah, we made the best of it. Seems like we kept it working." Then as an afterthought, I added, "Neal kept it working."

As if the reply instinctively waited, Monroe said, "Except Neal. He lost ... everything. Ironic, without him, I would have lost everything. I was too overwhelmed to thank him."

"And Skeads ... well, I can't say he lost," I added.

When I mentioned Skeads, neither Monroe nor I felt any remorse or sense that he could end any other way. Skeads' decisions seemed a fitting finish for him, an appropriate piece in the puzzles of his resolve.

Sitting in that renovated waypoint of our past lives, the clientele had filled the restaurant; their style blended well with the fugue in the background. They all appeared very chic, very casual, very oozing with social and cultural confidence. Though, as an afterthought, we now were not that much different than those taking the seats. We had changed; we were all suits by then.

"Uncanny. Neal was right all along. That crazy brilliant loon. He saw what we couldn't."

244

"To Skeads and Neal," I toasted, "Ordinary men." Again, we downed the shots like kids hiding behind a garage.

He waved his finger in a circle over our drinks, and the bartender, smiling, her fingernails flashing, set another round.

After a little silence, Monroe added, "Skeads made a decision, but Neal got screwed. And I stood by like a loser. You know, maybe we should have thrown Falin overboard. Maybe if I'd been strong enough ... maybe I blew the chance to do the right thing. An expression in situational ethics."

He stopped, hesitating as if seeing something swimming in his shot glass. "It was business after all. Not the end of the world. We all accepted the game. Made our choices."

I added, "I think we all thought that way ... except for Skeads. The man saw the game different."

Monroe played with his shot glass, twisting it in a circle on the bar. "Neal guessed right that Falin was the next skipper. I got fired at the dock and thought it was my last roundup. Damn if Falin wasn't a terrific skipper—for several years. The *Ambrosia* seemed to like him."

"Yeah, he was the man the women liked. You know, Skeads and I went up to the jail first light the next morning to visit Neal."

"Right, I still remember it." Monroe stared at his shot glass, and, looking away from me murmured, "Mean spirited, at best."

"Neal's cannery friend, the girl, was just leaving. Not a tear to that girl's eye. Face like carved beach rock. She was still wearing that field jacket and stocking cap like she'd just left a barracks. She looked through us like we didn't exist.

"She let us find out for ourselves. Native humor. We were too late. Neal was finished."

"You know, after all was said and done, I don't recall if anyone claimed his body ..." said Monroe, "we were all too busy. I'm not sure anyone cut him a check. I got fired at the dock. Falin took over the rig. The maggot couldn't help smiling at me."

The afternoon disappeared along with several rounds. We quit drinking. Monroe paid the tab, and we left the Place Pigalle.

In a few hours, Monroe would put on a suit and meet his business partners for dinner. He had become very successful and wealthy, but it didn't matter between us. I like to think we had shared a life bigger than money.

We walked out to First Avenue to say our goodbyes. Feeling the cognac and beer and the play on our faces of the evening chill coming off the sound, we talked a little about the strength of the foreign markets.

"You know, I have his journals ... Skeads' ... not Falin's?" I laughed at my joke. Monroe said nothing, but as we continued to walk, he shot glances at me waiting for more.

"Over the years I've read them several times. They're a testament, a meditation on his life. His thoughts about his life. He wrote in tight script, like a twelve font. He sketched pictures in steel-tip. Eyes of eagles, seagulls on bows, the details of the bark of a Sitka spruce, a few miniature landscapes. He had that night planned all out ... the night he broke loose hell. It's in the last journal like a briefing. All that etching on the tusk could be found in his journals, even the one of a gargoyle being hanged.

"On the last page of the journals, I found an ink sketch portrait of Billins, Gina, Paul, and Skeads. Like a family portrait. I found that same study etched on the tusk."

As we waited on First Avenue for the light to change, he asked, "How'd Skeads react ... at the jail when Neal hung himself?"

"At the jail? He said, 'Hell will pay. I should have thrown him overboard.' Had the same comments in the last journal. He never talked to me about Neal or Falin for that matter. Maybe to Mallary, but not to me."

"You think that was what tipped Skeads?" I asked.

"Yeah, maybe Billins. Who knows, and it doesn't much matter."

Monroe said nothing but, while waiting for a traffic light to change, his face involuntarily twisted in some emotion that men don't like showing. He looked up at the cloudy sky. A pigeon bobbled around the sidewalk, pecking at imperceptible refuse. Monroe looked at the bird scrounging the cracks in the soiled sidewalk. Cigarette butts waited for a sweeping or driving rain to flush them down the gutter. His face still twitching, he said, "Life works in mysterious ways, eh?"

I wasn't sure if he was talking about our life or the pigeon's, but I responded, "Yeah, but don't forget, it's great to be alive. Skeads said once back on the *Faith* that life was the only real miracle. The rest was smoke and mirrors."

When the light changed, Monroe said, "Skeads was different from us. Life, we still trust, its ... its goodness. For long or short, I guess guys like us don't have much choice."

We shook hands again; he held mine a little longer. Monroe had remained genuine over the years. Turning away, he said, "Before we're all dust, let's meet again. Hell, grab the wife and come down to my place in Phoenix. Remember Chief? He set up a helluva gated community. Helluva golf course country club. Who'd a thought?"

He added, "Hey ... you're the grammar guy; you should write a book about Skeads."

I had forgotten to ask, but I did suddenly, "Whatever happened to Falin? They find him hiding out down in Garberville someplace?"

247

In the middle of the crosswalk, Monroe turned around, "You never heard? Army of Engineers had to drain the lake for some reason. They found the sucker's bones anchored down at the bottom, trussed as tight as a turkey and with a survival knife stuck in his head. There wasn't much left of him but bones and those sunglasses duct-taped around his skull. I wouldn't put it past him. It fits."

The pigeon flew ten feet and landed, looking for a second course, and a drizzle began to fall. I heard a baby crying fearfully and turned to see a mother at a bus stop, bundling the child close to her breasts to protect him from the mounting sprays of chill from the sound as the wind kicked up a howl.

The End

## About the Author

I was very young when I was born. Mowed lawns, paperboy, bagboy, graduated high school, army infantry, busboy, washed dishes, bartender, busboy, did logging in the Pacific Northwest, commercial fishing in Alaska, married, carpenter and house painter, waiter, and, finally, busboy. At this writing, I moderately enjoy old age and excessively enjoy retirement. From my life's start to the present pre-finish, when peering back into the days gone, they clicked by exceptionally fast. Still married.

www.ingramcontent.com/pod-product-compliance
Lightning Source LLC
Chambersburg PA
CBHW020057180626
46812CB00006B/2369